ALIEN CONTACT

KU-728-242

'So these are the visitors from outer space!' The hyperman's propeller tail idled slowly as he spoke.

'Have they given you much trouble?'

'None at all. They're stupid, senseless brutes.'

'All right. I'll take over.'

As control passed from one weird being to the other, Seaton acted instinctively. With a twisting leap he whirled about, wrenching himself free from the punishing teeth of the grapple. Then he struck.

But the thing opposing him did not have the solid substance of a human, three-dimensional enemy. The body of the guard subsided instantly upon the floor, *a shapeless and mangled mass of oozing, dripping flesh* . . .

SKYLARK OF VALERON is the third stunning novel in the four-part 'Skylark' series by E. E. 'Doc' Smith, creator of the world-famous epic 'Lensman' series.*

* Also available in Panther Science Fiction

By the same author

The *Lensman* Series
Triplanetary
First Lensman
Second Stage Lensmen
Grey Lensman
Galactic Patrol
Children of the Lens
Masters of the Vortex

The *Skylark* Series
The Skylark of Space
Skylark Three
Skylark DuQuesne

The *Family d'Alembert* Series (with Stephen Goldin)
The Imperial Stars
Stranglers' Moon
The Clockwork Traitor
Getaway World
The Bloodstar Conspiracy
The Purity Plot
Planet of Treachery

Other Novels
Spacehounds of IPC
The Galaxy Primes
Subspace Explorers

E. E. 'DOC' SMITH

Skylark of Valeron

The third novel in the *Skylark* series

GRANADA
London Toronto Sydney New York

Published by Granada Publishing Limited in 1974
Reprinted 1976, 1978, 1979, 1981, 1982

ISBN 0 586 03948 1

Granada Publishing Limited
Frogmore, St Albans, Herts AL2 2NF
and
36 Golden Square, London W1R 4AH
866 United Nations Plaza, New York, NY 10017, USA
117 York Street, Sydney, NSW 2000, Australia
100 Skyway Avenue, Rexdale, Ontario, M9W 3A6, Canada
61 Beach Road, Auckland, New Zealand

Printed and bound in Great Britain by
Richard Clay (The Chaucer Press) Ltd,
Bungay, Suffolk
Set in Plantin

To
Lee Hawkins Garby

1 : Doctor DuQuesne's Ruse

Day after day a spherical space ship of Arenak tore through the illimitable reaches of the interstellar void. She had once been a war vessel of Osnome; now, rechristened the *Violet*, she was bearing two Tellurians and a Fenachrone – Dr. Marc C. Du-Quesne of World Steel, 'Baby Doll' Loring, his versatile and accomplished assistant, and the squat and monstrous engineer of the flagship Y427W – from the Green System toward the solar system of the Fenachrone. The mid-point of the stupendous flight had long since been passed; the *Violet* had long been braking down with a negative acceleration of five times the velocity of light.

Much to the surprise of both DuQuesne and Loring, their prisoner had not made the slightest move against them. He had thrown all the strength of his supernaturally powerful body and all the resources of his gigantic brain into the task of converting the atomic motors of the *Violet* into the space-annihilating drive of his own race. This drive, affecting alike as it does every atom of substance within the radius of action of the power bar, entirely nullifies the effect of acceleration, so that the passengers feel no motion whatever, even when the craft is accelerating at maximum.

The engineer had not shirked a single task, however arduous. And, once under way, he had nursed those motors along with every artifice known to his knowing clan; he had performed such prodigies of adjustment and tuning as to raise by a full two per cent their already inconceivable maximum acceleration. Nor was this all. After the first moment of rebellion, he did not even once attempt to bring to bear the almost irresistible hypnotic power of his eyes; the immense, cold, ruby-lighted projectors of mental energy which, both men knew, were awful weapons indeed. Nor did he even once protest against the attractors which were set upon his giant limbs.

Immaterial bands, these, whose slight force could not be felt unless the captor so willed. But let the prisoner make one false move, and those tiny beams of force would instantly become

5

copper-driven rods of pure energy, hurling the luckless weight against the wall of the control room and holding him motionless there, in spite of the most terrific exertions of his mighty body.

DuQuesne lay at ease in his seat; or rather, scarcely touching the seat, he floated at ease in the air above it. His black brows were drawn together, his black eyes were hard as he studied frowningly the Fenachrone engineer. As usual, that worthy was half inside the power plant, coaxing those mighty engines to do even better than their prodigious best.

Feeling his companion's eyes upon him, the doctor turned his inscrutable stare upon Loring, who had been studying his chief even as DuQuesne had been studying the outlander. Loring's cherubic countenance was as pinkly innocent as ever, his guileless blue eyes as calm and untroubled; but DuQuesne, knowing the man as he did, perceived an almost imperceptible tension and knew that the killer also was worried.

'What's the matter, Doll?' The saturnine scientist smiled mirthlessly. 'Afraid I'm going to let that ape slip one over on us?'

'Not exactly.' Loring's slight tenseness, however, disappeared. 'It's your party, and anything that's all right with you tickles me half to death. I have known all along you knew that that bird there isn't working under compulsion. You know as well as I do that nobody works that way because they're made to. He's working for himself, not for us, and I had just begun to wonder if you weren't getting a little late in clamping down on him.'

'Not at all – there are good and sufficient reasons for this apparent delay. I am going to clamp down on him in exactly' – DuQuesne glanced at his wrist watch – 'fourteen minutes. But you're keen – you've got a brain that really works – maybe I'd better give you the whole picture.'

DuQuesne, approving thoroughly of his iron-nerved, cold-blooded assistant, voiced again the thought he had expressed once before, a few hours out from Earth; and Loring answered as he had then, in almost the same words – words which revealed truly the nature of the man:

'Just as you like. Usually I don't want to know anything about anything, because what a man doesn't know he can't be accused of spilling. Out here, though, maybe I should know enough about things to act intelligently in case of a jam. But you're the doctor – if you'd rather keep it under your hat, that's all right with me, too. As I've said before, it's your party.'

'Yes; he certainly is working for himself.' DuQuesne scowled blackly. 'Or, rather, he thinks he is. You know I read his mind back there, while he was unconscious. I didn't get all I wanted to, by any means – he woke up too soon – but I got a lot more than he thinks I did.

'They have detector zones, 'way out in space, all around their world, that nothing can get past without being spotted; and patrolling those zones there are scout ships, carrying armament to stagger the imagination. I intend to take over one of those patrol ships and by means of it to capture one of their first-class battleships. As a first step I'm going to hypnotize that ape and find out absolutely everything he knows. When I get done with him, he'll do exactly what I tell him to, and nothing else.'

'Hypnotize him?' Curiosity was awakened in even Loring's incurious mind at this unexpected development. 'I didn't know that was one of your specialties.'

'It wasn't until recently, but the Fenachrone are all past masters, and I learned about it from his brain. Hypnosis is a wonderful science. The only drawback is that his mind is a lot stronger than mine. However, I have in my kit, among other things, a tube of something that will cut him down to my size.'

'Oh, I see – pentabarb.' With this hint, Loring's agile mind grasped instantly the essentials of DuQuesne's plan. 'That's why you had to wait so long, then, to take steps. Pentabarb kills in twenty-four hours, and he can't help us steal the ship after he's dead.'

'Right! One milligram, you know, will make a gibbering idiot out of any human being; but I imagine that it will take three or four times that much to soften *him* down to the point where I can work on him the way I want to. As I don't know the effects of such heavy dosages, since he's not really human, and since he must be alive when we go through their screens, I decided to give him the works exactly six hours before we are due to hit their outermost detector. That's about all I can tell you right now; I'll have to work out the details of seizing the ship after I have studied his brain more thoroughly.'

Precisely at the expiration of the fourteen allotted minutes, DuQuesne tightened the attractor beams, which had never been entirely released from their prisoner; thus pinning him helplessly, immovably, against the wall of the control room. He then filled a hypodermic syringe and moved the mechanical educator nearer the motionless, although violently struggling, creature. Then, avoiding carefully the baleful out-pourings of those flame-shot volcanoes of hatred that were the eyes of the Fenachrone, he set the dials of the educator, placed the headsets, and drove home the needle's hollow point. One milligram of the diabolical compound was absorbed, without appreciable lessening of the blazing defiance being hurled along the educator's wires. One and one-half – two milligrams – three – four – five —

That inhumanly powerful mind at last began to weaken, but it became entirely quiescent only after the administration of the seventh milligram of that direly potent drug.

'Just as well that I allowed only six hours.' DuQuesne sighed in relief as he began to explore the labyrinthine intricacies of the frightful brain now open to his gaze. 'I don't see how any possible form of life can hold together long under seven milligrams of that stuff.'

He fell silent and for more than an hour he studied the brain of the engineer, concentrating upon the several small portions which contained knowledge of most immediate concern. Finally he removed the headsets.

'His plans were all made,' he informed Loring coldly, 'and so are mine, now. Bring out two full outfits of clothing – one of yours and one of mine. Two guns, belts, and so on. Break out a bale of waste, the emergency candles, and all that sort of stuff you can find.'

DuQuesne turned to the Fenachrone, who stood utterly lax, and stared deep into those dull and expressionless eyes.

'You,' he directed crisply, 'will build at once, as quickly as you can, two dummies which will look exactly like Loring and myself. They must be lifelike in every particular, with faces capable of expressing the emotions of surprise and of anger, and with right arms able to draw weapons upon a signal – *my* signal. Also upon signal their heads and bodies will turn, they will leap toward the center of the room, and they will make certain noises

8

and utter certain words, the records of which I shall prepare. Go to it!'

'Don't you need to control him through the headsets?' asked Loring curiously.

'I may have to control him in detail when we come to the really fine work, later on,' DuQuesne replied absently. 'This is more or less in the nature of an experiment, to find out whether I have him thoroughly under control. During the last act he'll have to do exactly what I shall have told him to do, without supervision, and I want to be absolutely certain that he will do it without a slip.'

'What's the plan – or maybe it's something that is none of my business?'

'No; you ought to know it, and I've got time to tell you about it now. Nothing material can possibly approach the planet of the Fenachrone without being seen, as it is completely surrounded by never less than two full-sphere detector screens; and to make assurance doubly sure our engineer there has installed a mechanism which, at the first touch of the outer screen, will shoot a warning along a tight communicator beam directly into the receiver of the nearest Fenachrone scout ship. As you already know, the smallest of those scouts can burn this ship out of the ether in less than a second.'

'That's a cheerful picture. You still think we can get away?'

'I'm coming to that. We can't possibly get through the detectors without being challenged, even if I tear out all his apparatus, so we're going to use his whole plan, but for our benefit instead of his. Therefore his present hypnotic state and the dummies. When we touch that screen you and I are going to be hidden. The dummies will be in sole charge, and our prisoner will be playing the part I've laid out for him.

'The scout ship that he calls will come up to investigate. They will bring apparatus and attractors to bear to liberate the prisoner, and the dummies will try to fight. They will be blown up or burned to cinders almost instantly, and our little playmate will put on his space suit and be taken across to the capturing vessel. Once there, he will report to the commander.

'That officer will think the affair sufficiently serious to report it directly to headquarters. If he doesn't, this ape here will insist upon reporting it to general headquarters himself. As soon as that report is in, we, working through our prisoner here, will proceed to wipe out the crew of the ship and take it over.'

'And do you think he'll really do it?' Loring's guileless face showed doubt, his tone was faintly skeptical.

'I *know* he'll do it!' The chemist's voice was hard. 'He won't take any active part – I'm not psychologist enough to know whether I could drive him that far, even drugged, against an unhypnotizable subconscious or not – but he'll be carrying something along that will enable me to do it, easily and safely. But that's about enough of this chin music – we'd better start doing something.'

While Loring brought spare clothing and weapons, and rummaged through the vessel in search of material suitable for the dummies' fabrication, the Fenachrone engineer worked rapidly at his task. And not only did he work rapidly, he worked skillfully and artistically as well. This artistry should not be surprising, for to such a mentality as must necessarily be possessed by the chief engineer of a first-line vessel of the Fenachrone, the faithful reproduction of anything capable of movement was not a question of art – it was merely an elementary matter of line, form, and mechanism.

Cotton waste was molded into shape, reenforced, and wrapped in leather under pressure. To the bodies thus formed were attached the heads, cunningly constructed of masticated fiber, plastic, and wax. Tiny motors and many small pieces of apparatus were installed, and the completed effigies were dressed and armed.

DuQuesne's keen eyes studied every detail of the startlingly lifelike, almost microscopically perfect, replicas of himself and his traveling companion.

'A good job,' he commented briefly.

'Good?' exclaimed Loring. 'It's perfect! Why, that dummy would fool my own wife, if I had one – it almost fools me!'

'At least, they're good enough to pass a more critical test than any they are apt to get during this coming incident.'

Satisfied, DuQuesne turned from his scrutiny of the dummies and went to the closet in which had been stored the space suit of the captive. To the inside of its front protector flap he attached a small and inconspicuous flat-sided case. He then measured carefully, with a filar micrometer, the apparent diameter of the planet now looming so large beneath them.

'All right, Doll; our time's getting short. Break out our suits and test them, will you, while I give the big boy his final instructions?'

Rapidly those commands flowed over the wires of the mechanical educator, from DuQuesne's hard, keen brain into the now docile mind of the captive. The Earthly scientist explained to the Fenachrone, coldly, precisely, and in minute detail, exactly what he was to do and exactly what he was to say from the moment of encountering the detector screens of his native planet until after he had reported to his superior officers.

Then the two Tellurians donned their own armor and made their way into an adjoining room, a small armory in which were hung several similar suits and which was a veritable arsenal of weapons.

'We'll hang ourselves up on a couple of these hooks, like the rest of the suits,' DuQuesne explained. 'This is the only part of the performance that may be even slightly risky, but there is no real danger that they will spot us. That fellow's message to the scout ship will tell them that there are only two of us, and we'll be out there with him, right in plain sight.

'If by any chance they should send a party aboard us they would probably not bother to search the *Violet* at all carefully, since they will already know that we haven't got a thing worthy of attention; and they would of course suppose us to be empty space suits. Therefore keep your lens shields down, except perhaps for the merest crack to see through, and, above all, don't move a millimeter, no matter what happens.'

'But how can you manipulate your controls without moving your hands?'

'I can't; but my hands will not be in the sleeves, but inside the body of the suit – shut up! Hold everything – there's the flash!'

The flying vessel had gone through the zone of feeble radiations which comprised the outer detector screen of the Fenachrone. But, though tenuous, that screen was highly efficient, and at its touch there burst into frenzied activity the communicator built by the captive to be actuated by that very impulse. It had been built during the long flight through space, and its builder had thought that its presence would be unnoticed and would remain unsuspected by the Tellurians.

Now automatically put into action, it laid a beam to the nearest scout ship of the Fenachrone and into that vessel's receptors it passed the entire story of the *Violet* and her occupants. But DuQuesne had not been caught napping. Reading the engineer's brain and absorbing knowledge from it, he had installed a relay which would flash to his eyes an inconspicuous but unmistakable warning of the first touch of the screen of the enemy. The flash had come – they had penetrated the outer lines of the monstrous civilization of the dread and dreaded Fenachrone.

In the armory DuQuesne's hands moved slightly inside his shielding armor, and out in the control room the dummy, that was also to all outward seeming DuQuesne, moved and spoke. It tightened the controls of the attractors, which had never been entirely released from their prisoner, thus again pinning the Fenachrone helplessly against the wall.

'Just to be sure you don't try to start anything,' it explained coldly, in DuQuesne's own voice and tone. 'You have done well so far, but I'll run things myself from now on, so that you can't steer us into a trap. Now tell me exactly how to go about getting one of your vessels. After we get it I'll see about letting you go.'

'Fools, you are too late!' the prisoner roared exultantly. 'You would have been too late, even had you killed me out there in space and had fled at your utmost acceleration. Did you but know it you are as dead, even now – our patrol is upon you!'

The dummy that was DuQuesne whirled, snarling, and its automatic pistol and that of its fellow dummy were leaping out when an awful acceleration threw them flat upon the floor, a magnetic force snatched away their weapons, and a heat ray of prodigious power reduced the effigies to two small piles of gray ash. Immediately thereafter a beam of force from the patrolling cruiser neutralized the attractors bearing upon the captive and, after donning his space suit, he was transferred to the Fenachrone vessel.

Motionless inside his cubby, DuQuesne waited until the airlocks of the Fenachrone vessel had closed behind his erstwhile prisoner; waited until that luckless monster had told his story to Fenor, his emperor, and to Fenimol, his general in command; waited until the communicator circuit had been broken and the hypnotized, drugged, and already dying creature had turned as though to engage his fellows in conversation. Then only did the saturnine scientist act. His finger closed a circuit, and in the Fenachrone vessel, inside the front protector flap of the discarded space suit, the flat case fell apart noiselessly and from it there gushed forth volume upon volume of colorless and odorless, but intensely lethal, vapor.

'Just like killing goldfish in a bowl.' Callous, hard, and cold, DuQuesne exhibited no emotion whatever; neither pity for the vanquished foe nor elation at the perfect working out of his plans. 'Just in case some of them might have been wearing suits for emergencies, I had some explosive copper ready to detonate, but this makes it much better – the explosion might have damaged something we want.' ·

And aboard the vessel of the Fenachrone, DuQuesne's deadly gas diffused with extreme rapidity, and as it diffused, the hellish crew to the last man dropped in their tracks. They died not knowing what had happened to them; died with no thought of even attempting to send out an alarm; died not even knowing that they died.

'Can you open the airlocks of that scout ship from the outside, doctor?' asked Loring, as the two adventurers came out of the armory into the control room, where DuQuesne, by means of the attractors, began to bring the two vessels together.

'Yes. I know everything that the engineer of a first-class battleship knew. To him, one of these little scouts was almost beneath notice, but he did know that much about them – the outside controls of all Fenachrone ships work the same way.'

Under the urge of the attractors the two ships of space were soon door to door. DuQuesne set the mighty beams to lock the craft immovably together and both men stepped into the *Violet*'s airlock. Pumping back the air, DuQuesne opened the outer door, then opened both outer and inner doors of the scout.

As he opened the inner door the poisoned atmosphere of the vessel screamed out into space, and as soon as the frigid gale had subsided the raiders entered the control room of the enemy craft. Hardened and conscienceless killer though Loring was, the four bloated, ghastly objects that had once been men gave him momentary pause.

'Maybe we shouldn't have let the air out so fast,' he suggested, tearing his gaze away from the grisly sight.

'The brains aren't hurt, and that's all I care about.' Unmoved, DuQuesne opened the air valves wide, and not until the roaring blast had scoured every trace of the noxious vapor from the whole ship did he close the airlock doors and allow the atmosphere to come again to normal pressure and temperature.

'Which ship are you going to use – theirs or our own?' asked Loring, as he began to remove his cumbersome armor.

'I don't know yet. That depends largely upon what I find out from the brain of the lieutenant in charge of this patrol boat. There are two methods by which we can capture a battleship; one requiring the use of the *Violet*, the other the use of this scout. The information which I am about to acquire will enable me to determine which of the two plans entails the lesser amount of risk.

'There is a third method of procedure, of course; that is, to go back to Earth and duplicate one of their battleships ourselves, from the knowledge I shall have gained from their various brains concerning the apparatus, mechanisms, materials, and weapons of the Fenachrone. But that would take a long time and would be far from certain of success, because there would almost certainly be some essential facts that I would not have secured. Besides, I came out here to get one of their first-line space ships, and I intend to do it.'

With no sign of distaste DuQuesne coupled his brain to that of the dead lieutenant of the Fenachrone through the mechanical educator, and quite as casually as though he were merely giving Loring another lesson in Fenachrone matters did he begin systematically to explore the intricate convolutions of that fearsome brain. But after only ten minutes' study he was interrupted by the brazen clang of the emergency alarm. He flipped off the power of the educator, discarded his headset, acknowledged the call, and watched the recorder as it rapped out its short, insistent message.

'Something is going on here that was not on my program,' he announced to the alert but quiescent Loring. 'One should always be prepared for the unexpected, but this may run into something cataclysmic. The Fenachrone are being attacked from space, and all armed forces have been called into a defensive formation – Invasion Plan XB218, whatever that is. I'll have to look it up in the code.'

The desk of the commanding officer was a low, heavily built cabinet of metal. DuQuesne strode over to it, operated rapidly the levers and dials of its combination lock and took from one of the compartments the 'Code' – a polygonal framework of engraved metal bars and sliders, resembling somewhat an Earthly multiplex squirrel-cage slide rule.

'X – B – Two – One – Eight.' Although DuQuesne had never before seen such an instrument, the knowledge taken from the brains of the dead officers rendered him perfectly familiar with it, and his long and powerful fingers set up the indicated defense plan as rapidly and as surely as those of any Fenachrone could have done it. He revolved the mechanism in his hands, studying every plane surface, scowling blackly in concentration.

'Munition plants – shall – so-and-so — We don't care about that. Reserves – zones – ordnance – commissary – defensive screens ... Oh, here we are! Scout ships. Instead of patrolling a certain volume of space, each scout ship takes up a fixed post just inside the outer detector zone. Twenty times as many on duty, too – enough so that they will be only about ten thousand miles apart – and each ship is to lock high-power detector screens and visiplate and recorder beams with all its neighbors.

'Also, there is to be a first-class battleship acting as mother ship, protector, and reserve for each twenty-five scouts. The nearest one is to be — Let's see, from here that would be only about twenty thousand miles over that way and about a hundred thousand miles down.'

'Does that change your plans, chief?'

'Since my plans were not made, I cannot say that it does – it changes the background, however, and introduces an element of danger that did not previously exist. It makes it impossible to go out through the detector zone – but it was practically impossible before, and we have no intention of going out, anyway, until we possess a vessel powerful enough to go through any barrage they can lay down. On the other hand, there is bound to be a certain amount of confusion in placing so many vessels, and that fact will operate to make the capture of our battleship much easier than it would have been otherwise.'

'What danger exists that wasn't there before?' demanded Loring.

'The danger that the whole planet may be blown up,' DuQuesne returned bluntly. 'Any nation or race attacking from space would of course have atomic power, and any one with that power, could volatilize any planet by simply dropping a bomb on it from open space. They might want to colonize it, of course, in which case they wouldn't destroy it, but it is always safest to plan for the worst possible contingencies.'

'How do you figure on doing us any good if the whole world explodes?' Loring lighted a cigarette, his hand steady and his face pinkly unruffled. 'If she goes up, it looks as if we go out, like that – *puff!*' And he blew out the match.

'Not at all, Doll,' DuQuesne reassured him. 'An atomic explosion starting on the surface and propagating downward would hardly develop enough power to drive anything material much, if any, faster than light, and no explosion wave, however violent, can exceed that velocity. The *Violet*, as you know, although not to be compared with even this scout as a fighter, has an acceleration of five times that, so that we could outrun the explosion in her. However, if we stay in our own ship, we shall certainly be found and blown out of space as soon as this defensive formation is completed.

'On the other hand, this ship carries full Fenachrone power of offense and defense, and we should be safe enough from detection in it, at least for as long a time as we shall need it. Since these small ships are designed for purely local scout work, though, they are comparatively slow and would certainly be destroyed in any such cosmic explosion as is manifestly a possibility. That possibility is very remote, it is true, but it should be taken into consideration.'

'So what? You're talking yourself around a circle, right back to where you started from.'

'Only considering the thing from all angles.' DuQuesne was unruffled. 'We have lots of time, since it will take them quite a while to perfect this formation. To finish the summing up – we want to use this vessel, but is it safe? It is. Why? Because the Fenachrone, having had atomic energy themselves for a long time, are thoroughly familiar with its possibilities and have undoubtedly perfected screens through which no such bomb could penetrate.

'Furthermore, we can install the highspeed drive in this ship in a few days – I gave you all the dope on it over the educator, you know – so that we'll be safe, whatever happens. That's the safest plan, and it will work. So you move the stores and our most necessary personal belongings in here while I'm figuring out an orbit for the *Violet*. We don't want her anywhere near us, and yet we want her to be within reaching distance while we are piloting this scout ship of ours to the place where she is supposed to be in Plan XB218.'

'What are you going to do that for – to give them a chance to knock us off?'

'No. I need some time to study these brains, and it will take some time for that battleship mother ship of ours to get into her assigned position, where we can steal her most easily.' Du-Quesne, however, did not at once remove his headset, but remained standing, where he was, silent and thoughtful.

'Uh-huh,' agreed Loring. 'I'm thinking the same thing you are. Suppose that it *is* Seaton that's got them all hot and bothered this way?'

'The thought has occurred to me several times, and I have considered it at length,' DuQuesne admitted at last. 'However, I have concluded that it is not Seaton. For if it is, he must have a lot more stuff than I think he has. I do not believe that he can possibly have learned that much in the short time he has had to work in. I may be wrong, of course; but the immediately necessary steps toward the seizure of that battleship remain unchanged whether I am right or wrong; whether or not Seaton was the cause of this disturbance.'

The conversation definitely at an end, Loring again encased himself in his space suit and set to work. For hours he labored, silently and efficiently, at transferring enough of their Earthly possessions and stores to render possible an extended period of living aboard the vessel of the Fenachrone.

He had completed that task and was assembling the apparatus and equipment necessary for the rebuilding of the power plant before DuQuesne finished the long and complex computations involved in determining the direction and magnitude of the force required to give the *Violet* the exact trajectory he desired. The problem was finally solved and checked, however, and DuQuesne rose to his feet, closing his book of nine-place logarithms with a snap.

'All done with the *Violet*, Doll?' he asked, donning his armor. 'Yes.'

'Fine! I'll go aboard and push her off, after we do a little stage-setting here. Take that body there – I don't need it any more, since he didn't know much of anything, anyway – and toss it into the nose compartment. Then shut that bulkhead door, tight. I'm going to drill a couple of holes through there from the *Violet* before I give her the gun.'

'I see – going to make us *look* disabled, whether we are or not, huh?'

'Exactly! We've got to have a good excuse for our visirays

being out of order. I can make reports all right on the communicator, and send and receive code messages and orders, but we certainly couldn't stand a close-up inspection on a visiplate. Also, we've got to have some kind of an excuse for signaling to and approaching our mother battleship. We will have been hit and punctured by a meteorite. Pretty thin excuse, but it probably will serve for as long a time as we will need.'

After DuQuesne had made sure that the small compartment in the prow of the vessel contained nothing of use to them, the body of one of the Fenachrone was thrown carelessly into it, the air-tight bulkhead was closed and securely locked, and the chief marauder stepped into the airlock.

'As soon as I get her exactly on course and velocity, I'll step out into space and you can pick me up,' he directed briefly, and was gone.

In the *Violet*'s engine room DuQuesne released the anchoring attractor beams and backed off to a few hundred yards' distance. He spun a couple of wheels briefly, pressed a switch, and from the *Violet*'s heaviest needle-ray projector there flashed out against the prow of the scout patrol a pencil of incredibly condensed destruction.

Dunark, the crown prince of Kondal, had developed that stabbing ray as the culminating ultimate weapon of ten thousand years of Osnomian warfare: and, driven by even the comparatively feeble energies known to the denizens of the Green System before Seaton's advent, no known substance had been able to resist for more than a moment its corrosively, annihilatingly poignant thrust.

And now this furious stiletto of pure energy, driven by the full power of four hundred pounds of disintegrating atomic copper, at this point-blank range, was hurled against the mere inch of transparent material which comprised the skin of the tiny cruiser. DuQuesne expected no opposition, for with a beam less potent by far he had consumed utterly a vessel built of arenak – arenak, that Osnomian synthetic which is five hundred times as strong, tough, and hard as Earth's strongest, toughest, and hardest alloy steel.

Yet that annihilating needle of force struck that transparent surface and rebounded from it in scintillating torrents of fire.

Struck and rebounded, struck and clung; boring in almost imperceptibly as its irresistible energy tore apart, electron by electron, the surprisingly obdurate substance of the cruiser's wall. For that substance was the ultimate synthetic – the one limiting material possessing the utmost measure of strength, hardness, tenacity, and rigidity theoretically possible to any substance built up from the building blocks of ether-borne electrons. This substance, developed by the master scientists of the Fenachrone, was in fact identical with the Norlaminian synthetic metal, inoson, from which Rovol and his aids had constructed for Seaton his gigantic ship of space – *Skylark Three*.

For five long minutes DuQuesne held that terrific beam against the point of attack, then shut it off; for it had consumed less than half the thickness of the scout patrol's outer skin. True, the focal area of the energy was an almost invisibly violet glare of incandescence, so intensely hot that the concentric shading off through blinding white, yellow, and bright-red heat brought the zone of dull red far down the side of the vessel; but that awful force had had practically no effect upon the spaceworthiness of the stanch little craft.

'No use, Loring!' DuQuesne spoke calmly into the transmitter inside his face-plate. True scientist that he was, he neither expressed nor felt anger or bafflement when an idea failed to work, but abandoned it promptly and completely, without rancor or repining. 'No possible meteorite could puncture that shell. Stand by!'

He inspected the power meters briefly, made several readings through the filar micrometer of number six visiplate, and checked the vernier readings of the great circles of the gyroscopes against the figures in his notebook. Then, assured that the *Violet* was following precisely the predetermined course, he entered the airlock, waved a bloated arm at the watchful Loring, and coolly stepped off into space. The heavy outer door clanged shut behind him, and the globular ship of space rocketed onward; while DuQuesne fell with a sickening acceleration toward the mighty planet of the Fenachrone, so many thousands of miles below.

That fall did not long endure. Loring, now a space pilot

second to none, had held his vessel even with the *Violet*; matching exactly her course, pace, and acceleration at a distance of barely a hundred feet. He had cut off all his power as DuQuesne's right foot left the Osnomian vessel, and now falling man and plunging scout ship plummeted downward together at the same mad pace; the man drifting slowly toward the ship because of the slight energy of his step into space from the *Violet*'s side and beginning slowly to turn over as he fell. So good had been Loring's spacemanship that the scout did not even roll; DuQuesne was still opposite her starboard airlock when Loring stood in its portal and tossed a space line to his superior. This line – a small, tightly stranded cable of fiber capable of retaining its strength and pliability in the heatless depths of space – snapped out and curled around DuQuesne's bulging space suit.

'I thought you'd use an attractor, but this is probably better, at that,' DuQuesne commented, as he seized the line in a mailed fist.

'Yeah. I haven't had much practice with them on delicate and accurate work. If I had missed you with this line I could have thrown it again; but if I missed this opening with you on a beam and shaved your suit off on this sharp edge, I figured it'd be just too bad.'

The two men again in the control room and the vessel once more leveled out in headlong flight, Loring broke the silence:

'That idea of being punctured by a meteorite didn't pan out so heavy. How would it be to have one of the crew go space-crazy and wreck the boat from the inside? They do that sometimes, don't they?'

'Yes, they do. That's an idea – thanks. I'll study up on the symptoms. I have a lot more studying to do, anyway – there's a lot of stuff I haven't got yet. This metal, for instance – we couldn't possibly build a Fenachrone battleship on Earth. I had no idea that any possible substance could be as resistant as the shell of this ship is. Of course, there are many unexplored areas in these brains here, and quite a few high-class brains aboard our mother ship that I haven't even seen yet. The secret of the composition of this metal must be in some of them.'

'Well, while you're getting their stuff, I suppose I'd better fly at that job of rebuilding our drive. I'll have time enough all right, you think?'

'Certain of it. I have learned that their system is ample. It's automatic and foolproof. They have warning long before anything can possibly happen. They can, and do, spot trouble over a light-week away, so their plans allow one week to perfect their defenses. You can change the power plant over in three or four days, so we're well in the clear on that. I may not be done with my studies by that time, but I shall have learned enough to take effective action. You work on the drive and keep house. I will study Fenachrone science and so on, answer calls, make reports, and arrange the details of what is to happen when we come within the volume of space assigned to our mother ship.'

Thus for days each man devoted himself to his task. Loring rebuilt the power plant of the short-ranging scout patrol into the terric open-space drive of the first-line battleships and performed the simple routines of their Spartan housekeeping. DuQuesne cut himself short on sleep and spent every possible hour in transferring to his own brain every worthwhile bit of knowledge which had been possessed by the commander and crew of the patrol ship which he had captured.

Periodically, however, he would close the sending circuit and report the position and progress of his vessel, precisely on time and observing strictly all the military minutiae called for by the manual – the while watching appreciatively and with undisguised admiration the flawless execution of that stupendous plan of defense.

The change-over finished, Loring went in search of DuQuesne, whom he found performing a strenuous setting-up exercise. The scientist's face was pale, haggard, and drawn.

'What's the matter, chief?' Loring asked. 'You look kind of peaked.'

'Peaked is good – I'm just about bushed. This thing of getting a hundred and ninety years of solid education in a few days would hardly come under the heading of light amusement. Are you done?'

'Done and checked – O.K.'

'Good! I am, too. It won't take us long to get to our destination now; our mother ship should be just about at her post by this time.'

Now that the vessel was approaching the location assigned to it in the plan, and since DuQuesne had already taken from the brains of the dead Fenachrone all that he wanted of their knowledge, he threw their bodies into space and rayed them out of existence. The other corpse he left lying, a bloated and ghastly mass, in the forward compartment as he prepared to send in what was to be his last flight report to the office of the general in command of the plan of defense.

'His high-mightiness doesn't know it, but that is the last call he is going to get from this unit,' DuQuesne remarked, leaving the sender and stepping over to the control board. 'Now we can leave our prescribed course and go where we can do ourselves some good. First, we'll find the *Violet*. I haven't heard of her being spotted and destroyed as a menace to navigation, so we'll look her up and start her off for home.'

'Why?' asked the henchman. 'Thought we were all done with her.'

'We probably are, but if it should turn out that Seaton is back of all this excitement, our having her may save us a trip back to the Earth. Ah, there she is, right on schedule! I'll bring her alongside and set her controls on a distance-squared decrement, so that when she gets out into free space she'll have a constant velocity.'

'Think she'll get out into free space through those screens?'

'They will detect her, of course, but when they see that she is an abandoned derelict and headed out of their system they'll probably let her go. It will be no great loss, of course, if they do burn her.'

Thus it came about that the spherical cruiser of the void shot away from the then feeble gravitation of the vast but distant planet of the Fenachrone. Through the outer detector screens she tore. Searching beams explored her instantly and thoroughly; but since she was so evidently a deserted hulk and since the Fenachrone cared nothing now for impediments to navigation beyond their screens, she was not pursued.

On and on she sped, her automatic controls reducing her power in exact ratio to the square of the distance attained; on and on, her automatic deflecting detectors swinging her around suns and solar systems and back upon her original right line; on and on toward the Green System, the central system of this the First Galaxy – our own native island universe.

3 : DuQuesne Captures a Battleship

'Now we'll get ready to take that battleship.' DuQuesne turned to his aid as the *Violet* disappeared from their sight. 'Your suggestion that one of the crew of this ship could have gone space-crazy was sound, and I have planned our approach to the mother ship on that basis.

'We must wear Fenachrone space suits for three reasons: First, because it is the only possible way to make us look even remotely like them, and we shall have to stand a casual inspection. Second, because it is general orders that all Fenachrone soldiers must wear suits while at their posts in space. Third, because we shall have lost most of our air. You can wear one of their suits without any difficulty – the surplus circumference will not trouble you very much. I, on the contrary, cannot even get into one, since they're almost a foot too short.

'I must have a suit on, though, before we board the battle-ship; so I shall wear my own, with one of theirs over it – with the feet cut off so that I can get it on. Since I shall not be able to stand up or to move around without giving everything away because of my length, I'll have to be unconscious and folded up so that my height will not be too apparent, and you will have to be the star performer during the first act.

'But this detailed instruction by word of mouth takes altogether too much time. Put on this headset and I'll shoot you the whole scheme, together with whatever additional Fenachrone knowledge you will need to put the act across.'

A brief exchange of thoughts and of ideas followed. Then, every detail made clear, the two Tellurians donned the space suits of the very short, but enormously wide and thick, monstrosities in semihuman form who were so bigotedly working toward their day of universal conquest.

DuQuesne picked up in his doubly mailed hands a massive bar of metal. 'Ready, Doll? When I swing this we cross the Rubicon.'

'It's all right by me. All or nothing – shoot the works!'

DuQuesne swung his mighty bludgeon aloft, and as it

descended the telemental recorder sprang into a shower of shattered tubes, flying coils, and broken insulation. The visiray apparatus went next, followed in swift succession by the superficial air controls, the map cases, and practically everything else that was breakable; until it was clear to even the most casual observer that a madman had in truth wrought his frenzied will throughout the room. One final swing wrecked the controls of the airlocks, and the atmosphere within the vessel began to whistle out into the vacuum of space through the broken bleeder tubes.

'All right, Doll, do your stuff!' DuQuesne directed crisply, and threw himself headlong into a corner, falling into an inert, grotesque huddle.

Loring, now impersonating the dead commanding officer of the scout ship, sat down at the manual sender, which had not been seriously damaged, and in true Fenachrone fashion laid a beam to the mother ship.

'Scout ship K3296, Sublieutenant Grenimar commanding, sending emergency distress message,' he tapped out fluently. 'Am not using telemental recorder, as required by regulations, because nearly all instruments wrecked. Private 244C14, on watch, suddenly seized with space insanity, smashed air valves, instruments, and controls. Opened lock and leaped out into space. I was awake and got into suit before my room lost pressure. My other man, 397B42, was unconscious when I reached him, but believe I got him into his suit soon enough so that his life can be saved by prompt aid. 244C14 of course dead, but I recovered his body as per general orders and am saving it so that brain lesions may be studied by College of Science. Repaired this manual sender and have ship under partial control. Am coming toward you, decelerating to stop in fifteen minutes. Suggest you handle this ship with beam when approach as I have no fine controls. Signing off – K3296.'

'Superdreadnought Z12Q, acknowledging emergency distress message of scout ship K3296,' came almost instant answer. 'Will meet you and handle you as suggested. Signing off – Z12Q.'

Rapidly the two ships of space drew together; the patrol boat now stationary with respect to the planet, the huge battleship decelerating at maximum. Three enormous beams reached out and, held at prow, midsection, and stern, the tiny flier was drawn rapidly but carefully against the towering side of her mother ship. The double seals engaged and locked; the massive doors began to open.

Now came the most crucial point of DuQuesne's whole scheme. For that warship carried a complement of nearly a hundred men, and ten or a dozen of them – the lock commander, surgeons, and orderlies certainly, and possibly a corps of mechanics as well – would be massed in the airlock room behind those slowly opening barriers. But in that scheme's very audacity lay its great strength – its almost complete assurance of success. For what Fenachrone, with the inborn consciousness of superiority that was his heritage, would even dream that two members of any alien race would have the sheer, brazen effrontery to dare to attack a full-manned Class Z superdreadnought, one of the most formidable structures that had ever lifted its stupendous mass into the ether?

But DuQuesne so dared. Direct action had always been his forte. Apparently impossible odds had never daunted him. He had always planned his coups carefully, then followed those plans coldly and ruthlessly to their logical and successful conclusions. Two men could do this job very nicely, and would so do it. DuQuesne had chosen Loring with care. Therefore he lay at ease in his armor in front of the slowly opening portal, calmly certain that the iron nerves of his assassin aid would not weaken for even the instant necessary to disrupt his carefully laid plan.

As soon as the doors had opened sufficiently to permit ingress, Loring went through them slowly, carrying the supposedly unconscious man with care. But once inside the opaque walls of the lock room, that slowness became activity incarnate. DuQuesne sprang instantly to his full height, and before the clustered officers could even perceive that anything was amiss, four sure hands had trained upon them the deadliest hand weapons known to the science of their own race.

Since DuQuesne was overlooking no opportunity of acquiring knowledge, the heads were spared; but as the four furious blasts of vibratory energy tore through those massive bodies, making of their every internal organ a mass of disorganized protoplasmic pulp, every Fenachrone in the room fell lifeless to the floor before he could move a hand in self-defense.

Dropping his weapons, DuQuesne wrenched off his helmet, while Loring with deft hands bared the head of the senior officer of the group upon the floor. Headsets flashed out – were clamped into place – dials were set – the scientist shot power into the tubes, transferring into his own brain an entire section of the dead brain before him.

His senses reeled under the shock, but he recovered quickly, and even as he threw off the phones Loring slammed down over his head the helmet of the Fenachrone. DuQuesne was now commander of the airlocks, and the break in communication had been of such duration that not the slightest suspicion had been aroused. He snapped out mental orders to the distant power room, the side of the vessel opened, and the scout ship was drawn within.

'All tight, sir,' he reported to the captain, and the Z12Q began to retrace her path in space.

DuQuesne's first objective had been attained without untoward incident. The second objective, the control room, might present more difficulty, since its occupants would be scattered. However, to neutralize this difficulty, the Earthly attackers could work with bare hands and thus with the weapons with which both were thoroughly familiar. Removing their gauntlets, the two men ran lightly toward that holy of Fenachrone holies, the control room. Its door was guarded, but DuQuesne had known that it would be – wherefore the guards went down before they could voice a challenge. The door crashed open and four heavy, long-barreled automatics began vomiting forth a leaden storm of death. Those pistols were gripped in accustomed and steady hands; those hands in turn were actuated by the ruthless brains of heartless, conscienceless, and merciless killers.

His second and major objective gained, DuQuesne proceeded at once to consolidate his position. Pausing only to learn from the brain of the dead captain the exact technique of procedure, he summoned into the sanctum, one at a time, every member of the gigantic vessel's crew. Man after man they came, in answer to the summons of their all-powerful captain – and man after man they died.

'Take the educator and get some of their surgeon's skill,' DuQuesne directed curtly, after the last member of the crew had been accounted for. 'Take off the heads and put them where they'll keep. Throw the rest of the rubbish out. Never mind about this captain – I want to study him.'

Then, while Loring busied himself at his grisly task, Du-Quesne sat at the captain's bench, read the captain's brain, and sent in to general headquarters the captain's regular routine reports.

'All cleaned up. Now what?' Loring was as spick-and-span, as calmly unruffled, as though he were reporting in one of the private rooms of the Perkins Cafe. 'Start back to the Earth?'

'Not yet.' Even though DuQuesne had captured his battle-ship, thereby performing the almost impossible, he was not yet content. 'There are a lot of things to learn here yet, and I think that we had better stay here as long as possible and learn them; provided we can do so without incurring any extra risks. As far as actual flight goes, two men can handle this ship as well as a hundred, since her machinery is all automatic. Therefore we can run away any time.

'We could not fight, however, as it takes about thirty men to handle her weapons. But fighting would do no good, anyway, because they could outnumber us a hundred to one in a few hours. All of which means that if we go out beyond the detector screens we will not be able to come back – we had better stay here, so as to be able to take advantage of any favorable developments.'

He fell silent, frowningly concentrated upon some problem obscure to his companion. At last he went to the main control panel and busied himself with a device of photo cells, coils, and kino bulbs; whereupon Loring set about preparing a long-delayed meal.

'It's all hot, chief – come and get it,' the aid invited, when he saw that his superior's immediate task was done. 'What's the idea? Didn't they have enough controls there already?'

'The idea is, Doll, not to take any unnecessary chances. Ah, this goulash hits the spot!' DuQuesne ate appreciatively for a few minutes in silence, then went on: 'Three things may happen to interfere with the continuation of our search for knowledge. First, since we are now in command of a Fenachrone mother ship, I have to report to headquarters on the telemental recorder, and they may catch me in a slip any minute, which will mean a massed attack. Second, the enemy may break through the Fenachrone defenses and precipitate a general engagement. Third, there is still the bare possibility of that cosmic explosion I told you about.

'In that connection, it is quite obvious than an atomic explosion wave of that type would be propagated with the velocity of light. Therefore, even though our ship could run away from it, since we have an acceleration of five times that velocity, yet we could not see that such an explosion had occurred until the wave-front had reached us. Then, of course, it would be too late to do anything about it, because what an atomic explosion wave would do to the dense material of this battleship would be simply nobody's business.

'We might get away if one of us had his hands actually on the controls and had his eyes and his brain right on the job, but that is altogether too much to expect of flesh and blood. No brain can be maintained at its highest pitch for any length of time.'

'So what?' Loring said laconically. If the chief was not worried about these things, the henchman would not be worried either.

'So I rigged up a detector that is both automatic and instantaneous. At the first touch of any unusual vibration it will throw in the full space drive and will shoot us directly away from the point of disturbance. Now we shall be absolutely safe, no matter what happens.

'We are safe from any possible attack; neither the Fenachrone nor our common enemy, whoever they are, can harm us. We are safe even from the atomic explosion of the entire planet. We shall stay here until we get everything that we want. Then we shall go back to the Green System. We shall find Seaton.'

His entire being grew grim and implacable, his voice became harder and colder even than its hard and cold wont. 'We shall blow him clear out of the ether. The world – yes, whatever I want of the galaxy – shall be *mine*!'

4: A World is Destroyed

Only a few days were required for the completion of Du-Quesne's Fenachrone education, since not many of the former officers of the battleship could add much to the already vast knowledge possessed by the Terrestrial scientist. Therefore the time soon came when he had nothing to occupy either his vigorous body or his voracious mind, and the self-imposed idleness irked his active spirit sorely.

'If nothing is going to happen out here we might as well get started back; this present situation is intolerable,' he declared to Loring, and proceeded to lay spy rays to various strategic points of the enormous shell of defense, and even to the sacred precincts of headquarters itself.

'They will probably catch me at this, and when they do it will blow the lid off; but since we are all ready for the break we don't care now how soon it comes. There's something gone sour somewhere, and it may do us some good to know something about it.'

'Sour? Along what line?'

'The mobilization has slowed down. The first phase went off beautifully, you know, right on schedule; but lately things have slowed down. That doesn't seem just right, since their plans are all dynamic, not static. Of course general headquarters isn't advertising it to us outlying captains, but I think I can sense an undertone of uneasiness. That's why I am doing this little job of spying, to get the low-down ... Ah, I thought so! Look here, Doll! See those gaps on the defense map? Over half of their big ships are not in position – look at those tracer reports – not a battleship that was out in space has come back, and a lot of them are more than a week overdue. I'll say that's something we ought to know about —'

'Observation Officer of the Z12Q, attention!' snapped from the tight-beam headquarters communicator. 'Cut off those spy rays and report yourself under arrest for treason!'

'Not today,' DuQuesne drawled. 'Besides, I can't – I am in command here now.'

'Open your visiplate to full aperture!' The staff officer's voice was choked with fury; never in his long life had he been so grossly insulted by a mere captain of the line.

DuQuesne opened the plate, remarking to Loring as he did so; 'This is the blow-off, all right. No possible way of stalling him off now, even if I wanted to; and I really want to tell them a few things before we shove off.'

'Where are the men who should be at stations?' the furious voice demanded.

'Dead,' DuQuesne replied laconically.

'Dead! And you have reported nothing amiss?' He turned from his own microphone, but DuQuesne and Loring could hear his savage commands:

'K1427 – Order the twelfth squadron to bring in the Z12Q!'

He spoke again to the rebellious and treasonable observer: 'And you have made your helmet opaque to the rays of this plate, another violation of the code. Take it off!' The speaker fairly rattled under the bellowing voice of the outraged general. 'If you live long enough to get here, you will pay the full penalty for treason, insubordination, and conduct unbecom—'

'Oh, shut up, you yapping nincompoop!' snapped DuQuesne.

Wrenching off his helmet, he thrust his blackly forbidding face directly before the visiplate; so that the raging officer stared, from a distance of only eighteen inches, not into the cowed and frightened face of a guiltily groveling subordinate, but into the proud and sneering visage of Marc C. DuQuesne, of Earth.

And DuQuesne's whole being radiated open and supreme contempt, the most gallingly nauseous dose possible to inflict upon any member of that race of self-styled supermen, the Fenachrone. As he stared at the Earthman the general's tirade broke off in the middle of a word and he fell back speechless – robbed, it seemed, almost of consciousness by the shock.

'You asked for it – you got it – now just what are you going to do about it?' DuQuesne spoke aloud, to render even more trenchantly cutting the crackling mental comments as they leaped across space, each thought lashing the officer like the biting, tearing tip of a bull-whip.

'Better men than you have been beaten by overconfidence,' he went on, 'and better plans than yours have come to nothing through underestimating the resources in brain and power of the opposition. You are not the first race in the history of the universe to go down because of false pride, and you will not be the last. You thought that my comrade and I had been taken and killed. You thought so because *I* wanted you so to think. In reality we took that scout ship, and when we wanted it we took this battleship as easily.

'We have been here, in the very heart of your defense system for ten days. We have obtained everything that we set out to get; we have learned everything that we set out to learn. If we wished to take it, your entire planet could offer us no more resistance than did these vessels, but we do not want it.

'Also, after due deliberation, we have decided that the universe would be much better off without any Fenachrone in it. Therefore your race will of course soon disappear; and since we do not want your planet, we will see to it that no one else will want it, at least for some few eons of time to come. Think *that* over, as long as you are able to think. Good-bye!'

DuQuesne cut off the visiray with a vicious twist and turned to Loring. 'Pure boloney, of course!' he sneered. 'But as long as they don't know that fact it'll probably hold them for a while.'

'Better start drifting for home, hadn't we? They'll be coming out after us.'

'We certainly had.' DuQuesne strolled leisurely across the room toward the controls. 'We hit them hard, in a mighty tender spot, and they will make it highly unpleasant for us if we linger around here much longer. But we are in no danger. There is no tracer on this ship – they use them only on long-distance cruisers – so they'll have no idea where to look for us. Also, I don't believe that they'll even try to chase us, because I gave them a lot to think about for some time to come, even if it wasn't true.'

But DuQuesne had spoken far more truly than he knew – his 'boloney' was in fact a coldly precise statement of an awful truth even then about to be made manifest. For at that very moment Dunark of Osnome was reaching for the switch whose closing would send a detonating current through the thousands of tons of sensitized atomic copper already placed by Seaton in their deep-buried emplantments upon the noisome planet of the Fenachrone.

DuQuesne knew that the outlying vessels of the monsters had not returned to base, but he did not know that Seaton had destroyed them, one and all, in open space; he did not know that his arch-foe was the being who was responsible for the failure of the Fenachrone space ships to come back from their horrible voyages.

Upon the other hand, while Seaton knew that there were battleships afloat in the ether within the protecting screens of the planet, he had no inkling that one of those very battleships was manned by his two bitterest and most vindictive enemies, the official and completely circumstantial report of whose death by cremation he had witnessed such a few days before.

DuQuesne strolled across the floor of the control room, and in mid-step became weightless, floating freely in the air. The planet had exploded, and the outermost fringe of the wave-front of the atomic disintegration, propagated outwardly into spherical space with the velocity of light, had impinged upon the all-seeing and ever-watchful mechanical eye which DuQuesne had so carefully installed. But only that outermost fringe, composed solely of light and ultra-light, had touched that eye. The relay – an electronic beam – had been deflected instantaneously, demanding of the governors their terrific maximum of power, away from the doomed world. The governor had responded in a space of time to be measured only in fractional millionths of a second, and the vessel leaped effortlessly and almost instantaneously into an acceleration of five light-velocities, urged onward by the full power of the space-annihilating drive of the Fenachrone.

The eyes of DuQuesne and Loring had had time really to see nothing whatever. There was the barest perceptible flash of the intolerable brilliance of an exploding universe, succeeded in the very instant of its perception – yes, even before its real perception – by the utter blackness of the complete absence of all light whatever as the space drive automatically went into action and hurled the great vessel away from the all-destroying wave-front of the atomic explosion.

As has been said, there were many battleships within the

screens of the planet, supporting a horde of scout ships according to Invasion Plan XB218; but of all these vessels and of all things Fenachrone, only two escaped the incredible violence of the holocaust. One was the immense space ship of Ravindau the scientist, which had for days been hurtling through space upon its way to a far-distant galaxy; the other was the first-line battleship carrying DuQuesne and his killer aid, which had been snatched from the very teeth of that indescribable cosmic cataclysm by the instantaneous operation of DuQuesne's automatic relays.

Everything on or near the planet had of course been destoyed instantly, and even the fastest battleship, farthest removed from the disintegrating world, was overwhelmed. For to living eyes, staring however attentively into ordinary visiplates, there had been practically no warning at all, since the wave-front of atomic disruption was propagated with the velocity of light and therefore followed very closely indeed behind the narrow fringe of visible light which heralded its coming.

Even if one of the dazed commanders had known the meaning of the coruscant blaze of brilliance which was the immediate forerunner of destruction, he would have been helpless to avert it, for no hands of flesh and blood, human or Fenachrone, could possibly have thrown switches rapidly enough to have escaped from the advancing wave-front of disruption; and at the touch of that frightful wave every atom of substance, alike of vessel, contents, and hellish crew, became resolved into its component electrons and added its contribution of energy to the stupendous cosmic catastrophe.

Even before his foot had left the floor in free motion, however, DuQuesne realized exactly what had happened. His keen eyes saw the flash of blinding incandescence announcing a world's ending and sent to his keen brain a picture; and in the instant of perception that brain had analyzed that picture and understood its every implication and connotation. Therefore he only grinned sardonically at the phenomena which left the slower-minded Loring dazed and breathless.

He continued to grin as the battleship hurtled onward through the void at a pace beside which that of any ether-borne wave, even that of such a Titanic disturbance as the atomic explosion of an entire planet, was the veriest crawl.

At last, however, Loring comprehended what had happened. 'Oh, it exploded, huh?' he ejaculated.

'It most certainly did.' The scientist's grin grew diabolical. 'My statements to them came true, even though I did not have anything to do with their fruition. However, these events prove that caution is all right in its place – it pays big dividends at times. I'm very glad, of course, that the Fenachrone have been definitely taken out of the picture.'

Utterly callous, DuQuesne neither felt nor expressed the slightest sign of pity for the race of beings so suddenly snuffed out of existence. 'Their removal at this time will undoubtedly save me a lot of trouble later on,' he added, 'but the whole thing certainly gives me furiously to think, as the French say. It was done with a sensitized atomic copper bomb, of course; but I should like very much to know who did it, and why; and, above all, how they were able to make the approach.'

'Personally, I still think it was Seaton,' the baby-faced murderer put it calmly. 'No reason for thinking so, except that whenever anything impossible has been pulled off anywhere that I ever heard of, he was the guy that did it. Call it a hunch, if you want to.'

'It may have been Seaton, of course, even though I can't really think so.' DuQuesne frowned blackly in concentration. 'It may have been accidental – started by the explosion of an ammunition dump or something of the kind – but I believe that even less than I do the other. It couldn't have been any race of beings from any other planet of this system, since they are all bare of life, the Fenachrone having killed off all the other races ages ago and not caring to live on the other planets themselves. No; I still think that it was some enemy from outer space; although my belief that it could not have been Seaton is weakening.

'However, with this ship we can probably find out in short order who it was, whether it was Seaton or any possible outside race. We are far enough away now to be out of danger from that explosion, so we'll slow down, circle around, and find out whoever it was that touched it off.'

He slowed the mad pace of the cruiser until the firmament behind them once more became visible, to see that the system of the Fenachrone was now illuminated by a splendid double sun. Sending out a full series of ultra-powered detector screens, DuQuesne scanned the instruments narrowly. Every meter remained dead, its needle upon zero; not a sign of radiation could be detected upon any communicator or power band; the ether was empty for millions upon untold millions of miles. He then put on power and cruised at higher and higher velocities, describing a series of enormous looping circles throughout the space surrounding that entire solar system.

Around and around the flaming double sun, rapidly becoming first a double star and then merely a faint point of light, DuQuesne urged the Fenachrone battleship, but his screens remained cold and unresponsive. No ship of the void was operating in all that vast volume of ether; no sign of man or of any of his works was to be found throughout it.

DuQuesne then extended his detectors to the terrific maximum of their unthinkable range, increased his already frightful acceleration to its absolute limit, and cruised madly onward in already vast and ever-widening spirals until a grim conclusion forced itself upon his consciousness. Unwilling though he was to believe it, he was forced finally to recognize an appalling fact. The enemy, whoever he might have been, must have been operating from a distance immeasurably greater than any that even DuQuesne's new-found knowledge could believe possible; abounding though it was in astounding data concerning superscientific weapons of destruction.

He again cut their acceleration down to a touring rate, adjusted his automatic alarms and signals, and turned to Loring, his face grim and hard.

'They must have been farther away than even any of the Fenchrone physicists would have believed possible,' he stated flatly. 'It looks more and more like Seaton – he probably found some more high-class help somewhere. Temporarily, at least, I am stumped – but I do not stay stumped long. I shall find him if I have to comb the galaxy, star by star!'

Thus DuQuesne, not even dreaming what an incredibly inconceivable distance from their galaxy Seaton was to attain; nor what depths of extradimensional space Seaton was to traverse before they were again to stand face to face – cold black eyes staring straight into hard and level eyes of gray.

5: Thought – A Sixth-Order Wave

The mightiest space ship that had ever lifted her stupendous mass from any planet known to the humanity of this, the First Galaxy, was hurtling onward through the hard vacuum of intergalactic space. Around the *Skylark* there was nothing – no stars, no suns, no meteorites, no smallest particle of cosmic dust. The First Galaxy lay so far behind her that even its vast lens showed only as a dimly perceptible patch of light in the visiplates.

The Fenachrone space chart placed other galaxies to right of and to left of, above and below, the flying cruiser; but they were so infinitely distant that their light could scarcely reach the eyes of the Terrestrial wanderers.

So prodigious had been the velocity of the *Skylark*, when the last vessel of the Fenachrone had been destroyed, that she could not possibly have been halted until she had covered more than half the distance separating that galaxy from our own; and Seaton and Crane had agreed that this chance to visit it was altogether too good to be missed. Therefore the velocity of their vessel had been augmented rather than lessened, and for uneventful days and weeks, she had bored her terrific way through the incomprehensible nothingness of the intergalactic void.

After a few days of impatient waiting and of eager anticipation, Seaton had settled down into the friendly and companionable routine of the flight. But inaction palled upon his vigorous nature and, physical outlet denied, he began to delve deeper and deeper into the almost-unknown, scarcely plumbed recesses of his new mind – a mind stored with the accumulated knowledge of thousands of generations of the Rovol and of the Drasnik; generations of specialists in research in two widely separated fields of knowledge.

Thus it was that one morning Seaton prowled about aimlessly in brown abstraction, hands jammed deep into pockets, the while there rolled from his villainously reeking pipe blue clouds of fumes that might have taxed sorely a less efficient air-purifier than that boasted by the *Skylark*. Prowled, suddenly to dash across the control room to the immense keyboards of his fifth-order projector.

There he sat, hour after hour. Hands setting up incredibly complex integrals upon its inexhausible supply of keys and stops; gray eyes staring unseeingly into infinity he sat there; deaf, dumb, and blind to everything except the fascinatingly fathomless problem upon which he was so diligently at work.

Dinner time came and went, then supper time, then bedtime; and Dorothy strode purposefully toward the console, only to be led away, silently and quietly, by the watchful Crane.

'But he hasn't come up for air once today, Martin!' she protested, when they were in the private sitting room of the Cranes. 'And didn't you tell me yourself, that time back in Washington, to make him snap out of it whenever he started to pull off one of his wild marathon splurges of overwork?'

'Yes; I did,' Crane replied thoughtfully; 'but circumstances here and now are somewhat different from what they were then. I have no idea of what he is working out, but it is a problem of such complexity that in one process he used more than seven hundred factors, and it may well be that if he were to be interrupted now he could never recover that particular line of thought. Then, too, you must remember that he is now in such excellent physical condition that he is in no present danger. I would say to let him alone, for a while longer, at least.'

'All right, Martin, that's fine! I hated to disturb him, really – I would hate most awfully to derail an important train of thought.'

'Yes; let him concentrate a while,' urged Margaret. 'He hasn't indulged in one of those fits for weeks – Rovol wouldn't let him. I think it's a shame, too, because when he dives in like that after something he comes up with it in his teeth – when he really thinks, he does things. I don't see how those Norlaminians ever got anything done, when they always did their thinking by the clock and quit promptly at quitting time, even if it was right in the middle of an idea.'

'Dick can do more in an hour, the way he is working now, than Rovol of Rays could ever do in ten years!' Dorothy exclaimed with conviction. 'I'm going in to keep him company – he's more apt to be disturbed by my being gone than by having me there. Better come along, too, you two, just as though nothing was going on. We'll give him an hour or so yet, anyway.'

The trio then strolled back into the control room.

But Seaton finished his computations without interruption. Some time after midnight he transferred his integrated and assembled forces to an anchoring plunger, arose from his irksome chair, stretched mightily, and turned to the others, tired but triumphant.

'Folks, I think I've got something!' he cried. 'Kinda late, but it'll only take a couple of minutes to test it out, I'll put these nets over your heads, and then you all look into that viewing cabinet over there.'

Over his own head and shoulders Seaton draped a finely woven screen of silvery metal, connected by a stranded cable to a plug in his board; and after he had similarly invested his companions he began to manipulate dials and knobs.

As he did so the dark space of the cabinet became filled with a soft glow of light – a glow which resolved itself into color and form, a three-dimensional picture. In the background towered a snow-capped, beautifully symmetrical volcanic mountain; in the foreground were to be seen cherry trees in full bloom surrounding a small structure of unmistakable architecture; and through their minds swept fleeting flashes of poignant longing, amounting almost to nostalgia.

'Good heavens, Dick, what have you done now?' Dorothy broke out. 'I feel so homesick that I want to cry – and I don't care a bit whether I *ever* see Japan again or not!'

'These nets aren't perfect insulators, of course, even though I've got them grounded. There's some leakage. They'd have to be solid to stop all radiation. Leaks both ways, of course, so we're interfering with the picture a little too; but there's some outside interference that I can't discover yet.' Seaton thought aloud, rather than explained, as he shut off the power. 'Folks, we *have* got something! That's the sixth-order pattern, and *thought* is in that level! Those were *thoughts – Shiro's* thoughts.'

'But he's asleep, surely, by this time,' Dorothy protested.

'Sure he is, or he wouldn't be thinking those kind of thoughts. Must be dreaming – he's contented enough when he is awake.'

'How did you work it out?' asked Crane. 'You said, yourself, that it might well take lifetimes of research.'

'It would, ordinarily. Partly a hunch, partly dumb luck, but mostly a combination of two brains that upon Norlamin would ordinarily never touch the same subject anywhere. Rovol, who knows everything there is to be known about rays, and Drasnik, probably the greatest authority upon the mind that ever lived, both gave me a good share of their knowledge; and the combination turned out to be hot stuff, particularly in connection with this fifth-order keyboard. Now we can really do something!'

'But you had a sixth-order detector before,' Margaret put in. 'Why didn't we touch it off by thinking?'

'Too coarse – I see that, now. It wouldn't react to the extremely slight power of a thought-wave; only to the powerful impulses from a bar or from cosmic radiation. But I can build one now that will react to thought, and I'm going to; particularly since there was a little interference on that picture that I couldn't quite account for.' He turned back to the projector.

'You're coming to bed,' declared Dorothy with finality. 'You've done enough for one day.'

She had her way, but early the next morning Seaton was again at the keyboard, wearing a complex headset and driving a tenuous fabric of force far out into the void. After an hour or so he tensed suddenly, every sense concentrated upon something vaguely perceptible; something which became less and less nebulous as his steady fingers rotated micrometric dials in infinitesimal arcs.

'Come get a load of this!' he called at last. 'Mart, what would a planet – an inhabited planet, at that – be doing 'way out here, Heaven only knows how many light-centuries away from the nearest galaxy?'

The three donned headsets and seated themselves in their chairs in the base of the great projector. Instantly they felt projections of themselves hurled an incomprehensible distance out into empty space. But that weird sensation was not new; each was thoroughly accustomed to the feeling of duality incident to being in the *Skylark* in body, yet with a duplicate mentality carried by the projection to a point many light-years distant from his corporeal substance. Their mentalities, thus projected, felt a fleeting instant of unthinkable velocity, then hung poised above the surface of a small but dense planet, a planet utterly alone in that dreadful void.

But it was like no other planet with which the Terrestrial wanderers were familiar. It possessed neither air nor water, and it was entirely devoid of topographical features. It was merely a bare, mountainless, depthless sphere of rock and metal. Though sunless, it was not dark; it glowed with a strong, white light which emanated from the rocky soil itself. Nothing animate was visible, nor was there a sign that any form of life, animal or vegetable, had ever existed there.

'You can talk if you want to,' Seaton observed, noticing that Dorothy was holding back by main strength a torrent of words. 'They can't hear us – there's no audio in the circuit.'

'What do you mean by "they", Dick?' she demanded. 'You said it was an inhabited planet. That one isn't inhabited. It never was, and it can't possibly be, *ever!*'

'When I spoke I thought that it was inhabited, in the ordinary sense of the word, but I see now that it isn't,' he replied, quietly and thoughtfully. 'But they were there a minute ago, and they'll probably be back. Don't kid yourself, Dimples. It's inhabited, all right, and by somebody we don't know much about – or rather, by something that we knew once – altogether too well.'

'The pure intellectuals,' Crane stated, rather than asked.

'Yes; and that accounts for the impossible location of the planet, too. They probably materialized it out there, just for the exercise. There, they're coming back. Feel 'em?'

Vivid thoughts, for the most part incomprehensible, flashed from the headsets into their minds; and instantly the surroundings of their projections changed. With the speed of thought a building materialized upon that barren ground, and they found themselves looking into a brilliantly lighted and spacious hall. Walls of alabaster, giving forth a living, almost fluid light. Tapestries, whose fantastically intricate designs changed from moment to moment into ever new and ever more amazingly complex delineations. Gem-studded fountains, whose plumes and gorgeous sprays of dancing liquid obeyed no Earthly laws of mechanics. Chairs and benches, writhing, changing in form constantly and with no understandable rhythm. And in that hall were the intellectuals – the entities who had materialized those objects from the ultimately elemental radiant energy of open space.

Their number could not even be guessed. Sometimes only one was visible, sometimes it seemed that the great hall was crowded with them – ever-changing shapes varying in texture from the tenuousness of a wraith to a density greater than that of any Earthly metal.

So bewilderingly rapid were the changes in form that no one appearance could be intelligently grasped. Before one outlandish and unearthly shape could really be perceived it had vanished – had melted and flowed into one entirely different in form and in sense, but one equally monstrous to Terrestrial eyes. Even if grasped mentally, no one of those grotesque shapes could have been described in language, so utterly foreign were they to all human knowledge, history, and experience.

And now, the sixth-order projections in perfect synchronism, the thoughts of the Outlanders came clearly into the minds of the four watchers – thoughts cold, hard, and clear, diamond-like in polish and in definition; thoughts with the perfection of finish and detail possible only to the fleshless mentalities who for countless millions of years had done little save perfect themselves in the technique of pure and absolute thinking.

The four sat tense and strained as the awful import of those thoughts struck home; then, at another thought of horribly unmistakable meaning, Seaton snapped off his power and drove lightning fingers over his keyboard, while the two women slumped back, white-faced and trembling, into their seats.

'I thought it was funny, back there that time, that that fellow couldn't integrate in the ninety-seven dimensions necessary to dematerialize us, and I didn't know anything then.' Seaton, his preparations complete, leaned back in his operator's seat at the console. 'He was just kidding us – playing with us, just to see what we'd do, and as for not being able to think his way back – phooie! He can think his way through ninety-seven universes if he wants to. They're certainly extragalactic and very probably extrauniversal, and the one that played with us could have dematerialized us instantly if he had felt like it.'

'That is apparent, now,' Crane conceded. 'They are quite evidently patterns of sixth-order forces, and as such have a velocity of anything they want to use. They absorb force from the radiations in free space, and are capable of diverting and of utilizing those forces in any fashion they may choose. They would of course be eternal, and, so far as I can see, they would be indestructible. What are we going to do about it, Dick? What *can* we do about it?'

'We'll do *something*!' Seaton gritted. 'We're not as helpless as they think we are. I've got out five courses of six-ply screen, with full interliners of zones of force. I've got everything blocked, clear down to the sixth order. If they can think their way through those screens they're better than I think they are, and if they try anything else we'll do our darndest to block that, too – and with this Norlaminian keyboard and all the uranium we've got that'll be a mighty lot, believe me! After that last crack of theirs they'll hunt for us, of course, and I'm pretty sure they'll find us. I thought so here they are! Materialization, huh? I told him once that if he'd stick to stuff that I could understand, I'd give him a run for his money!'

6: Mind Versus Matter

Far out in the depths of the intergalactic void there sped along upon its strange course the newly materialized planet of the intellectuals. Desolate and barren it was, and apparently destitute of life; but life was there – eternal, disembodied life, unaffected by any possible extreme of heat or cold, requiring for its continuance neither water nor air, nor, for that matter, any material substance whatsoever. And from somewhere in the vacuum above that planet's forbidding surface there emanated a thought – a thought coldly clear, abysmally hopeless.

'I have but one remaining aim in this life. While I have failed again, as I have failed innumerable times in the past, I shall keep on trying until I succeed in assembling in sufficient strength the exact forces necessary to disrupt this sixth-order pattern which is I.'

'You speak foolishly, Eight, as does each of us now and again,' came instant response. 'There is much more to perceive, much more to do, much more to learn. Why be discouraged or disheartened? An infinity of time is necessary in which to explore infinite space and to acquire infinite knowledge.'

'Foolish I may be, but this is no simple recurrent outburst of melancholia. I am definitely weary of this cycle of existence, and I wish to pass on to the next, whatever of experience or of sheer oblivion it may bring. In fact, I wish that you, One, had never worked out the particular pattern of forces that liberated our eleven minds from the so-called shackles of our material bodies. For we cannot die. We are simply patterns of force eternal, marking the passage of time only by the life cycles of the suns of the galaxies.

'Why, I envy even the creatures inhabiting the planets throughout the galaxy we visited but a moment ago. Partially intelligent though they are, struggling and groping, each individual dying after only a fleeting instant of life; born, growing old, and passing on in a minute fraction of a millionth of one cycle – yet I envy even them.'

'That was the reason you did not dematerialize those you

45

accompanied briefly while they were flitting about in their crude space ship?'

'Yes. Being alive for such an infinitesimal period of time, they value life highly. Why hurry them into the future that is so soon to be theirs?'

'Do not dwell upon such thoughts, Eight,' advised One. 'They lead only to greater and greater depths of despondency. Consider instead what we have done and what we shall do.'

'I have considered everything, at length,' the entity known as Eight thought back stubbornly. 'What benefit or satisfaction do we get out of this continuous sojourn in the cycle of existence from which we should have departed aeons ago? We have power, it is true, but what of it? It is barren. We create for ourselves bodies and their material surroundings, like this' – the great hall came into being, and so vast was the mentality creating it that the flow of thought continued without a break – 'but what of it? We do not enjoy them as lesser beings enjoy the bodies which to them are synonymous with life.

'We have traveled endlessly, we have seen much, we have studied much; but what of it? Fundamentally we have accomplished nothing and we know nothing. We know but little more than we knew ourselves countless thousands of cycles ago, when our home planet was still substance. We know nothing of time; we know nothing of space; we know nothing even of the fourth dimension save that the three of us who rotated themselves into it have never returned. And until one of us succeeds in building a neutralizing pattern we can never die – we must face a drab and cheerless eternity of existence as we now are.'

'An eternity, yes, but an eternity neither drab nor cheerless. We know but little, as you have said, but in that fact lies a stimulus; we can and shall go on forever, learning more and ever more. Think of it! But hold – what is that? I feel a foreign thought. It must emanate from a mind powerful indeed to have come so far.'

'I have felt them. There are four foreign minds, but they are unimportant.'

'Have you analyzed them?'

'Yes. They are the people of the space ship which we just mentioned; projecting their mentalities to us here.'

'Projecting mentalities? Such a low form of life? They must have learned much from you, Eight.'

'Perhaps. I did give them one or two hints,' Eight returned, utterly indifferent, 'but they are of no importance to us.'

'I am not so sure of that,' One mused. 'We found no others in that galaxy capable of so projecting themselves, nor did we find any beings possessing minds strong enough to be capable of existence without the support of a material body. It may be that they are sufficiently advanced to join us. Even if they are not, if their minds should prove too weak for our company, they are undoubtedly strong enough to be of use in one of my researches.'

At this point Seaton cut off the projections and began to muster his sixth-order defenses, therefore he did not 'hear' Eight's outburst against the proposal of his leader.

'I will not allow it, One!' the disembodied intelligence protested intensely. 'Rather than have you inflict upon them the eternity of life that we have suffered I shall myself dematerialize them. Much as they love life, it would be infinitely better for them to spare a few minutes of it than to live forever.'

But there was no reply. One had vanished; had darted at utmost speed toward the *Skylark*. Eight followed him instantly.

Light-centuries of distance meant no more to them than to Seaton's own projector, and they soon reached the hurtling space ship; a space ship moving with all its unthinkable velocity, yet to them motionless – what is velocity when there are no reference points by which to measure it?

'Back, Eight!' commanded One abruptly. 'They are inclosed in a nullifying wall of the sixth-order. They are indeed advanced in mentality.'

'A complete stasis in the subether?' Eight marveled. 'That will do as well as the pattern...'

'Greetings, strangers!' Seaton's thought interrupted. Thoughts as clear as those require no interpretation of language. 'My projection is here, outside the wall, but I might caution you that one touch of your patterns will cut it off and stiffen that wall to absolute impenetrability. I assume that your visit is friendly?'

'Eminently so,' replied One. 'I offer you the opportunity of joining us; or, at least, the opportunity of being of assistance to science in the attempt at joining us.'

'They want us to join them as pure intellectuals, folks.' Seaton turned from the projector, toward his friends. 'How about it, Dottie? We've got quite a few things to do yet in the flesh, haven't we?'

'I'll say we have, Dickie – don't be an idiot!' she chuckled.

'Sorry, One!' Seaton thought again into space. 'Your invitation is appreciated to the full, and we thank you for it, but we have too many things to do in our own lives and upon our own world to accept it at this time. Later on, perhaps, we could do so with profit.'

'You will accept it *now*,' One declared coldly. 'Do you imagine that your puny wills can withstand *mine* for a single instant?'

'I don't know; but, aided by certain mechanical devices of ours, I do know that they'll do a terrific job of trying!' Seaton blazed back.

'There is one thing that I believe you can do,' Eight put in. 'Your barrier wall should be able to free me from this intolerable condition of eternal life!' And he hurled himself forward with all his prodigious force against that nullifying wall.

Instantly the screen flamed into incandescence; converters and generators whined and shrieked as hundreds of pounds of power uranium disappeared under that awful load. But the screens held, and in an instant it was over. Eight was gone, disrupted into the future life for which he had so longed, and the impregnable wall was once more merely a tenuous veil of sixth-order vibrations. Through that veil Seaton's projection crept warily; but the inhuman, monstrous mentality poised just beyond it made no demonstration.

'Eight committed suicide, as he has so often tried to do,' One commented coldly, 'but, after all, his loss will be felt with relief, if at all. His dissatisfaction was an actual impediment to the advancement of our entire group. And now, feeble intellect, I will let you know what is in store for you, before I direct against you the forces which will render your screens inoperative and therefore make further interchange of thought impossible. You shall be dematerialized; and, whether or not your minds are strong enough to exist in the free state, your entities shall be of some small assistance to me before you pass on to the next cycle of existence. What substance do you disintegrate for power?'

'That is none of your business, and since you cannot drive a ray through this screen you will never find out!' Seaton snapped.

'It matters little,' One rejoined, unmoved. 'Were you employing pure neutronium and were your vessel entirely filled with it, yet in a short time it would be exhausted. For, know you, I have summoned the other members of our group. We are able to direct cosmic forces which, although not infinite in magnitude, are to all intents and purposes inexhaustible. In a brief time your power will be gone, and I shall confer with you again.'

The other mentalities flashed up in response to the call of their leader, and at his direction arranged themselves all about the far-flung outer screen of the *Skylark*. Then from all space, directed inward, there converged upon the space ship gigantic streamers of force. Invisible streamers, and impalpable, but under their fierce impacts the defensive screens of the Terrestrial vessel flared into even more frenzied displays of pyrotechnic incandescence than they had exhibited under the heaviest beams of the superdreadnought of the Fenachrone. For thousands of miles space became filled with coruscantly luminous discharges as the uranium-driven screens of the *Skylark* dissipated the awful force of the attack.

'I don't see how they can keep that up for very long.' Seaton frowned at he read his meters and saw at what an appalling rate their store of metal was decreasing. 'But he talked as though he knew his stuff. I wonder if – um – um —' He fell silent, thinking intensely, while the others watched his face in strained attention; then went on: 'Uh-huh. I see – he can do it – he wasn't kidding us.'

'How?' asked Crane tensely.

'But how can he, possibly, Dick?' cried Dorothy. 'Why, they aren't *anything*, really!'

'They can't store up power in themselves, of course, but we know that all space is pervaded by radiation – theoretically a source of power that outclasses us as much as we outclass mule power. Nobody that I know of ever tapped it before, and I can't tap it yet; but they've tapped it and can direct it. The directing is easy enough to understand – just like a kid shooting a high-power rifle. He doesn't have to furnish energy for the bullet, you know – he merely touches off the powder and tells the bullet where to go.

'But we're not sunk yet. I see one chance; and even though it's pretty slim, I'd take it before I would knuckle down to his nibs out there. Eight said something a while ago, remember, about "rotating" into the fourth dimension? I've been mulling the idea around in my mind. I'd say that as a last resort we might give it a whirl and take a chance on coming through. See anything else that looks at all feasible, Mart?'

'Not at the present moment,' Crane replied calmly. 'How much time have we?'

'About forty hours at the present rate of dissipation. It's constant, so they've probably focused everything they can bring to bear on us.'

'You cannot attack them in any way? Apparently the sixth-order zone of force kills them?'

'Not a chance. If I open a slit one kilocycle wide anywhere in the band they'll find it instantly and it'll be curtains for us. And even if I could fight them off and work through that slit I couldn't drive a zone into them – their velocity is the same as that of the zone, you know, and they'd simply bounce back with it. If I could pen them up into a spherical – um – um – no use, can't do it with this equipment. If we had Rovol and Caslor and a few others of the Firsts of Norlamin here, and had a month or so of time, maybe we could work out something, but I couldn't even start it alone in the time we've got.'

'But even if we decide to try the fourth dimension, how could you do it? Surely that dimension is merely a mathematical concept, with no actual existence in nature?'

'No; it's actual enough, I think – nature's a big field, you know, and contains a lot of unexplored territory. Remember how casually that Eight thing out there discussed it? It isn't how to get there that's biting me; it's only that those intellectuals can stand a lot more grief than we can, and conditions in the region of the fourth dimension probably wouldn't suit us any too well.

'However, we wouldn't have to be there for more than a hundred thousandth of a second to dodge this gang, and we could stand almost anything that long, I imagine. As to how to do it – rotation. Three pairs of rotating, high-amperage currents, at mutual right angles, converging upon a point. Remembering that any rotating current exerts its force at a right angle, what would happen?'

'It might, at that,' Crane conceded, after minutes of narrow-eyed concentration; then, Crane-wise, began to muster objections. 'But it would not so affect this vessel. She is altogether too large, is of the wrong shape, and —'

'And you can't pull yourself up by your own boot straps,' Seaton interrupted. 'Right – you've got to have something to work from, something to anchor your forces to. We'd make the trip in little old *Skylark Two*. She's small, she's spherical and she has so little mass compared to *Three* that rotating her out of space would be easy – it wouldn't even shift *Three*'s reference planes.'

'It might prove successful,' Crane admitted at last, 'and, if so, it could not help but be a very interesting and highly informative experience. However, the chance of success seems to be none too great, as you have said, and we must exhaust every other possibility before we decide to attempt it.'

For hours then the two scientists went over every detail of their situation, but could evolve no other plan which held out even the slightest gleam of hope for a successful outcome; and Seaton seated himself before the banked and tiered keyboards of his projector.

There he worked for perhaps half an hour, then called to Crane: 'I've got everything set to spin *Two* out to where we're going, Mart. Now if you and Shiro' – for Crane's former "man" and the *Skylark*'s factotum was now quite as thoroughly familiar with Norlaminian forces as he had formerly been with Terrestrial tools – 'will put some forces onto the job of getting her ready for anything you think we may meet up with, I'll put in the rest of the time trying to figure out a way of taking a good stiff poke at those jaspers out there.'

He knew that the zones of force surrounding his vessel were absolutely impenetrable to any wave propagated through the ether, and to any possible form of material substance. He knew also that the subether was blocked, through the fifth and sixth orders. He knew that it was hopeless to attempt to solve the problem of the seventh order in the time at his disposal.

If he were to open any of his zones, even for an instant, in order to launch a direct attack, he knew that the immense mentalities to which he was opposed would perceive the opening and through it would wreak the Terrestrials' dematerialization before he could send out a single beam.

Last and worst, he knew that not even his vast console afforded any combination of forces which could possibly destroy the besieging intellectuals. What *could* he do?

For hours he labored with all the power of his wonderful brain, now stored with all the accumulated knowledge of thousands upon thousands of years of Norlaminian research. He stopped occasionally to eat, and once, at his wife's insistence, he snatched a little troubled and uneasy sleep; but his mind drove him back to his board and at that board he worked. Worked – while the hands of the chronometer approached more and ever more nearly the zero hour. Worked – while the *Skylark*'s immense stores of uranium dwindled visibly away in the giving up of their inconceivable amounts of intra-atomic energy to brace the screens which were dissipating the inexhaustible flood of cosmic force being directed against them. Worked – in vain. At last he glanced at the chronometer and stood up. 'Twenty minutes now – time to go,' he announced. 'Dot, come here a minute!'

'Sweetheart!' Tall though Dorothy was, the top of her auburn head came scarcely higher than Seaton's chin. Tightly but tenderly held in his arms she tipped her head back, and her violet eyes held no trace of fear as they met his. 'It's all right, lover. I don't know whether it's because I think we're going to get away, or because we're together; but I'm not in the least bit afraid.'

'Neither am I, dear. Some way, I simply can't believe that we're passing out; I've got a hunch that we're going to come through. We've got a lot to live for yet, you and I, together. But I want to tell you what you already know – that, whatever happens, I love you.'

'Hurry it up, Seatons!'

Margaret's voice recalled them to reality, and all five were wafted upon beams of force into the spherical launching space of the craft in which they were to venture into the unknown.

That vessel was *Skylark Two*, the forty-foot globe of arenak which from Earth to Norlamin had served them so well and which had been carried, lifeboatlike, well inside the two-mile-long torpedo which was *Skylark Three*. The massive doors were clamped and sealed, and the five human beings strapped themselves into their seats against they knew not what emergency.

'All ready, folks?' Seaton grasped the ebonite handle of his master switch. 'I'm not going to tell you Cranes good-bye, Mart – you know my hunch. You got one, too?'

'I cannot say that I have. However, I have always had a great deal of confidence in your ability. Then, too, I have always been something of a fatalist; and, most important of all, like you and Dorothy, Margaret and I are together. You may start any time now, Dick.'

'All right – hang on. On your marks! Get set! Go!'

As the master switch was thrown, a set of gigantic plungers drove home, actuating the tremendous generators in the holds of the massive cruiser of space above and around them; generators which, bursting into instantaneous and furious activity, directed upon the spherical hull of their vessel three opposed pairs of currents of electricity; madly spinning currents, of a potential and of a density never before brought into being by human devices.

DuQuesne did not find Seaton, nor did he quite comb the galaxy star by star, as he had declared that he would do in that event. He did, however, try; he prolonged the vain search to distances of so many light-years and through so many weeks of time that even the usually complacent Loring was moved to protest.

'Pretty much like hunting the proverbial needle in the haystack, isn't it, chief?' that worthy asked at last. 'They could be clear back home by this time, whoever they are. It looks as though maybe we could do ourselves more good by doing something else.'

'Yes; I probably am wasting time now, but I hate to give it up,' the scientist replied. 'We have pretty well covered this section of the galaxy. I wonder if it really was Seaton, after all? If he could blow up that planet through those screens he must have a lot more stuff than I have ever thought possible – certainly a lot more than I have, even now – and I would like very much to know how he did it. I couldn't have done it, nor could the Fenachrone, and if he did it without coming closer to it than a thousand light-years...'

'He may have been a lot closer than that,' Loring interrupted. 'He has had lots of time to make his get-away, you know.'

'Not so much as you think, unless he has an acceleration of the same order of magnitude as ours, which I doubt,' DuQuesne countered. 'Although it is of course possible, in the light of what we know must have happened, that he may have an acceleration as large as ours, or even larger. But the most vital question now is, where did he get his dope? We'll have to consider the probabilities and make our own plans accordingly.'

'All right! That's your dish – you're the doctor.'

'We shall have to assume that it was Seaton who did it, because if it was any one else, we have nothing whatever to work on. Assuming Seaton, we have four very definite leads. Our first lead is that it must have been Seaton in the *Skylark* and Dunark in the *Kondal* that destroyed the Fenachrone ship from the wreck of which we rescued the engineer. I couldn't learn anything about the actual battle from his brains, since he didn't know much except that it was a zone of force that did the real damage, and that the two strange ships were small and spherical.

'The *Skylark* and the *Kondal* answer that description and, while the evidence is far from conclusive, we shall assume as a working hypothesis that the *Skylark* and the *Kondal* did in fact attack and cut up a Fenachrone battleship fully as powerful as the one we are now in. That, as I do not have to tell you, is a disquieting thought.

'If it is true, however, Seaton must have left the Earth shortly after we did. That idea squares up, because he could very well have had an object-compass on me – whose tracer, by the way, would have been cut by the Fenachrone screens, so we needn't worry about it, even if he did have it once.

'Our second lead lies in the fact that he must have got the data on the zone of force sometime between the time when we left the Earth and the time when he cut up the battleship. He either worked it out himself on Earth, got it en route, or else got it on Osnome, or at least somewhere in the Green System. If my theory is correct, he worked it out by himself, before he left the Earth. He certainly did not get it on Osnome, because they did not have it.

'The third lead is the shortness of the period of time that elapsed between his battle with the Fenachrone warship and the destruction of their planet.

'The fourth lead is the great advancement in ability shown; going as he did from the use of a zone of force as an offensive weapon, up to the use of some weapon as yet unknown to us that works *through* defensive screens fully as powerful as any possible zone of force.

'Now, from the above hypothesis, we are justified in concluding that Seaton succeeded in enlisting the help of some ultrapowerful allies in the Green System, on some planet other than Osnome...'

'Why? I don't quite follow you there,' put in Loring.

'He didn't have this new stuff, whatever it is, when he met the battleship, or he would have used it instead of the dangerous, almost hand-to-hand fighting entailed by the use of a zone of force,' DuQuesne declared flatly. 'Therefore, he got it some time after that, but before the big explosion; and you can take it from me that no one man worked out a thing that big in such a short space of time. It can't be done. He had help, and high-class help at that.

'The time factor is also an argument in favor of the idea that he got it somewhere in the Green System – he didn't have time to go anywhere else. Also, the logical thing for him to do would be to explore the Green System first, since it has a very large number of planets, many of which undoubtedly are inhabited by highly advanced races. Does that make it clearer?'

'I've got it straight so far,' assented the aid.

'We must plan our course of action in detail before we leave this spot,' DuQuesne decided. 'Then we will be ready to start back for the Green System, to find out who Seaton's friends were and to persuade them to give us all the stuff they gave him. Now listen – carefully.

'We are not nearly as ready nor as well equipped as I thought we were – Seaton is about three laps ahead of us yet. Also, there is a lot more to psychology than I ever thought there was before I read those brains back there. Both of us had better get in training mentally to meet Seaton's friends, whoever they may be, or else we probably will not be able to get away with a thing.

'Both of us, you especially, want to clear our minds of every thought inimical to Seaton in any way or in even the slightest degree. You and I are, and always have been, two of the best friends Seaton ever had on earth – or anywhere else, for that matter. And of course I cannot be Marc DuQuesne, for reasons that are self-evident. From now on I am Stewart Vaneman, Dorothy's brother ... No, forget all that – too dangerous. They may know all about Seaton's friends and Mrs. Seaton's family. Our best line is to be humble cogs in Seaton's great machine. We worship him from afar as the world's greatest hero, but we are not of sufficient importance for him to know personally.'

'Isn't that carrying caution to extremes?'

'It is not. The only thing that we are certain of concerning these postulated beings is that they know immensely more than we do; therefore our story cannot have even the slightest flaw in it – it must be bottle-tight. So I will be Stewart Donovan – fortunately I haven't my name, initials, or monogram on anything I own – and I am one of the engineers of the Seaton-Crane Co., working on the power-plant installation.

'Seaton may have given them a mental picture of DuQuesne, but I will grow a mustache and beard, and with this story they will never think of connecting Donovan with DuQuesne. You can keep your own name, since neither Seaton nor any of his crowd ever saw or heard of you. You are also an engineer – my technical assistant at the works – and my buddy.

'We struck some highly technical stuff that nobody but Seaton could handle, and nobody had heard anything from him for a long time, so we came out to hunt him up and ask him some questions. You and I came together because we are just like Damon and Pythias. That story will hold water, I believe – do you see any flaws in it?'

'Perhaps not flaws, but one or two things you forgot to mention. How about this ship? I suppose you could call her an improved model, but suppose they are familiar with Fenachrone space-ship construction?'

'We shall not be in this ship. If, as we are assuming, Seaton and his new friends were the star actors in the late drama, those friends certainly have mentalities and apparatus of high caliber and they would equally certainly recognize this vessel. I had that in mind when I shoved the *Violet* off.'

'Then you will have the *Violet* to explain – an Osnomian ship. However, the company could have imported a few of them, for runabout work, since Seaton left. It would be quicker than building them, at that, since they already have all the special tools and stuff on Osnome.'

'You're getting the idea. Anything else?'

'All this is built around the supposition that he will not be there when we arrive. Suppose he *is* there?'

'The chances are a thousand to one that he will be gone somewhere, exploring – he never did like to stick around in any one place. And even in the remote possibility that he should be on the planet, he certainly will not be at the dock when we land, so the story is still good. If he should be there, we shall simply have to arrange matters so that our meeting him face to face is delayed until after we have got what we want; that's all.'

'All right; I've got it down solid.'

'Be sure that you have. Above all, remember the mental attitude toward Seaton – hero worship. He is not only the greatest man that Earth ever produced; he is the king-pin of the entire galaxy, and we rate him just a hair below God Himself. Think that thought with every cell of your brain. Concentrate on it with all your mind. Feel it – act it – really believe it until I tell you to quit.'

'I'll do that. Now what?'

'Now we hunt up the *Violet*, transfer to her, and set this cruiser adrift on a course toward Earth. And while I think of it, we want to be sure not to use any more power than the *Skylark* could, anywhere near the Green System, and cover up anything that looks peculiar about the power plant. We're not supposed to know anything about the five-light drive of the Fenachrone, you know.'

'But suppose that you can't find the *Violet*, or that she has been destroyed?'

'In that case we'll go on to Osnome and steal another one just like her. But I'll find her – I know her exact course and velocity, we have ultrarange detectors, and her automatic instruments and machinery make her destructionproof.'

DuQuesne's chronometers were accurate, his computations were sound, and his detectors were sensitive enough to have revealed the presence of a smaller body than the *Violet* at a distance vastly greater than the few millions of miles which constituted his unavoidable error. Therefore the Osnomian cruiser was found without trouble and the transfer was effected without untoward incident.

Then for days the *Violet* was hurled at full acceleration toward the center of the galaxy. Long before the Green System was reached, however, the globular cruiser was swung off her course and, mad acceleration reversed, was put into a great circle, so that she would approach her destination from the direction of our own solar system. Slower and slower she drove onward, the bright green star about which she was circling resolving itself first into a group of bright-green points and finally into widely spaced, tiny green suns.

Although facing the completely unknown and about to do battle, with their wits certainly, and with their every weapon possibly, against overwhelming odds, neither man showed or felt either nervousness or disorganization. Loring was a fatalist. It was DuQuesne's party; he was merely the hired help. He would do his best when the time came to do something; until that time came there was nothing to worry about.

DuQuesne's, on the other hand, was the repose of conscious power. He had laid his plans as best he could with the information then at hand. If conditions changed he would change those plans; otherwise he would drive through with them ruthlessly, as was his wont. In the meantime he awaited he knew not what, poised, cool, and confident.

Since both men were really expecting the unexpected, neither betrayed surprise when something that was apparently a man materialized before them in the air of the control room. His skin was green, as was that of all the inhabitants of the Green System. He was tall and well proportioned, according to Earthly standards, except for his head, which was overlarge and particularly massive above the eyes and backward from the ears. He was evidently of advanced years, for his face was seamed and wrinkled, and both his long, heavy hair and his yard-long, square-cut beard were a snowy white, only faintly tinged with green.

The Norlaminian projection thickened instantly, with none of the oscillation and 'hunting' which had been so noticeable in the one which had visited *Skylark Two* a few months earlier, for at that comparatively short range the fifth-order keyboard handling it could hold a point, however moving, as accurately as a Terrestrial photographic telescope holds a star. And in the moment of materialization of his projection the aged Norlaminian spoke.

'I welcome you to Norlamin, Terrestrials,' he greeted the two marauders with the untroubled serenity and calm courtesy of his race. 'Since you are quite evidently of the same racial stock as our very good friends the doctors Seaton and Crane, and since you are traveling in a ship built by the Osnomians, I assume that you speak and understand the English language which I am employing. I suppose that you are close friends of

Seaton and Crane and that you have come to learn why they have not communicated with you of late?'

Self-contained as DuQuesne was, this statement almost took his breath away, squaring almost perfectly as it did with the tale he had so carefully prepared. He did not show his amazed gratification, however, but spoke as gravely and as courteously as the other had done:

'We are very glad indeed to see you, sir; particularly since we know neither the name nor the location of the planet for which we are searching. Your assumptions are correct in every particular save one...'

'You do not know even the name of Norlamin?' the Green scientist interrupted. 'How can that be? Did not Dr. Seaton send the projections of all his party to you upon Earth, and did he not discuss matters with you?'

'I was about to explain that.' DuQuesne lied instantly, boldly, and convincingly. 'We heard that he had sent a talking, three-dimensional picture of his group to Earth, but after it had vanished all the real information that any one seemed to have obtained was that they were here in the Green System somewhere, but not upon Osnome, and that they had been taught much of science. Mrs. Seaton did most of the talking, I gather, which may account for the dearth of pertinent details.

'Neither my friend Loring, here nor I – I am Stewart Donovan, by the way – saw the picture, or rather, projection. You assumed that we are Seaton's close friends. We are engineers in his company, but we have not the honor of his personal acquaintance. His scientific knowledge was needed so urgently that it was decided that we should come out here after him, since the chief of construction had heard nothing from him for so long.'

'I see.' A shadow passed over the seamed green face. 'I am very sorry indeed at what I have to tell you. We did not report anything of it to Earth because of the panic that would have ensued. We shall of course send the whole story as soon as we can learn what actually did take place and can deduce therefrom the probable sequence of events yet to occur.'

'What's that – an accident? Something happened to Seaton?' DuQuesne snapped. His heart leaped in joy and relief, but his face showed only strained anxiety and deep concern. 'He isn't here now? Surely nothing serious could have happened to him.'

'Alas, young friend, none of us knows yet what really occurred. It is highly probable, however, that their vessel was destroyed in intergalactic space by forces about which we have as yet been able to learn nothing; forces directed by some intelligence as yet to us unknown. There is a possibility that Seaton and his companions escaped in the vessel you knew as *Skylark Two*, but so far we have not been able to find them.

'But enough of talking; you are strained and weary and you must rest. As soon as your vessel was detected the beam was transferred to me – the student Rovol, perhaps the closest to Seaton of any of my race – so that I could give you this assurance. With your permission I shall direct upon your controls certain forces which shall so govern your flight that you shall alight safely upon the grounds of my laboratory in a few minutes more than twelve hours of your time, without any further attention or effort upon your part.

'Further explanations can wait until we meet in the flesh. Until that time, my friends, do nothing save rest. Eat and sleep without care or fear, for your flight and your landing shall be controlled with precision. Farewell!'

The projection vanished instantaneously, and Loring expelled his pent-up breath in an explosive sigh.

'Whew! But what a break, chief, what a ...'

He was interrupted by DuQuesne, who spoke calmly and quietly, yet insistently: 'Yes, it is a singularly fortunate circumstance that the Norlaminians detected us and recognized us; it probably would have required weeks for us to have found their planet unaided.' DuQuesne's lightning mind found a way of covering up his companion's betraying exclamation and sought some way of warning him that could not be overheard. 'Our visitor was right in saying that we need food and rest badly, but before we eat let us put on the headsets and bring the record of our flight up to date – it will take only a minute or two.'

'What's biting you, chief?' thought Loring as soon as the power was on. 'We didn't have any ...'

'Plenty!' DuQuesne interrupted him viciously. 'Don't you realize that they can probably hear every word we say, and that they can see every move we make, even in the dark? In fact, they may be able to read thoughts, for all I know; so *think straight* from now on, if you never did before! Now let's finish up this record.'

He then impressed upon a tape the record of everything that had just happened. They ate. Then they slept soundly – the first really untroubled sleep they had enjoyed for weeks. And at last, exactly as the projection had foretold, the *Violet* landed without a jar upon the spacious grounds beside the laboratory of Rovol, the foremost physicist of Norlamin.

When the door of the space ship opened, Rovol in person was standing before it, waiting to welcome the voyagers and to escort them to his dwelling. But DuQuesne, pretending a vast impatience, would not be dissuaded from the object of his search merely to satisfy the Norlaminian amenities of hospitality and courtesy. He poured forth his prepared story in a breath, concluding with a flat demand that Rovol tell him everything he knew about Seaton, and that he tell it at once.

'It would take far too long to tell you anything in words,' the ancient scientist replied placidly. 'In the laboratory, however, I can and will inform you fully in a few minutes concerning everything that has happened.'

Utter stranger himself to deception in any form, as was his whole race, Rovol was easily and completely deceived by the consummate acting, both physical and mental, of DuQuesne and Loring. Therefore, as soon as the three had donned the headsets of the wonderfully efficient Norlaminian educator, Rovol gave to the Terrestrial adventurers without reserve his every mental image and his every stored fact concerning Seaton and his supposedly ill-fated last voyage.

Even more clearly than as if he himself had seen them all happen, DuQuesne beheld and understood Seaton's visit to Norlamin, the story of the Fenachrone peril, the building of the fifth-order projector, the demolition of Fenor's space fleet, the revenge-purposed flight of Ravindau the scientist, and the complete volatilization of the Fenachrone planet.

He saw Seaton's gigantic space cruiser *Skylark Three* come into being and, uranium-driven, speed out into the awesome void of intergalactic space in pursuit of the last survivors of the

Fenachrone race. He watched the mighty *Three* overtake the fleeing vessel, and understood every detail of the epic engagement that ensued, clear to its cataclysmic end. He watched the victorious battleship speed on and on, deeper and deeper into the intergalactic void, until she began to approach the limiting range of even the stupendous fifth-order projector by means of which he knew the watching had been done.

Then, at the tantalizing limit of visibility, something began to happen; something at the very incomprehensibility of which DuQuesne strained both mind and eye, exactly as had Rovol when it had taken place so long before. The immense bulk of the *Skylark* disappeared behind zone after impenetrable zone of force, and it became increasingly evident that from behind those supposedly impervious and impregnable shields Seaton was waging a terrific battle against some unknown opponent, some foe invisible even to fifth-order vision.

For nothing was visible – nothing, that is, save the released energies which, leaping through level after level reached at last even to the visible spectrum. Yet forces of such unthinkable magnitude were warring there that space itself was being deformed visibly, moment by moment. For a long time the space strains grew more and more intense, then they disappeared instantly. Simultaneously the *Skylark*'s screens of force went down and she was for an instant starkly visible before she exploded into a vast ball of appallingly radiant, flaming vapor.

In that instant of clear visibility, however, Rovol's stupendous mind had photographed every salient visible feature of the great cruiser of the void. Being almost at the limit of range of the projector, details were of course none too plain; but certain things were evident. The human beings were no longer aboard; the little lifeboat that was *Skylark Two* was no longer in her spherical berth; and there were unmistakable signs of a purposeful and deliberate departure.

'And,' Rovol spoke aloud as he removed the headset, 'although we searched minutely and most carefully all the surrounding space we could find nothing tangible. From these observations it is all too plain that Seaton was attacked by some intelligence wielding dirigible forces of the sixth order; that he was able to set up a defensive pattern; that his supply of power uranium was insufficient to cope with the attacking forces; and that he took the last desperate means of escaping from his foes by rotating *Skylark Two* into the unknown region of the fourth dimension.'

DuQuesne's stunned mind groped for a moment in an amazement akin to stupefaction, but he recovered quickly and decided upon his course.

'Well, what are you doing about it?'

'We have done and are doing everything possible for us, in our present state of knowledge and advancement, to do,' Rovol replied placidly. 'We sent out forces, as I told you, which obtained and recorded all the phenomena to which they were sensitive. It is true that a great deal of data escaped them, because the primary impulses originated in a level beyond our present knowledge, but the fact that we cannot understand it has only intensified our interest in the problem. It shall be solved. After its solution we shall know what steps to take and those steps shall then be taken.'

'Have you any idea how long it will take to solve the problem?'

'Not the slightest. Perhaps one lifetime, perhaps many – who knows? However, rest assured that it shall be solved, and that the condition shall be dealt with in the manner which shall best serve the interest of humanity as a whole.'

'But good God!' exclaimed DuQuesne. 'In the meantime, what of Seaton and Crane?' He was now speaking his true thoughts. Upon this, his first encounter, he could in nowise understand the deep, calm, timeless trend of mind of the Norlaminians; not even dimly could he grasp or appreciate the seemingly slow but inexorably certain method in which they pursued relentlessly any given line of research to its ultimate conclusion.

'If it should be graven upon the Sphere that they shall pass they may – and will – pass in all tranquility, for they know full well that it was not in idle gesture that the massed intellect of Norlamin assured them that their passing should not be in vain. You, however, youths of an unusually youthful and turbulent race, could not be expected to view the passing of such a one as Seaton from our own mature viewpoint.'

'I'll tell the universe that I don't look at things the way you do!' barked DuQuesne scathingly. 'When I go back to Earth – if I go – I shall at least have tried. I've got a life-sized picture of myself standing idly by while someone else tries for seven hundred years to decipher the indecipherable!'

'There speaks the impetuousness of youth,' the old man chided. 'I have told you that we have proved that at present we can do nothing whatever for the occupants of *Skylark Two*. Be warned, my rash young friend; do not tamper with powers entirely beyond your comprehension.'

'Warning be damned!' DuQuesne snorted. 'We're shoving off. Come on, Loring – the quicker we get started the better our chance of getting something done. You'll be willing to give me the exact bearing and the distance, won't you Rovol?'

'We shall do more than that, son,' the patriarch replied, while a shadow came over his wrinkled visage. 'Your life is your own, to do with as you see fit. You have chosen to go in search of your friends, scorning the odds against you. But before I tell you what I have in mind, I must try once more to make you see that the courage which dictates the useless sacrifice of a life ceases to be courage at all, but becomes sheerest folly.

'Since we have had sufficient power several of our youths have been studying the fourth dimension. They rotated many inanimate objects into that region, but could recover none of them. Instead of waiting until they had derived the fundamental equations governing such phenomena they rashly visited that region in person, in a vain attempt to achieve a short cut to knowledge. Not one of them has come back.

'Now I declare to you in all solemnity that the quest you wish to undertake, involving as it does not only that entirely unknown region but also the equally unknown sixth order of vibrations, is to you at present utterly impossible. Do you still insist upon going?'

'We certainly do. You may as well save your breath.'

'Very well; so be it. Frankly, I had but little hope of swerving you from your purpose by reason. But before you go we shall supply you with every resource at our command which may in any way operate to increase your infinitesimal chance of success. We shall build for you a duplicate of Seaton's own *Skylark*

Three, equipped with every device known to our science, and we shall instruct you fully in the use of those devices before you set out.'

'But the time . . . DuQuesne began to object.

'A matter of hours only,' Rovol silenced him. 'True, it took us some little time to build *Skylark Three*, but that was because it had not been done before. Every force employed in her construction was of course recorded, and to reproduce her in every detail, without attention or supervision, it is necessary only to thread this tape, thus, into the integrator of my master keyboard. The actual construction will of course take place in the area of experiment, but you may watch it, if you wish, in this visiplate. I must take a short series of observations at this time. I will return in ample time to instruct you in the operation of the vessel and of everything in it.'

In stunned amazement the two men stared into the visiplate, so engrossed in what they saw there that they scarcely noticed the departure of the aged scientist. For before their eyes there had already sprung into being an enormous structure of laced and latticed members of purple metal, stretching over two miles of level plain. While it was very narrow for its length, yet its fifteen hundred feet of diameter dwarfed into insignificance the many outlandish structures near by, and under their staring eyes the vessel continued to take form with unbelievable rapidity. Gigantic girders appeared in place as though by magic; skin after skin of thick, purple inoson was welded on; all without the touch of a hand, without the thought of a brain, without the application of any visible force.

'Now you can say it, Doll; there's no spy ray on us here. What a break – what a break!' exulted DuQuesne. 'The old fossil swallowed it bodily, hook, line, and sinker!'

'It may not be so good, though, at that, chief, in one way. He's going to watch us, to help us out if we get into a jam, and with that infernal telescope, or whatever it is, the Earth is right under his nose.'

'Simpler than taking milk away from a blind kitten,' the saturnine chemist gloated. 'We'll go out to where Seaton went, only farther – out beyond the reach of his projector. There,

66

completely out of touch with him, we'll circle around the galaxy back to Earth and do our stuff. Easier than dynamiting fish in a bucket – the old sap's handing me everything I want, right on a silver platter!'

8: Into the Fourth Dimension

Six mighty rotating currents of electricity impinged simultaneously upon the spherical hull of *Skylark Two* and she disappeared utterly. No exit had been opened and the walls remained solid, but where the forty-foot globe of arenak had rested in her cradle an instant before there was nothing. Pushed against by six balancing and gigantic forces, twisted cruelly by six couples of angular force of unthinkable magnitude, the immensely strong arenak shell of the vessel had held and, following the path of least resistance – the only path in which she could escape from those irresistible forces – she had shot out of space as we know it and into the impossible reality of that hyperspace which Seaton's vast mathematical knowledge had enabled him so dimly to perceive.

As those forces smote his vessel, Seaton felt himself compressed. He was being driven together irresistibly in all three dimensions, and in those dimensions at the same time he was as irresistibly being twisted – was being corkscrewed in a monstrously obscure fashion which permitted him neither to move from his place nor to remain in it. He hung poised there for interminable hours, even though he knew that the time required for that current to build up to its inconceivable value was to be measured only in fractional millionths of a single second.

Yet he waited strainingly while that force increased at an all but imperceptible rate, until at last the vessel and all its contents were squeezed out of space, in a manner somewhat comparable to that in which an orange pip is forced out from between pressing thumb and resisting finger.

At the same time Seaton felt a painless, but unutterably horrible, transformation of his entire body – a rearrangement, a writhing, crawling distortion; a hideously revolting and incomprehensibly impossible extrusion of his bodily substance as every molecule, every atom, every ultimate particle of his physical structure was compelled to extend itself into that unknown new dimension.

He could not move his eyes, yet he saw every detail of the

grotesquely altered space ship. His Earthly mentality could not understand anything he saw, yet to his transformed brain everything was as usual and quite in order. Thus the four-dimensional physique that was Richard Seaton perceived, recognized, and admired as of yore his beloved Dorothy, in spite of the fact that her normally solid body was now quite plainly nothing but a three-dimensional surface, solid only in that logically impossible new dimension which his now four-dimensional brain accepted as a matter of course, but which his thinking mentality could neither really perceive nor even dimly comprehend.

He could not move a muscle, yet in some obscure and impossible way he leaped toward his wife. Immobile though tongue and jaws were, yet he spoke to her reassuringly, remonstratingly, as he gathered up her trembling form and silenced her hysterical outbursts.

'Steady on, girl, it's all right – everything's jake. Hold everything, dear. Pipe down, I tell you! This is nothing to let get your goat. Snap out of it, Red-Top!'

'But, Dick, it's ... it's too perfectly outrageous!' Dorothy had been on the verge of hysteria, but she regained a measure of her customary spirit under Seaton's ministrations. 'In some ways it seems to be all right, but it's so ... so ... oh, I can't ...'

'Hold it!' he commanded. 'You're going off the deep end again. I can't say that I expected anything like this, either, but when you think about things it's natural enough that they should be this way. You see, while we've apparently got four-dimensional bodies and brains now, our intellects are still three-dimensional which complicates things considerably. We can handle things and recognize them, but we can't think about physical forms, understand them, or express them either in words or in thoughts. Peculiar, and nerve-wracking enough, especially for you girls, but quite normal – see?'

'Well, maybe – after a fashion. I was afraid that I had really gone crazy back there, at first, but if you feel that way, too, I know it's all right. But you said that we'd be gone only a skillionth of a second, and we've been here a week already, at the very least.'

'All wrong, Dot – at least, partly wrong. Time does go faster here, apparently, so that we seem to have been here quite a while; but as far as our own time is concerned we haven't been here anywhere near a millionth of a second yet. See that plunger? It's still moving in – it has barely made contact. Time is purely relative, you know, and it moves so fast here that that plunger switch, traveling so fast that the eye cannot follow it at all ordinarily, seems to us to be perfectly stationary.'

'But it *must* have been longer than that, Dick! Look at all the talking we've done. I'm a fast talker, I know, but even I can't talk that fast!'

'You aren't talking – haven't you discovered that yet? You are thinking, and we are getting your thoughts as speech; that's all. Don't believe it? All right; there's your tongue, right there – or better, take your heart. It's that funny-looking object right there – see it? It isn't beating – that is, it would seem to us to take weeks, or possibly months, to beat. Take hold of it – feel it for yourself.'

'Take *hold* of it! My own heart? Why, it's inside me, between my ribs – I couldn't possibly!'

'Sure you can! That's your intellect talking now, not your brain. You're four-dimensional now, remember, and what you used to call your body is nothing but the three-dimensional hypersurface of your new hyperbody. You can take hold of your heart or your gizzard just as easily as you used to pat yourself on the nose with a powder puff.'

'Well, I won't, then – why, I wouldn't touch that thing for a million dollars!'

'All right; watch me feel mine, then. See, it's perfectly motionless, and my tongue is, too. And there's something else that I never expected to look at – my appendix. Good thing you're in good shape, old vermiform, or I'd take a pair of scissors and snick you off while I've got such a good chance to do it without . . .'

'Dick!' shrieked Dorothy. 'For the love of Heaven . . .'

'Calm down, Dottie, calm down. I'm just trying to get you used to this mess – I'll try something else. Here, you know what this is – a new can of tobacco, with the lid soldered on tight. In three dimensions there's no way of getting into it without breaking metal – you've opened lots of them. But out here I simply reach *past* the metal of the container, like this, see, and put it into my pipe, thus. The can is still soldered tight, no holes in it anywhere, but the tobacco is out, nevertheless. Inexplicable in three-dimensional space, impossible for us really to understand mentally, but physically perfectly simple and perfectly natural after you get used to it. That'll straighten you out some, perhaps.'

'Well, maybe – I guess I won't get frantic again, Dickie – but just the same, it's altogether too perfectly darn weird to suit me. Why don't you pull that switch back out and stop us?'

'Wouldn't do any good – wouldn't stop us, because we have already had the impulse and are simply traveling on momentum now. When that is used up – in some extremely small fraction of a second of our time – we'll snap back into our ordinary space, but we can't do a thing about it until then.'

'But how can we move around so fast?' asked Margaret from the protecting embrace of the monstrosity that they knew to be Martin Crane. 'How about inertia? I should think we'd break our bones all to pieces.'

'You can't move a three-dimensional body that fast, as we found out when the force was coming on,' Seaton replied. 'But I don't think that we are ordinary matter any more, and apparently our three-dimensional laws no longer govern, now that we are in hyperspace. Inertia is based upon time, of course, so our motion might be all right, even at that. Mechanics seem to be different here, though, and, while we seem solid enough, we certainly aren't matter at all in the three-dimensional sense of the term, as we used it back where we came from. But it's all over my head like a circus tent – I don't know any more about most of this stuff than you do. I thought of course – if I thought at all, which I doubt – that we'd go *through* hyperspace in an instant of time, without seeing it or feeling it in any way, since a three-dimensional body cannot exist, of course, in four-dimensional space. How did we get this way, Mart? Is this space coexistent with ours or not?'

'I believe that it is.' Crane, the methodical, had been thinking deeply, considering every phase of their peculiar predicament. 'Coexistent, but different in all its attributes and properties. Since we may be said to be experiencing two different time rates simultaneously, we cannot even guess at what our velocity relation is, in either system of coordinates. As to what happened, that is now quite clear. Since a three-dimensional object cannot exist in hyperspace, it of course cannot be thrown or forced through hyperspace.

'In order to enter this region, our vessel and everything in it had to acquire the property of extension in another dimension. Your forces, calculated to rotate us here, in reality forced us to assume that extra extension, which process automatically moved us from the space in which we could no longer exist into the only one in which it is possible for us to exist. When that force is no longer operative, our extension into the fourth dimension will vanish and we shall as automatically return to our customary three-dimensional space, but probably not to our original location in that space. Is that the way you understand it?'

'That's a lot better than I understood it, and it's absolutely right, too. Thanks, old thinker! And I certainly hope we don't land back there where we took off from – that's why we left, because we wanted to get away from there. The farther the better,' Seaton laughed. 'Just so we don't get so far away that the whole galaxy is out of range of the object-compasses we've got focused on it. We'd be lost for fair, then.'

'That is a possibility, of course.' Crane took the light utterance far more seriously than did Seaton. 'Indeed, if the two time rates are sufficiently different, it becomes a probability. However, there is another matter which I think is of more immediate concern. It occurred to me, when I saw you take that pinch of tobacco without opening the tin, that everywhere we have gone, even in intergalactic space, we have found life, some friendly, some inimical. There is no real reason to suppose that hyperspace is devoid of animate and intelligent life.'

'Oh, Martin!' Margaret shuddered. 'Life! Here? In this horrible, this utterly impossible place?'

'Certainly, dearest,' he replied gravely. 'It all goes back to the conversation we had long ago, during the first trip of the old *Skylark*. Remember? Life need not be comprehensible to us to exist – compared to what we do not know and what we can never either know or understand, our knowledge is infinitesimal.'

She did not reply and he spoke again to Seaton:

'It would seem to be almost a certainty that four-dimensional life does in fact exist. Postulating its existence, the possibility of an encounter cannot be denied. Such beings could of course enter this vessel as easily as your fingers entered that tobacco can. The point of these remarks is this – would we not be at a serious disadvantage? Would they not have fourth-dimensional shields or walls about which we three-dimensional intelligences would know nothing?'

'Sweet spirits of niter!' Seaton exclaimed. 'Never thought of that at all, Mart. Don't see how they could – and yet it does stand to reason that they'd have some way of locking up their horses so they couldn't run away, or so that nobody else could steal them. We'll have to do a job of thinking on that, big fellow, and we'd better start right now. Come on – let's get busy!'

Then for what seemed hours the two scientists devoted the power of their combined intellects to the problem of an adequate fourth-dimensional defense, only and endlessly to find themselves butting helplessly against a blank wall. Their three dimensional brains in their now four-dimensional bodies told them that such extra-dimensional bulwarks and safeguards must, and in fact did, exist; that they were not only possible, but necessary in the humanly incomprehensible actuality in which the Terrestrials now found themselves: but still the immaterial and thus unaltered intelligences of the human beings, utterly unable to cope with any save three-dimensional concepts, failed miserably to envisage anything which promised to be of the slightest service.

Baffled, they drifted on through the unknowable reaches of hyperspace. All they knew of time was that it was hopelessly distorted; of space that it was hideously unrecognizable; of matter that it obeyed no familiar laws. They drifted. And drifted. Futilely.

Timelessly ... aimlessly ... endlessly ...

The take-off of Norlamin's second immense space ship was not at all like that of its first. When *Skylark Three* left Norlamin in pursuit of the fleeing vessel of Ravindau, the Fenachrone scientist, the occasion had been made an event of world-wide interest. From their tasks everywhere had come the mental laborers to that portentous launching. To it had come also, practically en masse, the 'youngsters' from the Country of Youth; and even those who, their life work done, had betaken themselves to the placid Nirvana of the Country of Age, returned briefly to the Country of Study to speed upon its epoch-making way that stupendous messenger of civilization.

But in sharp contrast to the throngs of Norlaminians who had witnessed the take-off of *Three*, Rovol alone was present when DuQuesne and Loring wafted themselves into the control room of its gigantic counterpart. DuQuesne had been in a hurry, and in the driving urge of his haste to go to the rescue of his 'friend' Seaton he had so completely occupied the mind of Rovol that that aged scientist had had no time to do anything except transfer to the brain of the Terrestrial pirate the knowledge which he would so soon require.

Of the real reason for this overwhelming haste, however, Rovol had not had the slightest inkling. DuQuesne well knew what the ancient physicist did not even suspect – that if any one of several Norlaminians, particularly one Drasnik, First of Psychology, should become informed of the proposed flight, that flight would not take place. For Drasnik, that profound student of the mind, would not be satisfied with DuQuesne's story without a thorough mental examination – an examination which, DuQuesne well knew, he could not pass. Therefore Rovol alone saw them off, but what he lacked in numbers he made up in sincerity.

'I am very sorry that the exigencies of the situation did not permit a more seemly leave-taking,' he said in parting, 'but I can assure you of the cooperation of every one of us whose brain can be of any use. We shall watch you, and shall aid you in any way we can. May the Unknowable Force direct your minor forces to the successful conclusion of your task. If, however, it is graven upon the Sphere that you are to pass in this venture, you may pass in all tranquility, for I affirm in the name of all Norlamin that this problem shall not be laid aside short of complete solution. For all my race I bid you farewell.'

'Farewell to you, Rovol, my friend and my benefactor, and to all Norlamin,' DuQuesne replied solemnly. 'I thank you from the bottom of my heart for everything you have done for us and for Seaton, and for what you may yet be called upon to do for all of us.'

He touched a stud and in each of the many skins of the great cruiser a heavy door drove silently shut, establishing a manifold seal.

His hand moved over the controls, and the gigantic vessel tilted slowly upward until her narrow prow pointed almost directly into the zenith. Then, easily as a wafted feather, the unimaginable mass of the immense cruiser of space floated upward with gradually increasing velocity. Faster and faster she flew, out beyond measurable atmospheric pressure, out beyond the outermost limits of the Green System, swinging slowly into a right line toward the point in space where Seaton, his companions, and both their space ships had disappeared.

On and on she drove, now at high acceleration; the stars, so widely spaced at first, crowding closer and closer together as her speed, long since incomprehensible to any finite mind, mounted to a value almost incalculable. Past the system of the Fenachrone she hurtled; past the last outlying fringe of stars of our galaxy; on and on into the unexplored, awesome depths of open and absolute space.

Behind her the vast assemblage of stars comprising our island universe dwindled to a huge, flaming lens, to a small but bright lenticular nebula, and finally to a mere patch of luminosity.

For days communication with Rovol had been difficult, since as the limit of projection was approached it became impossible for the most powerful forces at Rovol's command to hold a projection upon the flying vessel. In order to communicate, Rovol had to send out a transmitting and receiving projection.

As the distance grew still greater, DuQuesne had done the

same thing. Now it was becoming evident, by the wavering and fading of the signals, that even the two projections, reaching out toward each other though they were, would soon be out of touch, and DuQuesne sent out his last message:

'There is no use in trying to keep in communication any longer, as our beams are falling apart fast. I am on negative acceleration now, of an amount calculated to bring us down to maneuvering velocity at the point to which the inertia of *Skylark Two* would have carried her, without power, at the time when we shall arrive there. Please keep a listening post established out this way as far as you can, and I will try to reach it if I find out anything. If I fail – good-bye!'

'The poor, dumb cluck!' DuQuesne sneered as he shut off his sender and turned to Loring. 'That was so easy that it was a shame to take it, but we're certainly set to go now.'

'I'll say so!' Loring agreed enthusiastically. 'That was a nice touch, chief, telling him to keep a lookout out here. He'll do it with forces, of course, not in person; but at that it'll keep him from thinking about the Earth until you're all set.'

'You've got the idea, Doll. If they had any suspicion at all that we were heading back for the Earth they could block us yet, easily enough; but if we can get back inside the Solar System before they smell a rat it will be too late for them to do anything.'

He rotated his ship through an angle of ninety degrees upon her longitudinal axis and applied enough 'downward' acceleration to swing her around in such an immense circle that she would approach the galaxy from the side opposite to that from which she had left it.

Then, during days that lengthened into weeks and months of dull and monotonous flight, the two men occupied themselves, each in his own individual fashion. There was no piloting to do and no need of vigilance, for space to a distance of untold billions of miles was absolutely and utterly empty.

Loring, unemotional and incurious, performed what simple routine house-keeping there was to do, ate, slept, and smoked. During the remainder of the time he simply sat still, stolidly doing nothing whatever until the time should come when DuQuesne would tell him to perform some specific act.

DuQuesne, on the other hand, dynamic and energetic to his ultimate fiber, found not a single idle moment. His newly acquired knowledge was so vast that he needs must explore and catalogue his own brain, to be sure that he would be able instantly to call upon whatever infinitesimal portion of it might be needed in some emergency.

The fifth-order projector, with its almost infinitely complicated keyboard, must needs be studied until its every possible resource of integration, permutation, and combination held from him no more secrets than does his console from a master of the pipe organ. Thus it was that the galaxy loomed ahead, a stupendous lens of flame, before DuQuesne had really realized that the long voyage was almost over.

To his present mentality, working with his newly acquired fifth-order projector, the task of locating our Solar System was but the work of a moment; and to the power and speed of his new space ship the distance from the galaxy's edge to the Earth was merely a longish jaunt.

When they approached the Earth it appeared as a softly shining greenish half moon. With fleecy wisps of cloud obscuring its surface here and there, with gleaming ice caps making of its poles two brilliant areas of white, it presented an arrestingly beautiful spectacle indeed; but DuQuesne was not interested in beauty. Driving down from the empty reaches of space north of the ecliptic, he observed that Washington was in the morning zone, and soon his great vessel was poised motionless, invisibly high above the city.

His first act was to throw out an ultra-powered detector screen, with automatic trips and tighteners, around the entire Solar System; out far beyond the outermost point of the orbit of Pluto. Its every part remained unresponsive. No foreign radiation was present in all that vast volume of space, and DuQuesne turned to his henchman with cold satisfaction stamped upon his every hard lineament.

'No interference at all, Doll. No ships, no projections, no spy rays, nothing,' he said. 'I can really get to work now. I won't be needing you for a while, and I imagine that, after being out in space so long, you would like to circulate around with the boys and girls for a couple of weeks or so. How are you fixed for money?'

'Well, chief, I could do with a small binge and a few nights out among 'em, if it's all right with you,' Loring admitted. 'As for money, I've got only a couple of hundred on me, but I can get some at the office – we're quite a few pay days behind, you know.'

'Never mind about going to the office. I don't know exactly how well Brookings is going to like some of the things I'm going to tell him, and you're working for *me*, you know, not for the office. I've got plenty. Here's five thousand, and you can have three weeks to spend it in. Three weeks from today I'll tell you what to do. Until then, do as you please. Where do you want me to set you down? Perhaps the Perkins roof will be clear at this hour.'

'Good as any. Thanks, chief,' and without even a glance to assure himself that DuQuesne was at the controls Loring made his way through the manifold airlocks and calmly stepped out into ten thousand feet of empty air.

DuQuesne caught the falling man neatly with an attractor and lowered him gently to the now-deserted roof of the Perkins Cafe – that famous restaurant which had been planned and was maintained by the World Steel Corporation as a blind for its underground activities. He then seated himself at his console and drove his projection down into the innermost private office of Steel. He did not at first thicken the pattern into visibility, but remained invisible, studying Brookings, now president of that industrial octopus.

The magnate was seated as of yore in a comfortably padded chair at his massive and ornate desk, the focus and center of a maze of secret private communication bands and even more secret private wires. For Steel was a growing octopus and its voraciously insatiable maw must be fed.

Brookings had but one motto, one tenet – 'get it.' By fair play at times, although this method was employed but seldom; by bribery, corruption, and sabotage as the usual thing; by murder, arson, mayhem, and all other known forms of foul play if necessary or desirable – Steel GOT IT.

To be found out was the only sin, and that was usually only venial instead of cardinal; for it was because of that sometimes unavoidable contingency that Steel not only retained the shrewdest legal minds in the world, but also wielded subterranean forces sufficiently powerful to sway even supposedly incorruptible courts of justice.

Occasionally, of course, the sin was cardinal; the transgression irremediable; the court unreachable. In that case the octopus lost a very minor tentacle; but the men really guilty had never been brought to book.

Into the center of this web, then, DuQuesne drove his projection and listened. For a whole long week he kept at Brookings' elbow, day and night. He listened and spied, studied and planned until his now gigantic mentality not only had grasped every detail of everything that had developed during his long absence and of everything that was then going on, but also had planned meticulously the course which he would pursue. Then, late one afternoon, he cut in his audio and spoke.

'I knew of course that you would try to double-cross me, Brookings, but even I had no idea that you would make such an utter fool of yourself as you have.'

As he heard the sneering, cutting tone of the scientist's well-remembered voice, the magnate seemed to shrink bodily, his face turning a pasty gray as the blood receded from it.

'DuQuesne!' he gasped. 'Where – are you?'

'I'm right beside you, and I have been for over a week.' DuQuesne thickened his image to full visibility and grinned sardonically as the man at the desk reached hesitantly toward a button. 'Go ahead and push it – and see what happens. Surely even you are not dumb enough to suppose that a man with my brain – even the brain I had when I left here – would take any chances with such a rat as you have always shown yourself to be?'

Brookings sank back into his chair, shaking visibly. 'What are you, anyway? You look like DuQuesne, and yet...' His voice died away.

'That's better, Brookings. Don't ever start anything that you can't finish. You are and always were a physical coward. You're one of the world's best at bossing dirty work from a distance, but as soon as it gets close to you, you fold up like an accordion.

'As to what this is that I am talking and seeing from, it is technically known as a projection. You don't know enough to understand it even if I should try to explain it to you, which I have no intention of doing. It's enough for you to know that it is something that has all the advantages of an appearance in person, and none of the disadvantages. *None* of them – remember that word.

'Now I'll get down to business. When I left here I told you to hold your cockeyed ideas in check – that I would be back in less than five years, with enough stuff to do things in a big way. You didn't wait five days, but started right in with your pussyfooting and gumshoeing around, with the usual result – instead of cleaning up the mess, you made it messier than ever. You see, I've got all the dope on you – I even know that you were going to try to gyp me out of my back pay.'

'Oh, no, doctor; you are mistaken, really,' Brookings assured him, oilily. He is fast regaining his usual poise, and his mind was again functioning in its wonted devious fashion. 'We have really been trying to carry on until you got back, exactly as you told us to. And your salary has been continued in full, of course – you can draw it all at any time.'

'I know I can, in spite of you. However, I am no longer interested in money. I never cared for it except for the power it gave, and I have brought back with me power far beyond that of money. Also I have learned that knowledge is even greater than power. I have also learned, however, that in order to increase my present knowledge – yes, even to protect that which I already have – I shall soon need a supply of energy a million times greater than the present peak output of all the generators of Earth. As a first step in my project I am taking control of Steel right now, and I am going to do things the way they should be done.'

'But you can't do that, doctor!' protested Brookings volubly. 'We will give you anything you ask, of course, but . . .'

'But nothing!' interrupted DuQuesne. 'I'm not asking a thing of you, Brookings – I'm *telling* you!'

'You think you are!' Brookings, goaded to action at last, pressed a button, savagely, while DuQuesne looked on in calm contempt.

Behind the desk, ports flashed open and rifles roared thunderously in the confined space. Heavy bullets tore through the peculiar substance of the projection and smashed into the plastered wall behind it, but DuQuesne's contemptuous grin did not change. He moved slowly forward, hands outthrust. Brookings screamed once – a scream that died away to a gurgle as fingers of tremendous strength closed about his flabby neck.

There had been four riflemen on guard. Two of them threw down their guns and fled in panic, amazed and terrified at the failure of their bullets to take effect. Those guards died in their tracks as they ran. The other two rushed upon DuQuesne with weapons clubbed. But steel barrel and wooden stock alike rebounded harmlessly from that pattern of force, fiercely driven knives penetrated it but left no wound, and the utmost strength of the two brawny men could not even shift the position of the weird being's inhumanly powerful fingers upon the throat of their employer. Therefore they stopped their fruitless attempts at a rescue and stood, dumbfounded.

'Good work, boys,' DuQuesne commended. 'You've got nerve – that's why I didn't bump you off. You can keep on guarding this idiot here after I get done teaching him a thing or two. As for you, Brookings,' he continued, loosening his grip sufficiently so that his victim could retain consciousness, 'I let you try that to show you the real meaning of futility. I told you particularly to remember that this projection has *none* of the disadvantages of a personal appearance, but apparently you didn't have enough brain power to grasp the thought. Now, are you going to work with me the way I want you to or not?'

'Yes, yes – I'll do anything you say,' Brookings promised.

'All right, then.' DuQuesne resumed his former position in front of the desk. 'You are wondering why I didn't finish choking you to death, since you know that I am not at all squeamish about such things. I'll tell you. I didn't kill you because I may be able to use you. I am going to make World Steel the real government of the Earth, and its president will therefore be dictator of the world. I do not want the job myself because I will be too busy extending and consolidating my authority, and with other things, to bother about the details of governing the planet. As I have said before, you are probably the best manager alive today; but when it comes to formulating policies you're a complete bust. I am giving you the job of world dictator under one condition – that you run it *exactly* as I tell you to.'

'Ah, a wonderful opportunity, doctor! I assure you that...'

'Just a minute, Brookings! I can read your mind like an open book. You are still thinking that you can slip one over on me. Know now, once and for all, that it can't be done. I am keeping on you continuously automatic devices that are recording every order that you give, every message that you receive or send, and every thought that you think. The first time that you try any more of your funny work on me, I will come back here and finish up the job I started a few minutes ago. Play along with me and you can run the Earth as you please, subject only to my direction in broad matters of policy; try to double-cross me and you pass out of the picture. Get me?'

'I understand you thoroughly.' Brookings' agile mind flashed over the possibilities of DuQuesne's stupendous plan. His eyes sparkled as he thought of his own place in that plan, and he became his usual blandly alert self. 'As world dictator, I would of course be in a higher place than any that World Steel, as at present organized, could possibly offer. Therefore I will be glad to accept your offer, without reservations. Now, if you will, go ahead and give me an outline of what you propose. I will admit that I did harbor a few mental reservations at first, but you have convinced me that you actually can deliver the goods.'

'That's better. I have prepared full plans for the rebuilding of all our stations and Seaton's into my new type of power plant, for the erection of a new plant at every strategic point throughout the world, and for interlocking all these stations into one system. Here they are.' A bound volume of data and a mass of blueprints materialized in the air and dropped upon the desk. 'As soon as I have gone you can call in the chiefs of the engineering staff and put them to work.'

'I perceive what seem to me to be obstacles,' Brookings remarked, after his practiced eye had run over the salient points of the project and he had leafed over the pile of blueprints. 'We have not been able to do anything with Seaton's plants because of their enormous reserves of power, and his number one plant is to be the key station of our new network. Also, there simply are not men enough to do this work. These are slack times, I know, but even if we could get every unemployed man we still would not have enough. And, by the way, what became of Seaton? He apparently has not been around for some time.'

'You needn't worry about Seaton's plants – I'll line them up for you myself. As for Seaton, he was chased into the fourth dimension. He hasn't got back yet, and he probably won't; as I will explain to his crowd when I take them over. As for men, we shall have the combined personnel of all the armies and navies of the world. You think that even that force won't be enough, but it will. As you go over those plans in detail, you will see that by the proper use of dirigible forces we shall have plenty of man power.'

'How do you intend to subdue the armies and navies of the world?'

'It would take too long to go into detail. Turn on that radio there and listen, however, and you'll get it all – in fact, being on the inside, you'll be able to do a lot of reading between the lines that no one else will. Also, what I am going to do next will settle the doubt that is still in your mind as to whether I've really got the stuff.'

The projection vanished, and in a few minutes every radio receiving set throughout the world burst into stentorian voice. DuQuesne was broadcasting simultaneously upon every channel from five meters to five thousand, using a wave of such tremendous power that even two-million-watt stations were smothered at the very bases of their own transmitting towers.

'People of Earth, attention!' the speakers blared. 'I am speaking for the World Steel Corporation. From this time on the governments of all nations of the Earth will be advised and guided by the World Steel Corporation. For a long time I have sought some method of doing away with the stupidities of the present national governments. I have studied the possibilities of doing away with war and its attendant horrors. I have considered all feasible methods of correcting your present economic system, under which you have had constantly recurring cycles of boom and panic.

'Most of you have thought for years that something should be done about all these things. You are not only unorganized, however; you are and always have been racially distrustful and hence easily exploited by every self-seeking demagogue who has arisen to proclaim the dawn of a new day. Thus you have been able to do nothing to improve world conditions.

'It was not difficult to solve the problem of the welfare of mankind. It was quite another matter, however, to find a way of enforcing that solution. At last I have found it. I have developed a power sufficiently great to compel world-wide disarmament and to inaugurate productive employment of all men now bearing arms, as well as all persons now unemployed, at shorter hours and larger wages than any heretofore known. I have also developed means whereby I can trace with absolute certainty the perpetrators of any known crime, past or present; and I have both the power and the will to deal summarily with habitual criminals.

'The revolution which I am accomplishing will harm no one except parasites upon the body politic. National boundaries and customs shall remain as they are now. Governments will be overruled only when and as they impede the progress of civilization. War, however, will not be tolerated. I shall prevent it, not by killing the soldiers who would do the actual fighting, but by putting out of existence every person who attempts to foment strife. Those schemers I shall kill without mercy, long before their plans shall have matured.

'Trade shall be encouraged, and industry. Prosperity shall be world-wide and continuous, because of the high level of employment and remuneration. I do not ask you to believe all this, I am merely telling you. Wait and see – it will come true in less than thirty days.

'I shall now demonstrate my power by rendering the navy of the United States helpless, without taking a single life. I am now poised low over the city of Washington. I invite the Seventieth Bombing Squadron, which I see has already taken to the air, to drop their heaviest bombs upon me. I shall move out over the Potomac, so that the fragments will do no damage, and I shall not retaliate. I could wipe out that squadron without effort, but I have no desire to destroy brave men who are only obeying blindly the dictates of an outworn system.'

The space ship, which had extended across the city from Chevy Chase to Anacostia, moved out over the river, followed by the relatively tiny bombers. After a time the entire country-side was shaken by the detonations of the world's heaviest pro-jectiles, but DuQuesne's cold, clear voice went on:

'The bombers have done their best, but they have not even marred the outer plating of my ship. I will now show you what I can do if I should decide to do it. There is an obsolete battle-ship anchored off the Cape, which was to have been sunk by naval gunfire. I direct a force upon it – it is gone; volatilized almost instantly.

'I am now over Sandy Hook, I am not destroying the installa-tions, as I cannot do so without killing men. Therefore I am simply uprooting them and am depositing them gently upon the mud flats of the Mississippi River, at St. Louis, Missouri. Now I am sending out a force to each armed vessel of the United States navy, wheresoever situated upon the face of the globe.

'At such speed as is compatible with the safety of the per-sonnel, I am transporting those vessels through the air toward Salt Lake City, Utah. Tomorrow morning every unit of the American navy will float in Great Salt Lake. If you do not believe that I am doing this, read in your own newspaper to-morrow that I have done it.

'Tomorrow I shall treat similarly the navies of Great Britain, France, Italy, Japan, and the other maritime nations. I shall deal then with the military forces and their fortifications.

'I have already taken steps to abate the nuisance of certain widely known criminals and racketeers who have been conduct-ing, quite openly and flagrantly, a reign of terror for profit. Seven of those men have already died, and ten more are to die tonight. Your homes shall be safe from the kidnapper; your busi-nesses shall be safe from the extortioner and his skulking aid, the dynamiter.

'In conclusion, I tell you that the often-promised new era is here; not in words, but in actuality. Good-bye until tomorrow.'

DuQuesne flashed his projection down into Brookings' office. 'Well, Brookings, that's the start. You understand now what I am going to do, and you know that I can do it.'

'Yes. You undoubtedly have immense power, and you have taken exactly the right course to give us the support of a great number of people who would ordinarily be bitterly opposed to anything we do. But that talk of wiping out gangsters and racketeers sounded funny, coming from you.'

'Why should it? We are now beyond that stage. And, while public opinion is not absolutely necessary to our success it is always a potent force. No program of despotism, however benevolent, can expect to be welcomed unanimously; but the course I have outlined will at least provide the opposition.'

DuQuesne cut off his forces and sat back at the controls, relaxed, his black eyes staring into infinity. Earth was his, to do with as he wished; and he would soon have it so armed that he could hold it against the universe. Master of Earth! His highest ambition had been attained – or had it? The world, after all, was small – merely a mote in space. Why not be master of the entire galaxy? There was Norlamin to be considered, of course...

Norlamin!

Norlamin would not like the idea and would have to be pacified.

As soon as he got the Earth straightened out he would have to see what could be done about Norlamin.

10 : Captured!

'Dick!' Dorothy shrieked, flashing to Seaton's side; and, abandoning his fruitless speculations, he turned to confront two indescribable, yet vaguely recognizable, entities who had floated effortlessly into the control room of the *Skylark*. Large they were, and black — a dull, lusterless black — and each was possessed of four huge, bright lenses which apparently were eyes. 'Dick! What are they, anyway?'

'Life, probably; the intelligent, four-dimensional life that Mart fully expected to find here,' Seaton answered. 'I'll see if I can't send them a thought.'

Staring directly into those expressionless lenses the man sent out wave after wave of friendly thought, without result or reaction. He then turned on the power of the mechanical educator and donned a headset, extending another toward one of the weird visitors and indicating as clearly as he could by signs that it was to be placed back of the outlandish eyes. Nothing happened, however, and Seaton snatched off the useless phones.

'Might have known they wouldn't work!' he snorted. 'Electricity! Too slow — and those tubes probably won't be hot in less than ten years of this hypertime, besides. Probably wouldn't have been any good, anyway — their minds would of course be four-dimensional, and ours most distinctly are not. There may be some point — or rather, plane — of contact between their minds and ours, but I doubt it. They don't act warlike, though; we'll simply watch them a while and see what they do.'

But if, as Seaton had said, the intruders did not seem inimical, neither were they friendly. If any emotion at all affected them, it was apparently nothing more nor less than curiosity. They floated about, gliding here and there, their great eyes now close to this article, now that; until at last they floated *past* the arenak wall of the spherical space ship and disappeared.

Seaton turned quickly to his wife, ready to minister again to overstrained nerves, but much to his surprise he found Dorothy calm and intensely interested.

'Funny-looking things, weren't they, Dick?' she asked animatedly. 'They looked just like highly magnified chess knights with four hands; or like those funny little sea horses they have in the aquarium, only on a larger scale. Were those propellers they had instead of tails natural or artificial – could you tell?'

'Huh? What're you talking about? I didn't see any such details as that!' Seaton exclaimed.

'I couldn't, either, really,' Dorothy explained, 'until after I found out how to look at them. I don't know whether my method would appeal to a strictly scientific mind or not. I can't understand any of this fourth-dimensional, mathematical stuff of yours and Martin's anyway, so when I want to see anything out here I just pretend that the fourth dimension isn't there at all. I just look at what you call the three-dimensional surface and it looks all right. When I look at you that way, for instance, you look like my very own Dick, instead of like a cubist's four-dimensional nightmare.'

'You have hit it, Dorothy.' Crane had been visualizing four-dimensional objects as three-dimensional while she was speaking. 'That is probably the only way in which we can really perceive hyperthings at all.'

'It *does* work, at that!' Seaton exclaimed. 'Congratulations, Dot; you've made a contribution to science – but say, what's coming off now? We're going somewhere.'

For the *Skylark*, which had been floating freely in space – a motion which the senses of the wanderers had long since ceased to interpret as a sensation of falling – had been given an acceleration. Only a slight acceleration, barely enough to make the floor of the control room seem 'down,' but any acceleration at all in such circumstances was to the scientists cause for grave concern.

'Nongravitational, of course, or we would have felt it before – what's the answer, Mart, if any?' Seaton demanded. 'Suppose that they've taken hold of us with a tractor and are taking us for a ride?'

'It would appear that way. I wonder if the visiplates are still practical?' Crane moved over to number one visiplate and turned it in every direction. Nothing was visible in the abysmal, all-engulfing, almost palpable darkness of the absolute black outside the hull of the vessel.

'It wouldn't work, hardly,' Seaton commented. 'Look at our time here – we must be 'way beyond light. I doubt if we could see anything, even if we had a sixth-order projector – which of course we haven't.'

'But how about our light inside here, then?' asked Margaret. 'The lamps are burning, and we can see things.'

'I don't know, Peg,' Seaton replied. 'All this stuff is 'way past me. Maybe it's because the lights are traveling with us – no, that's out. Probably, as I intimated before, we aren't seeing things at all – just feeling them, some way or other. That must be it, I think – it's sure that the light-waves from those lamps are almost perfectly stationary, as far as we're concerned.'

'Oh, there's something!' Dorothy called. She had remained at the visiplate, staring into the impenetrable darkness. 'See, it just flashed on! We're falling toward ground of some kind. It doesn't look like any planet I ever saw before, either – it's perfectly endless and it's perfectly flat.'

The others rushed to the plates and saw, instead of the utter blackness of a moment before, an infinite expanse of level, uncurving hyperland. Though so distant from it that any planetary curvature should have been evident, they could perceive none. Flat that land was – a geometrical plane – and sunless, but apparently self-luminous; glowing with a strong, somewhat hazy, violet light. And now they could also see the craft which had been towing them. It was a lozenge-shaped affair, glowing fiercely with the peculiarly livid 'light' of the hyperplanet; and was now apparently exerting its maximum tractive effort in a vain attempt to hold the prodigious mass of *Skylark Two* against the seemingly slight force of gravitation.

'Must be some kind of hyperlight that we're seeing by,' Seaton cogitated. 'Must be sixth- or seventh-order velocity, at least, or we'd be . . .'

'Never mind the light or our seeing things!' Dorothy interrupted. 'We are falling, and we shall probably hit hard. Can't you do something about it?'

'Afraid not, Kitten.' He grinned at her. 'But I'll try it – Nope, everything's dead. No power, no control, no nothing, and there won't be until we snap back where we belong. But don't worry about a crash. Even if that ground is solid enough to crash us, and I don't think it is, everything out here, including gravity seems to be so feeble that it won't hurt us any.'

Scarcely had he finished speaking when the *Skylark* struck – or rather, floated gently downward into the ground. For, slight as was the force of gravitation, and partially counteracted as well by the pull of the towing vessel, the arenak globe did not even pause as it encountered the apparently solid rock of the surface of the planet – if planet it was. That rock billowed away upon all sides as the *Skylark* sank into it and through it, to come to a halt only after her mass had driven a vertical, smooth-sided well some hundreds of feet in depth.

Even though the Osnomian metal had been rendered much less dense than normal by its extrusion and expansion into the fourth dimension, yet it was still so much denser than the unknown material of the hyperplanet that it sank into that planet's rocky soil as a bullet sinks into thick jelly.

'Well, that's that!' Seaton declared. 'Thinness and tenuosity, as well as feebleness, seem to be characteristics of this hyper-material. Now we'll camp here peacefully for a while. Before they succeed in digging us out – if they try it, which they probably will – we'll be gone.'

Again, however, the venturesome and impetuous chemist was wrong. Feeble the hypermen were, and tenuous, but their curiosity was whetted even sharper than before. Derricks were rigged, and slings; but even before the task of hoisting the *Skylark* to the surface of the planet was begun, two of the peculiar denizens of the hyperworld were swimming down through the atmosphere of the four-dimensional well at whose bottom the Earth vessel lay. Past the arenak wall of the cruiser they dropped, and into the control room they floated.

'But I do not understand it at all, Dick,' Crane had been arguing. 'Postulating the existence of a three-dimensional object in four-dimensional space, a four-dimensional being could of course enter it at will, as your fingers entered that tobacco can. But since all objects here are in fact and of necessity four-dimensional, that condition alone should bar any such proceeding. Therefore, since you actually *did* take the contents out of that can without opening it, and since our recent visitors actually *did* enter and leave our vessel at will, I can only conclude that we must still be essentially three-dimensional in nature, even though constrained temporarily to occupy four-dimensional space.'

'Say, Mart, that's a thought! You're still the champion thinker of the universe, aren't you? That explains a lot of things I've been worrying myself black in the face about. I think I can explain it, too, by analogy. Imagine a two-dimensional man, one centimeter wide and ten or twelve centimeters long; the typical flatlander of the classical dimensional explanations. There he is, in a plane, happy as a clam and perfectly at home. Then some force takes him by one end and rolls him up into a spiral, or sort of semisolid cylinder, one centimeter long. He won't know what to make of it, but in reality he'll be a two-dimensional man occupying three-dimensional space.

'Now imagine further that we can see him, which of course is a pretty tall order, but necessary since this is a very rough analogy. We wouldn't know what to make of him, either, would we? Doesn't that square up with what we're going through now? We'd think that such a thing was quite a curiosity and want to find out about it, wouldn't we? That, I think, explains the whole thing, both our sensations and the actions of those sea horses – huh! Here they are again. Welcome to our city, strangers!'

But the intruders made no sign of understanding the message. They did not, could not, understand.

Their four-dimensional minds, conceived and reared in hyperspace and knowing nothing save hyperthings, were of course utterly incapable of receiving or of comprehending any thoughts emanating from the fundamentally three-dimensional Terrestrials.

The human beings, now using Dorothy's happily discovered method of dimensional reduction, saw that the hypermen did indeed somewhat resemble overgrown sea horses – the *hippocampus heptagonus* of Earthly zoology – but sea horses each equipped with a writhing, spinning, air-propeller tail and with four long and sinuous arms, terminating in many dexterous and prehensile fingers.

Each of those hands held a grappling trident; a peculiar, four-dimensional hyperforceps whose insulated, interlocking teeth were apparently electrodes – conductors of some hyper-equivalent of our Earthly electricity. With unmoved, expressionless 'faces' the two visitors floated about the control room, while Seaton and Crane sent out wave after wave of friendly thought and made signs of friendship in all the various pantomimic languages at their command.

'Look out, Mart, they're coming this way! I don't want to start anything hostile, but I don't particularly like the looks of those toad-stabbers of theirs, and if they start any funny business with them maybe we'd better wring their fishy little necks!'

But there was to be no neck-wringing – then. Slight of strength the hypermen were, and of but little greater density than the thin air through which they floated so easily; but they had no need of physical strength – then. Indeed, some little time was to elapse before they were even to suspect the undreamed-of potentialities inherent in the, to them, incomprehensible Terrestrial physiques.

Four tridents shot out, and in a monstrously obscure fashion reached *past* clothing skin, and ribs; seizing upon and holding firmly, but painlessly and gently, the vital nervous centers of the human bodies. Seaton tried to leap to the attack, but even his quickness was of no avail – even before he moved, a wave of intolerable agony surged throughout his being, ceasing only and completely when he relaxed, relinquishing his pugnacious attempt. Shiro, leaping from the galley with cleaver upraised, was similarly impaled and similarly subdued.

Then a hoisting platform appeared, and Seaton and Margaret were forced to board it. They had no choice; the first tensing of the muscles to resist the will of the hypermen was quelled instantly by a blast of such intolerable torture that no human body could possibly defy it for even the slightest perceptible instant of time.

'Take it easy, Dot – Mart,' Seaton spoke rapidly as the hoist started upward. 'Do whatever they say – no use taking much of that stuff – until Peg and I get back. We'll get back, too, believe me! They'll *have* to take these meat hooks out of us sometime, and when they do they'll think a cyclone has broken loose.'

11: Hyperland

Raging but impotent, Seaton stood motionless beside his friend's wife upon the slowly rising lift; while Crane, Dorothy, and Shiro remained in the control room of the *Skylark*. All were helpless, incapable alike of making a single movement not authorized by their grotesque captors. Feeble the hypermen were, as has been said; but at the first tensing of a human muscle in revolt there shot from the insulated teeth of the grappling hypertrident such a terrific surge of unbearably poignant torture that any thought of resistance was out of the question.

Even Seaton – fighter by instinct though he was, and reckless as he was and desperate at the thought of being separated from his beloved Dorothy – had been able to endure only three such shocks. The unimaginable anguish of the third rebuke, a particularly vicious and long-continued wrenching and wringing of the most delicate nerve centers of his being, had left him limp and quivering. He was still furious, still bitterly humiliated. His spirit was willing, but he was physically unable to drive his fiendishly tortured body to further acts of rebellion.

Thus it was that the improvised elevator of the hypermen carried two docile captives as it went *past* not *through* – the spherical arenak shell of *Skylark Two* and up the mighty well which the vessel had driven in its downward plunge. The walls of that pit were glassily smooth; or, more accurately, were like slag; as though the peculiarly unsubstantial rock of the hyperplanet had been actually melted by the force of the cruiser's descent, easy and gradual as the fall had seemed to the senses of the Terrestrials.

It was apparent also that the hypermen were having difficulty in lifting the, to them, tremendous weight of the two human bodies. The platform would go up a few feet, then pause. Up and pause, up and pause; again and again. But at last they reached the top of the well, and, wretched as he was, Seaton had to grin when he perceived that they were being hoisted by a derrick, whose over-driven engine, attended though it was by a veritable corps of mechanics, could lift them only a few feet at a time. Coughing and snorting, it ran slower and slower until, released from the load, it burst again into free motion to build up sufficient momentum to lift them another foot or so.

And all about the rim of that forty-foot well there were being erected other machines. Trusses were rising into the air, immense chains were being forged, and additional motors were being assembled. It was apparent that the *Skylark* was to be raised; and it was equally evident that to the hypermen that raising presented an engineering problem of no small magnitude.

'She'll be right here when we get back, Peg, as far as those jaspers are concerned,' Seaton informed his companion. 'If they have to slip their clutches to lift the weight of just us two, they'll have one sweet job getting the old *Skylark* back up here. They haven't got the slightest idea of what they're tackling – they can't begin to pile enough of that kind of machinery in this whole part of the country to budge her.'

'You speak as though you were quite certain of our returning.' Margaret spoke somberly. 'I wish that I could feel that way.'

'Sure I'm certain of it,' Seaton assured her. 'I've got it all figured out. Nobody can maintain one hundred per cent vigilance forever, and as soon as I get back into shape from that last twisting they gave me, I'll be fast enough to take advantage of the break when it comes.'

'Yes, but suppose it doesn't come?'

'It's bound to come sometime. The only thing that bothers me is that I can't even guess at when we're due to snap back into our own three-dimensional space. Since we couldn't detect any motion in an ether wave, though, I imagine that we'll have lots of time, relatively speaking, to get back here before the *Skylark* leaves. Ah! I wondered if they were going to make us walk to wherever it is they're taking us, but I see we ride – there comes something that must be an airship. Maybe we can make our break now instead of later.'

But the hyperman did not relax his vigilance for an instant as the vast, vague bulk of the flier hovered in the air beside their elevator. A port opened, a short gangplank shot out, and under the urge of the punishing tridents the two human beings stepped aboard. A silent flurry ensued among the weird crew of the vessel as its huge volume sank downward under the unheard-of-mass of the two captives, but no opportunity was afforded for escape – the gripping tridents did not relax, and at last the amazed officers succeeded in driving their motors sufficiently to lift the prodigious load into the air of the hyperplanet.

'Take a good long look around, Peg, so that you can help find our way back,' Seaton directed, and pointed out through the peculiarly transparent wall of their conveyance. 'See those three peaks over there, the only hills in sight? Our course is about twelve or fifteen degrees off the line of the right-hand two – and there's something that looks like a river down below us. The bend there is just about on line – see anything to mark it by?'

'Well, there's a funny-looking island, kind of heart-shaped, with a reddish-colored spire of rock – see it?'

'Fine – we ought to be able to recognize that. Bend, heart-island, red obelisk on what we'll call the upstream end. Now from here, what? Oh, we're turning – going upstream. Fine business! Now we'll have to notice when and where we leave this river, lake, or whatever it is.'

They did not, however, leave the course of the water. For hundreds of miles, apparently, it was almost perfectly straight, and for hours the airship of the hypermen bored through the air only a few hundred feet above its gleaming surface. Faster and faster the hypership flew onward, until it became a whistling, yelling projectile, tearing its way at a terrific but constant velocity through the complaining air.

But while that which was beneath them was apparently the fourth-dimensional counterpart of an Earthly canal, neither water nor landscape was in any sense familiar. No sun was visible, nor moon, nor the tiniest twinkling star. Where the heavens should have been there was merely a void of utter, absolute black, appalling in its uncompromising profundity. Indeed, the Terrestrials would have thought themselves blind were it not for the forbidding, Luciferean vegetation which, self-luminous with a ghastly bluish-violet pseudo-light, extended outward – flat – in every direction to infinity.

'What's the matter with it, Dick?' demanded Margaret, shivering. 'It's horrible, awful, unsettling. Surely anything that is actually seen must be capable of description? But this...' Her voice died away.

'Ordinarily, three-dimensionally, yes; but this, no,' Seaton assured her. 'Remember that our brains and eyes, now really pseudo-fourth-dimensional, are capable of seeing those things as they actually are; but that our entities – intelligences – whatever you like – are still three-dimensional and can neither comprehend nor describe them. We can grasp them only very roughly by transposing them into our own three-dimensional concepts, and that is a poor subterfuge that fails entirely to convey even an approximate idea. As for that horizon – or lack of it – it simply means that this planet is so big that it looks flat. Maybe it *is* flat in the fourth-dimension – I don't know!'

Both fell silent, staring at the weird terrain over which they were being borne at such an insane pace. Along its right line above that straight watercourse sped the airship, a shrieking arrow; and to the right of the observers and to left of them spread, as far as the eye could reach, a flatly unbroken expanse of the ghostly, livid, weirdly self-luminous vegetation of the unknowable hyperworld. And, slinking, leaping, or perchance flying between and among the boles and stalks of the rank forest growth could be glimpsed monstrous forms of animal life.

Seaton strained his eyes, trying to see them more clearly; but owing to the speed of the ship, the rapidity of the animals' movements, the unsatisfactory illumination, and the extreme difficulty of translating at all rapidly the incomprehensible four-dimensional forms into their three-dimensional equivalents, he could not even approximate either the size or the appearance of the creatures with which he, unarmed and defenseless, might have to deal.

'Can you make any sense out of those animals down there, Peg?' Seaton demanded. 'See, there's one just jumped out of the river and seemed to fly into that clump of bamboo-like stuff there. Get any details?'

'No. What with the poor light and everything being so awful and so distorted, I can hardly see anything at all. Why – what of them?'

'This of 'em. We're coming back this way, and we may have to come on foot. I'll try to steal a ship, of course, but the chance that we'll be able to get one – or to run it after we do get it – is mighty slim. But assuming that we are afoot, the more we know about what we're apt to go up against the better we'll be able to meet it. Oh, we're slowing down – been wondering what that thing up ahead of us is. It looks like a cross between the Pyramid of Cheops and the old castle of Bingen on the Rhine, but I guess it's a city – it seems to be where we're headed for.'

'Does this water actually flow out from the side of that wall, or am I seeing things?' the girl asked.

'It seems to – your eyes are all right, I guess. But why shouldn't it? There's a big archway, you notice – maybe they use it for power or something, and this is simply an outfall...'

'Oh, we're going in!' Margaret exclaimed, her hand flashing out to Seaton's arm.

'Looks like it, but they probably know their stuff.' He pressed her hand reassuringly. 'Now, Peg, no matter what happens, stick to me as long as you possibly can!'

As Seaton had noticed, the city toward which they were flying resembled somewhat an enormous pyramid, whose component units were themselves mighty buildings, towering one above and behind the other in crenelated majesty to an awe-inspiring height. In the wall of the foundation tier of buildings there yawned an enormous opening, spanned by a noble arch of metaled masonry, and out of this gloriously arched aqueduct there sprang the stream whose course the airship had been following so long. Toward that forbidding opening the hyper-ship planed down, and into it she floated slowly and carefully.

Much to the surprise of the Terrestrials, however, the great tunnel of the aqueduct was not dark. Walls and arched ceiling alike glowed with the livid, bluish-violet ultra-light which they had come to regard as characteristic of all hyperthings, and through that uncanny glare the airship stole along. Once inside the tunnel its opening vanished – imperceptible, indistinguishable from its four-dimensional, black-and-livid-blue background.

Unending that tunnel stretched before and behind them. Walls and watery surface alike were smooth, featureless, and so uniformly and weirdly luminous that the eye could not fix upon any point firmly enough to determine the rate of motion of the vessel – or even to determine whether it was moving at all. No motion could be perceived or felt and the time-sense had long since failed. Seaton and Margaret may have traveled in that gigantic bore for inches or for miles of distance; for seconds or for weeks of hypertime; they did not then and never did know. But with a slight jar the hypership came to rest at last upon a metallic cradle which had in some fashion appeared beneath her keel. Doors opened and the being holding the tridents, who had not moved a muscle during the, to the Terrestrials, interminable journey, made it plain to them that they were to precede him out of the airship. They did so, quietly and without protest, utterly helpless to move save at the behest of their unhuman captor-guide.

Through a maze of corridors and passages the long way led. Each was featureless and blank, each was lighted by the same eerie, bluish light, each was paved with a material which, although stone-hard to the hypermen, yielded springily, as yields a soft peat bog, under the feet of the massive Terrestrials. Seaton, although now restored to full vigor, held himself rigorously in check. Far from resisting the controlling impulses of the trident he sought to anticipate those commands.

Indeed, recognizing the possibility that the captor might be aware, through those electrical connections, of his very ideas, he schooled his outward thoughts to complete and unquestioning submission. Yet never had his inner brain been more active, and now the immense mentality given him by the Norlaminians stood him in good stead. For every doorway, every turn, every angle and intersection of that maze of communicating passageways was being engraved indelibly upon his brain – he knew that no matter how long or how involved the way, he could retain his orientation with respect to the buried river up which they had sailed.

And, although quiescent enough and submissive enough to all outward seeming, his inner brain was keyed up to its highest pitch, ready and eager to drive his muscles into furious activity at the slightest lapse of the attention of the wielder of the mastering trident.

But there was no such lapse. The intelligence of the hyperman seemed to be concentrated in the glowing tips of the forceps and did not waver for an instant, even when an elevator into which he steered his charges refused to lift the immense weight put upon it.

A silent colloquy ensued, then Seaton and Margaret walked endlessly up a spiral ramp. Climbed, it seemed, for hours, their feet sinking to the ankles into the resilient material of the rock-and-metal floor, while their alert guardian floated effortlessly in the air behind them, propelled and guided by his swiftly revolving tail.

Eventually the ramp leveled off into a corridor. Straight ahead, two aisles – branch half right – branch half left – first turn left – third turn right – second doorway on right. They stopped. The door opened. They stepped into a large, office-like room, thronged with the peculiar, sea-horselike hypermen of this four-dimensional civilization. Everything was indescribable, incomprehensible, but there seemed to be desks, mechanisms, and tier upon tier of shelf-like receptacles intended for the storage of they knew not what.

Most evident of all, however, were the huge, goggling, staring eyes of the creatures as they pressed in, closer and closer to the helplessly immobile bodies of the man and the woman. Eyes dull, expressionless, and unmoving to Earthly, three-dimensional intelligences; but organs of highly intelligible, flashing language, as well as of keen vision, to their possessors.

Thus it was that the very air of the chamber was full of speech and of signs, but neither Margaret nor Seaton could see or hear them. In turn the Earthman tried, with every resource at his command of voice, thought, and pantomime, to bridge the gap – in vain.

Then strange, many-lensed instruments were trundled into the room and up to the helpless prisoners. Lenses peered; multi-colored rays probed; planimeters, pantographs, and plotting points traced and recorded every bodily part; the while the two sets of intelligences, each to the other so foreign, were at last compelled to acknowledge frustration. Seaton of course knew what caused the impasse and, knowing the fundamental incompatibility of the dimensions involved, had no real hope that communication could be established, even though he knew the hypermen to be of high intelligence and attainment.

The natives, however, had no inkling of the possibility of

three-dimensional actualities. Therefore, when it had been made plain to them that they had no point of contact with their visitors – that the massive outlanders were and must remain unresponsive to their every message and signal – they perforce ascribed that lack of response to a complete lack of intelligence.

The chief of the council, who had been conducting the examination, released the forces of his mechanisms and directed his flashing glance upon the eyes of the Terrestrials' guard, ordering him to put the specimens away.

'... and see to it that they are watched very carefully,' the ordering eye concluded. 'The Fellows of Science will be convened and will study them in greater detail than we have been able to do here.'

'Yes, sir; as you have said, so shall it be,' the guard acknowledged, and by means of the trident he guided his captives through a high-arched exit and into another labyrinth of corridors.

Seaton laughed aloud as he tucked Margaret's hand under his arm and marched along under the urge of the admonishing trident.

' "Nobody 'ome – they ain't got no sense," says his royal nibs. "Tyke 'em awye!" ' he exclaimed.

'Why so happy all of a sudden, Dick? I can't see very much change in our status.'

'You'd be surprised.' He grinned. 'There's been a lot of change. I've found out that they can't read our thoughts at all, as long as we don't express them in muscular activity. I've been guarding my thoughts and haven't been talking to you much for fear they could get my ideas some way. But now I can tell you that I'm going to start something pretty quick. I've got this trident thing pretty well solved. This bird's taking us to jail now, I think, and when he gets us there his grip will probably slip for an instant. If it does he'll never get it back, and we'll be merrily on our way.'

'To jail!' Margaret exclaimed. 'But suppose they put us – I hope they put us in the same cell!'

'Don't worry about that. If my hunch is right it won't make a bit of difference – I'll have you back before they can get you out of sight. Everything around here is thin almost to the point of being immaterial, you know – you could whip an army of them in purely physical combat, and I could tear this whole joint up by the roots.'

'À la Samson? I believe that you could, at that.' Margaret smiled.

'Yeah; or rather, you can play you're Paul Bunyan, and I'll be Babe, the big blue ox. We'll show this flock of proptailed gilli-wimpuses just how we gouged out Lake Superior to make a he-man's soup bowl!'

'You make me feel a lot better, Dick, even if I do remember that Babe was forty-seven ax handles across the horns.' Margaret laughed, but sobered quickly. 'But here we are – oh, I *do* hope that he leaves me with you!'

They stopped beside a metal grill, in front of which was poised another hyperman, his propeller tail idling slowly. He had thought that he was to be Seaton's jailer, and as he swung the barred gate open he engaged the Terrestrial's escort in optical conversation – a conversation which gave Seaton the mere instant of time for which he had been waiting.

'So these are the visitors from outer space, whose bodies are so much denser than solid metal?' he asked curiously. 'Have they given you much trouble?'

'None at all. I touched that one only once, and this one, that you are to keep here, wilted at only the third step of force. The orders are to keep them under control every minute, however. They are stupid, senseless brutes, as is of course to be expected from their mass and general make-up. They have not given a single sign of intelligence of even the lowest order, but their strength is apparently enormous, and they might do a great deal of damage if allowed to break away from the trident.'

'All right; I'll hold him constantly until I am relieved,' and the jailer, lowering his own trident, extended a long, tentacular arm toward the grooved and knobbed shaft of the one whose teeth were already imbedded in Seaton's tissues.

Seaton had neither perceived nor sensed anything of this conversation, but he was tense and alert; tight-strung to take advantage of even the slightest slackening of the grip of the grappling fingers of the controller. Thus in the bare instant of transfer of control from one weird being to the other he acted –

instantaneously and highly effectively.

With a twisting leap he whirled about, wrenching himself free from the punishing teeth of the grapple. Lightning hands seized the shaft and swung the weapon in a flashing arc. Then, with all the quickness of his highly trained muscles and with all the power of his brawny right arm, Seaton brought the controller down full upon the grotesque head of the hyperman.

He had given no thought to the material character of weapon or of objective; he had simply wrenched himself free and struck instinctively, lethally, knowing that freedom had to be won then or never. But he was not wielding an Earthly club or an Osnomian bar; nor was the flesh opposing him the solid substance of a human and three-dimensional enemy.

At impact the fiercely driven implement flew into a thousand pieces, but such was the power behind it that each piece continued on, driving its relentless way through the tenuous body substance of the erstwhile guard. That body subsided instantly upon the floor, a shapeless and mangled mass of oozing, dripping flesh. Weaponless now, holding only the shattered butt of the ex-guard's trident, Seaton turned to front the other guard who, still holding Margaret helpless, was advancing upon him, wide-open trident to the fore.

He hurled the broken stump; then as the guard nimbly dodged the flying missile, he leaped to the barred door of the cell. He seized it and jerked mightily; and as the anchor bolts of the hinges tore out of the masonry he swung the entire gate in a full-sweeping circle. Through the soft body the interlaced bars tore, cutting it into grisly, ghastly dice, and on, across the hall, tearing into and demolishing the opposite wall.

'All right, Peg, or did he shock you?' Seaton demanded.

'All right, I guess – he didn't have time to do much of anything.'

'Fine, let's snap it up, then. Or wait a minute. I'd better get us a couple of shields. We've got to keep them from getting those stingarees into us again – as long as we can keep them away from us we can do about as we please around here, but if they ever get hold of us again it'll be just too bad.'

While Seaton was speaking he had broken away and torn out two great plates or doors of solid metal, and, handing one of them to his companion, he went on: 'Here, carry this in front of you and we'll go places and do things.'

But in that time, short as it was, the alarm had been given, and up the corridor down which they must go was advancing a corps of heavily armed beings. Seaton took one quick step forward, then realizing the impossibility of forcing his way through such a horde without impalement, he leaped backward to the damaged wall and wrenched out a huge chunk of masonry. Then, while the upper wall and the now unsupported ceiling collapsed upon him, their fragments touching his hard body lightly and bouncing off like so many soft pillows, he hurled that chunk of material down the hall and into the thickest ranks of the attackers.

Through the close-packed phalanx it tore as would a plunging tank through massed infantry, nor was it alone.

Mass after mass of rock was hurled as fast as the Earthman could bend and straighten his mighty back, and the hypermen broke ranks and fled in wild disorder.

For to them Seaton was not a man of flesh and blood, lightly tossing pillows of eiderdown along a corridor, through an assemblage of wraithlike creatures. He was to them a monstrous being, constructed of something harder, denser, and tougher than any imaginable metal. A being driven by engines of unthinkable power, who stood unharmed and untouched while masses of stone, brickwork, and structural steel crashed down upon his bare head. A being who caught those falling masses of granite and concrete and steel and hurled them irresistibly through rank after rank of flesh-and-blood men!

'Let's go, Peg!' Seaton gritted. 'The way's clear now, I guess – we'll show those horse-faced hippocampuses that what it takes to do things, we've got!'

Through the revolting, reeking shambles of the corpse-littered corridor they gingerly made their way. Past the scene of the battle, past intersection after intersection they retraced their course, warily and suspiciously at first. But no ambush had been laid – the hypermen were apparently only too glad to let them go in peace – and soon they were hurrying along as fast as Margaret could walk.

They were soon to learn, however, that the denizens of this

city of four-dimensional space had not yet given up the chase. Suddenly the yielding floor dropped away beneath their feet and they fell, or rather, floated, easily and slowly downward. Margaret shrieked in alarm, but the man remained unmoved and calm.

''Sall right, Peg,' he assured her. 'We want to go clear down to the bottom of this dump, anyway, and this'll save us the time and trouble of walking down. All right; that is, if we don't sink into the floor so deep when we hit that we won't be able to get ourselves out of it. Better spread out that shield so you'll fall on it – it won't hurt you, and it may help a lot.'

So slowly were they falling that they had ample time in which to prepare for the landing; and, since both Seaton and Margaret were thoroughly accustomed to weightless maneuvering in free space, their metal shields were flat beneath them when they struck the lowermost floor of the citadel. Those shields were crushed, broken, warped and twisted as they were forced into the pavement by the force of the falling bodies – as would be the steel doors of a bank vault upon being driven broadside on, deep into a floor of solid concrete.

But they served their purpose; they kept the bodies of the Terrestrials from sinking beyond their depth into the floor of the hyperdungeon. As they struggled to their feet, unhurt, and saw that they were in a large, cavernous room, six searchlight-like projectors came into play, enveloping them in a flood of soft, pinkish-white light.

Seaton stared about him, uncomprehending, until he saw that one of the hypermen, caught accidentally in the beam, shriveled horribly and instantly into a few floating wisps of luminous substance which in a few seconds disappeared entirely.

'Huh! Death rays!' he exclaimed then. ''Sa good thing for us we're essentially three-dimensional yet, or we'd probably never have known what struck us. Now let's see – where's our river? Oh, yes; over this way. Wonder if we'd better take these shields along? Guess not, they're pretty well shot – we'll pick us up a couple of good ones on the way, and I'll get you a grill like this one to use as a flail.'

'But there's no door on that side!' Margaret protested.

'So what? We'll roll our own as we go along.'

His heavy boot crashed against the wall before them, and a section of it fell outward. Two more kicks and they were through, hurrying along passages which Seaton knew led toward the buried river, breaking irresistibly through solid walls whenever the corridor along which they were moving angled away from his chosen direction.

Their progress was not impeded. The hyperbeings were willing – yes, anxious – for their unmanageable prisoners to depart and made no further attempts to bar their path. Thus the river was soon reached.

The airship in which they had been brought to the hypercity was nowhere to be seen, and Seaton did not waste time looking for it. He had been unable to understand the four-dimensional controls even while watching them in operation, and he realized that even if he could find the vessel the chance of capturing it and of escaping in it were slight indeed. Therefore throwing an arm around his companion, he leaped without ado into the speeding current.

'But, Dick, we'll drown!' Margaret protested. 'This stuff is altogether too thin for us to swim in – we'll sink like rocks!'

'Sure we will, but what of it?' he returned. 'How many times have you actually breathed since we left three-dimensional space?'

'Why, thousands of times, I suppose – or, now that you mention it, I don't really know whether I'm breathing at all or not – but we've been gone so long ... Oh, I don't believe that I really know *anything*!'

'You aren't breathing at all,' he informed her then. 'We have been expending energy, though, in spite of that fact, and the only way I can explain it is that there must be fourth-dimensional oxygen or we would have suffocated long ago. Being three-dimensional, of course we wouldn't have to breathe it in for the cells to get the benefit of it – they grab it direct. Incidentally, that probably accounts for the fact that I'm hungry as a wolf, but that'll have to wait until we get back into our own space again.'

True to Seaton's prediction, they suffered no inconvenience as they strode along the metaled pavement of the river's bottom, Seaton still carrying the bent and battered grating with which he had wrought such havoc in the corridor so far above.

Almost at the end of the tunnel, a sharklike creature darted upon them, dreadful jaws agape. With his left arm Seaton threw Margaret behind him, while with his right he swung the four-dimensional grating upon the monster of the deeps. Under the fierce power of the blow the creature became a pulpy mass, drifting inertly away upon the current, and Seaton stared after it ruefully.

'That particular killing was entirely unnecessary, and I'm sorry I did it,' he remarked.

'Unnecessary? Why, it was going to bite me!' she cried.

'Yeah, it *thought* it was, but it would have been just like one of our own real sharks trying to bite the chilled-steel prow off a battleship,' he replied. 'Here comes another one. I'm going to let him gnaw on my arm, and see how he likes it.'

On the monster came with a savage rush, until the dreadful outthrust snout almost touched the man's bare, extended arm. Then the creature stopped, dead still in mid-rush, touched the arm tentatively, and darted away with a quick flirt of its powerful tail.

'See, Peg, he knows we ain't good to eat. None of these hyperanimals will bother us – it's only these men with their meat hooks that we have to fight shy of. Here's the jump-off. Better we hit it easylike – I wouldn't wonder if that sandy bottom would be pretty tough going. I think maybe we'd better take to the beach as soon as we can.'

From the metaled pavement of the brilliantly lighted aqueduct they stepped out upon the natural sand bottom of the open river. Above them was only the somberly sullen intensity of velvety darkness; a darkness only slightly relieved by the bluely luminous vegetation upon the river's either bank. In spite of their care they sank waist-deep into that sand, and it was only with great difficulty that they fought their way up to the much firmer footing of the nearer shore.

Out upon the margin at last, they found that they could make good time, and they set out downstream at a fast but effortless pace. Mile after mile they traveled, until, suddenly, as though some universal switch had been opened, the ghostly radiance of all the vegetation of the countryside disappeared in an instant, and utter and unimaginable darkness descended as a pall. It was not the ordinary darkness of an Earthly night, nor yet the darkness of even an Earthly dark room; it was indescribable, completely perfect darkness of the total absence of every ray of light.

'Dick!' shrieked Margaret. 'Where are you?'

'Right here, Peg – take it easy,' he advised, and groping fingers touched and clung. 'They'll probably light up again. Maybe this is their way of having night. We can't do much, anyway, until it gets light again. We couldn't possibly find the *Skylark* in this darkness; and even if we could feel our way downriver we'd miss the island that marks our turning-off point. Here, I feel a nice soft rock. I'll sit down with my back against it and you can lie down, with my lap for a pillow, and we'll take us a nap. Wasn't it Porthos, or some other one of Dumas' characters that said, "He who sleeps, eats"?'

'Dick, you're a perfect peach to take things the way you do.' Margaret's voice was broken. 'I know what you're thinking of, too. Oh, I *do* hope that nothing has become of them!' For she well knew that, true and loyal friend though Seaton was, yet his every thought was for beloved Dorothy, presumably still in *Skylark Two* – just as Martin Crane came first with her in everything.

'Sure they're all right, Peg.' An instantly suppressed tremor shook his giant frame. 'They're figuring on keeping them in the *Lark* until they raise her, I imagine. If I had known as much then as I know now they'd never have got away with any of this stuff – but it can't be helped now. I wish I could do something, because if we don't get back to *Two* pretty quick it seems as though we may snap back into our own three dimensions and land in empty space. Or would we, necessarily? The time coordinates would change, too, of course, and that change might very well make it obligatory for us to be back in our exact original locations in the *Lark* at the instant of transfer, no matter where we happen to be in this hyperspace–hypertime continuum. Too deep for me – I can't figure it. Wish Mart was here, maybe he could see through it.'

'You don't wish half as much as I do!' Margaret exclaimed feelingly.

'Well, anyway, we'll pretend that *Two* can't run off and leave us here. That certainly is a possibility, and it's a cheerful thought to dwell on while we can't do anything else. Now close your eyes and go bye-bye.'

They fell silent. Now and again Margaret dozed, only to start awake at the coughing grunt of some near-by prowling hyper-denizen of that unknown jungle, but Seaton did not sleep. He did not even half believe in his own hypothesis of their auto-matic return to their space ship; and his vivid imagination in-sisted upon dwelling lingeringly upon every hideous possibility of their return to three-dimensional space outside their vessel's sheltering walls. And the same imagination continually conjured up visions of what might be happening to Dorothy – to the beloved bride who, since their marriage upon far distant Os-nome, had never before been separated from him for so long a time. He had to struggle against an insane urge to do something, anything; even to dash madly about in the absolute darkness of hyperspace in a mad attempt – doomed to certain failure before it was begun – to reach *Skylark Two* before she should vanish from four-dimensional space.

Thus, while Seaton grew more and more tense momently, more and ever more desperately frustrated, the abysmally op-pressive hypernight wore illimitably on. Creeping – plodding – d-r-a-g-g-i-n-g endlessly along; extending itself fantastically into the infinite reaches of all eternity.

12 : Reunion

As suddenly as the hyperland had become dark it at last became light. There was no gradual lightening, no dawning, no warning – in an instant, blindingly to eyes which had for so long been strained in vain to detect even the faintest ray of visible light in the platinum-black darkness of the hypervoid, the entire countryside burst into its lividly glowing luminescence. As the light appeared Seaton leaped to his feet with a yell.

'Yowp! I was never so glad to see a light before in all my life, even if it *is* blue! Didn't sleep much either, did you, Peg?'

'Sleep? I don't believe that I'll *ever* be able to sleep again! It seemed as though I was lying there for weeks!'

'It did seem long, but time is meaningless to us here, you know.'

The two set out at a rapid pace, down the narrow beach beside the hyperstream. For a long time nothing was said, then Margaret broke out, half hysterically:

'Dick, this is simply driving me mad! I think probably I *am* mad, already. We seem to be walking, yet we aren't, really; we're going altogether too fast, and yet we don't seem to be getting anywhere. Besides, it's taking forever and ever...'

'Steady, Peg! Keep a stiff upper lip! Of course we really aren't walking, in a three-dimensional sense, but we're getting there, just the same. I'd say that we are traveling almost half as fast as that airship was, which is a distinctly cheerful thought. And don't try to think of anything in detail, because equally of course we can't understand it. Try not to think of anything at all, out here, because you can't get to first base. You can *do* it, physically – let it go at that.

'And as for time, forget it. Just remember that, as far as we are concerned, this whole episode is occupying only a thousandth of a second of our own real time, even if it seems to last a thousand years. Paste that idea in your hat and stick to it. Think of a thousandth of a second and snap your fingers at anything that happens. And, above all, get it down solid that you're not nutty – it's just that everything else around here is.

109

It's like that wild one Sir Eustace pulled on me that time, remember? "I say, Seaton old chap, the chaps hereabout seem to regard me as a foreigner. Now really, you know, they should realize that I am simply alone in a nation of foreigners." '

Margaret laughed, recovering a measure of her customary poise at Seaton's matter-of-fact explanations and reassurance, and the seemingly endless journey went on. Indeed, so long did it seem that the high-strung and apprehensive Seaton was every moment expecting the instantaneous hypernight again to extinguish all illumination long before they came within sight of the little island, with its unmistakably identifying obelisk of reddish stone.

'Woof, but that's a relief!' he exploded at sight of the marker. 'We'll be there in a few minutes more – here's hoping it holds off for those few minutes!'

'It will,' Margaret said confidently. 'It'll have to, now that we're so close. How are you possibly going to get a line on those three peaks? We cannot possibly see over or through that jungle.'

'Easy – just like shooting fish down a well. That's one reason I was so glad to see that tall obelisk thing over there – it's big enough to hold my weight and high enough so that I can see the peaks from its top. I'm going to climb up it and wigwag you onto the line we want. Then we'll set a pole on that line and crash through the jungle, setting up back-sights as we go along. We'll be able to see the peaks in a mile or so, and once we see them it'll be easy to find *Two*.'

'But climbing Cleopatra's Needle comes first, and it's straight up and down,' Margaret objected practically. 'How are you going to do that?'

'With a couple of hypergrab-hooks – watch me!'

He wrenched off three of the bars of his cell grating and twisted them together, to form a heavy rod. One end of this rod he bent back upon itself, sharpening the end by squeezing it in his two hands. It required all of his prodigious strength, but in his grasp the metal slowly flowed together in a perfect weld and he waved in the air a sharply pointed hook some seven feet in length. In the same way he made another, and, with a word to the girl, he shot away through the almost intangible water toward the island.

He soon reached the base of the obelisk, and into its rounded surface he drove one of his hyperhooks. But he struck too hard. Though the hook was constructed of the most stubborn metal known to the denizens of that strange world, the obelisk was of hyperstone and the improvised tool rebounded, bent out of all semblance and useless.

It was quickly reshaped, however, and Seaton went more gently about his task. He soon learned exactly how much pressure his hooks would stand, and also the best method of imbedding the sharp metal points in the rock of the monument. Then, both hooks holding, he drove the toe of one heavy boot into the stone and began climbing.

Soon, however, his right-hand hook refused to bite; the stone had so dulled the point of the implement that it was useless. After a moment's thought Seaton settled both feet firmly, and, holding the shaft of the left-hand hook under his left elbow, bent the free end around behind his back. Then, both hands free, he essayed the muscle-tearing task of squeezing that point again into serviceability.

'Watch out, Dick – you'll fall!' Margaret called.

'I'll try not to,' he called back cheerfully. 'Took too much work and time to get up this far to waste it. Wouldn't hurt me if I did fall – but you might have to come over and pull me out of the gound.'

He did not fall. The hook was repointed without accident and he continued up the obelisk – a human fly walking up a vertical column. Four times he had to stop to sharpen his climbers, but at last he stood atop the lofty shaft. From that eminence he could see not only the three peaks, but even the scene of confused activity which he knew marked the mouth of the gigantic well at whose bottom the *Skylark* lay. Margaret had broken off a small tree, and from the obelisk's top Seaton directed its placing as a transitman directs the setting of his head flag.

'Left – 'way left!' His arm waved its hook in great circles. 'Easy now!' Left arm poised aloft. 'All right for line!' Both arms swept up and down, once. A careful recheck ... 'Back a hair.' Right arm out, insinuatingly. 'All right for tack – down she goes!' Both arms up and down, twice, and the feminine flagman drove the marker deep into the sand.

'You might come over here, Peg!' Seaton shouted, as he began his hasty descent. 'I'm going to climb down until my hooks get too dull to hold, and then fall the rest of the way – no time to waste sharpening them – and you may have to rally round with a helping hand.'

Scarcely a third of the way down, one hook refused to function. A few great plunging steps downward and the other also failed – would no longer even scratch the stubborn stone. Already falling, Seaton gathered himself together, twisted bars held horizontally beneath him, and floated gently downward. He came to the ground no harder than he would have landed after jumping from a five-foot Earthly fence; but even his three-ply bars of hypermetal did not keep him from plunging several feet into that strangely unsubstantial hyperground.

Margaret was there, however, with her grating and her plate of armor. With her aid Seaton struggled free, and together they waded through the river and hurried to the line post which Margaret had set. Then, along the line established by the obelisk and the post, the man crashed into the thick growth of the jungle, the woman at his heels.

Though the weirdly peculiar trees, creepers, and bamboo-like shoots comprising the jungle's vegetation were not strong enough to bar the progress of the dense, hard, human bodies, yet they impeded that progress so terribly that the trail-breaker soon halted.

'Not so good this way, Peg,' he reflected. 'These creepers will soon pull you down, I'm afraid; and, besides, we'll be losing our line pretty quickly. What to do? Better I knock out a path with this magic wand of mine, I guess – none of this stuff seems to be very heavy.'

Again they set out; Seaton's grating, so bent and battered now that it could not be recognized as once having been the door of a prison cell, methodically sweeping from side to side; a fiercely driven scythe against which no hyperthing could stand. Vines and creepers still wrapped around and clung to the struggling pair; shattered masses drifted down upon them from above, exuding in floods a viscous, gluey sap; and both masses of broken vegetation and floods of adhesive juices reenforced and rendered even more impassable the already high-piled wilderness of debris which had been accumulating there during time unthinkable. All hypernature seemed to be in league against them; feebly but clingingly attempting to hold them back and devour them.

Thus hampered, but driven to highest effort by the fear of imminent darkness and consequent helplessness, they struggled indomitably on. On and on; while behind them stretched an ever-lengthening, straight, sharply cut streak of blackness in the livid hyperlight of the jungle. On and on; Seaton flailing a path through the standing jungle, Margaret plowing along in his wake, fighting, struggling through and over the matted tangle of underbrush and the grasping, clinging tentacles of its parasitic inhabitants.

Seaton's great mass and prodigious strength enabled him to force his way through that fantastically inimical undergrowth, but the unremitting pull and drag of the attacking vines wore down the woman's slighter physique.

'Just a minute, Dick!' She stopped, strength almost spent. 'I hate to admit that I can't stand the pace, especially since you are doing all the work, as well as wading through the same mess that I am, but I don't believe that I can go on much longer without a rest.'

'All right...' Seaton began, but broke off, staring ahead. 'No; keep on coming one minute more, Peg – three more jumps and we're through.'

'I can go that much farther, of course. Lead on, MacDuff!' and they struggled on.

In a few more steps they broke out of the thick growth of the jungle and into the almost-palpable darkness of a great, roughly circular area which had been cleared of the prolific growth. In the center of this circle could be seen the bluely illuminated works of the engineers who were raising *Skylark Two*. The edge of the great well was surrounded by four-dimensional machinery; and that well's wide apron and its towering derricks were swarming with hypermen.

'Stay behind me, Peg, but as close as you can without getting hit,' the man instructed his companion after a hasty but comprehensive study of the scene. 'Keep your shield up and have your grating in good swinging order. I'll be able to take care of most of them, I think, but you want to be ready to squash any of them that may get around me or who may rush us from behind. Those stickers of theirs are bad medicine, girl, and we don't want to take any chances at all of getting stuck again.'

'I'll say we don't!' she agreed feelingly, and Seaton started off over the now unencumbered ground. 'Wait a minute, Dick – where are you, anyway? I can't see you at all!'

'That's right, too. Never thought of it, but there's no light. The glimmer of those plants is pretty faint at best, and doesn't reach out here at all. We'd better hold hands, I guess, until we get close enough to the works out there so that we can see what we're doing and what's going on.'

'But I've got only two hands – I'm not a hippocampus – and they're both full of doors and clubs and things. But maybe I can carry this shield under my arm – it isn't heavy – there, where are you, anyway?'

Seeking hands found each other, and, hand in hand, the two set out boldly toward the scene of activity so starkly revealed in the center of that vast circle of darkness. So appalling was the darkness that it was a thing tangible – palpable. Seaton could not see his companion, could not see the weapons and the shield he bore, could not even faintly discern the very ground upon which he walked. Yet he plunged forward, almost dragging the girl along bodily, eyes fixed upon the bluely gleaming circle of structures which was his goal.

'But Dick!' Margaret panted. 'Let's not go so fast; I can't see a thing – not even my hand right in front of my eyes – and I'm afraid we'll bump into something – anything!'

'We've got to snap it up, Peg,' the man replied, not slackening his pace in the slightest, 'and there's nothing very big between us and the *Skylark*, or we could see it against those lights. We may stumble over something, of course, but it'll be soft enough so that it won't hurt us any. But suppose that another night clamps down on us before we get out there?'

'Oh, that's right; it did come awfully suddenly,' and Margaret leaped ahead; dread of the abysmally horrible hypernight so far outweighing her natural fear of unseen obstacles in her

114

path that the man was hard put to it to keep up with her. 'Suppose they'll know we're coming?'

'Maybe – probably – I don't know. I don't imagine they can see us, but since we cannot understand anything about them, it's quite possible thay they may have other senses that we know nothing about. They'll have to spot us mighty quick, though, if they expect to do themselves any good.'

The hypermen could not see them, but it was soon made evident that the weird beings had indeed, in some unknown fashion, been warned of their coming. Mighty searchlights projected great beams of livid blue light, beams which sought eagerly the human beings – probing, questing, searching.

As he perceived the beams Seaton knew that the hypermen could not see without lights any better than he could; and knowing what to expect, he grinned savagely into the darkness as he threw an arm around Margaret and spoke – or thought – to her.

'One of those beams'll find us pretty quick, and they may send something along it. If so, and if I yell jump, do it quick. Straight up; high, wide, and handsome – jump!'

For even as he spoke, one of the stabbing beams of light found them and had stopped full upon them. And almost instantly had come flashing along that beam a horde of hypermen, armed with peculiar weapons at whose use the Terrestrials could not even guess.

But also almost instantly had Seaton and Margaret jumped – jumped with the full power of Earthly muscles which, opposed by only the feeble gravity of hyperland, had given their bodies such a velocity that to the eyes of the hypermen their intended captives had simply and instantly disappeared.

'They knew we were there, all right, some way or other – maybe our mass jarred the ground – but they apparently can't see us without lights, and that gives us a break,' Seaton remarked conversationally, as they soared interminably upward. 'We ought to come down just about where that tallest derrick is – right where we can go to work on them.'

But the scientist was mistaken in thinking that the hypermen had discovered them through tremors of the ground. For the searching cones of light were baffled only for seconds; then, guided by some sense or by some mechanism unknown and unknowable to any three-dimensional intelligence, they darted aloft and were once more outlining the fleeing Terrestrials in the bluish glare of their livid radiance. And upward, along those illuminated ways, darted those living airplanes, the hypermen; and this time the man and the woman, with all their incredible physical strength could not leap aside.

'Not so good,' said Seaton, 'better we'd stayed on the ground, maybe. They *could* trace us, after all; and of course this air is their natural element. But now that we're up here, we'll just have to fight them off; back to back, until we land.'

'But how can we stay back to back?' asked Margaret sharply. 'We'll drift apart at our first effort. Then they'll be able to get behind us and they'll have us again!'

'That's so, too – never thought of that angle, Peg. You've got a belt on, haven't you?'

'Yes.'

'Fine! Loosen it up and I'll run mine through it. The belts and an ankle-and-knee lock'll hold us together and in position to play tunes on those sea-horses' ribs. Keep your shield up and keep that grating swinging and we'll lay them like a carpet.'

Seaton had not been idle while he was talking, and when the attackers drew near, vicious tridents outthrust, they encountered an irresistibly driven wall of crushing, tearing dismembering, and all-destroying metal. Back to back the two unknown monstrosities floated through the air; interlaced belts holding their vulnerable backs together, gripped legs holding their indestructibly dense and hard bodies in alignment.

For a time the four-dimensional creatures threw themselves upon the Terrestrials, only to be hurled away upon all sides, chopped literally to bits. For Margaret protected Seaton's back, and he himself took care of the space in front of him, to right and to left of them, above and below them; driving the closely spaced latticework of his metal grating throughout all that space so viciously and so furiously that it seemed to be omnipresent as well as omnipotent. For a time the hypermen tried, as has been said; only to be sliced by that fearsomely irresistible weapon into such grisly fragments that the appalled survivors of the hyperhorde soon abandoned the futile and suicidal attack.

116

Then, giving up hope of recapturing the specimens alive, the hyperbeings turned upon them their lethal beams. Soft, pinkly glowing beams which turned to a deep red and then flamed through the spectrum and into the violet as they were found to have no effect upon the human bodies. But the death rays of the hypermen, whatever the frequency, were futile – the massed battalions at the pit's mouth were as impotent as had been the armed forces of the great hypercity, whose denizens had also failed either to hold or to kill the supernatural Terrestrials.

During the hand-to-hand encounter the two had passed the apex of their flight; and now, bathed in the varicolored beams, they floated gently downward, directly toward the great derrick which Seaton had pointed out as marking their probable landing place. In fact, they grazed one of the massive corner members of the structure; but Seaton interposed his four-dimensional shield and, although the derrick trembled notice-ably under the impact, neither he nor Margaret was hurt as they drifted lightly to the ground.

'Just like jumping off of and back into a feather bed!' Seaton exulted, as he straightened up, disconnected the hampering belts, and guided Margaret toward the vast hole in the ground, un-opposed now save for the still-flaring beams. 'Wonder if any more of them want to argue the right of way with us? Guess not.'

'But how are we going to get down there?' asked Margaret.

'Fall down – or, better yet, we'll slide down those chains they've already got installed. You'd better carry all this junk, and I'll kind of carry you. That way you won't have to do anything – just take a ride.'

Scarcely encumbered by the girl's weight, Seaton stepped outward to the great chain cables, and hand under hand he went down, down past the huge lifting cradles which had been placed around the massive globe of arenak.

'But we'll go right through it – there's nothing to stop us in this dimension!' protested Margaret.

'No, we won't; and yes, there is,' Seaton replied. 'We swing *past* it and down, around onto level footing, on this loose end of chain – like this, see?' and they were once more in the control room of *Skylark Two*.

There stood Dorothy, Crane, and Shiro, exactly as they had left them so long before. Still held in the grip of the tridents, they were silent, immobile; their eyes were vacant and expressionless. Neither Dorothy nor Crane gave any sign of recognition, neither seemed even to realize that their loved ones, gone so long, had at last returned.

Seaton's glance leaped to his beloved Dorothy. Drooping yet rigid she stood there, unmoving, corpselike. Accustomed now to seeing four-dimensional things by consciously examining only their three-dimensional surfaces, he perceived instantly the waxen, utterly inhuman vacuity of her normally piquant and vivacious face – perceived it, and at that perception went mad.

Clutching convulsively the length of hyperchain by which he had swung into the control room he leaped, furious and elementally savage; forgetting weapons and armor, heedless of risk and of odds, mastered completely by a seething, searing urge to wreak vengeance upon the creature who had so terribly outraged his Dorothy, the woman in whom centered his Universe.

So furious was his action that the chain snapped apart at the wall of the control room; so rapid was it that the hyperguard had no time to move, nor even to think.

That guard had been peacefully controlling with his trident the paralyzed prisoner. All had been quiet and calm. Suddenly – in an instant – had appeared the two monstrosities who had been taken to the capital. And in that same fleeting instant one of the monsters was leaping at him. And ahead of that monster there came lashing out an enormous anchor chain, one of whose links of solid steel no ordinary mortal could lift; an anchor chain hurtling toward him with a velocity and a momentum upon that tenuous hyperworld unthinkable.

The almost-immaterial flesh of the hyperman could no more withstand that fiercely driven mass of metal than can a human body ward off an armor-piercing projectile in full flight. Through his body the great chain tore; cutting, battering, rending it into ghastly, pulpily indescribable fragments unrecognizable as ever having been anything animate. Indeed, so fiercely had the chain been urged that the metal itself could not stand the strain. Five links broke off at the climax of the chain's blacksnake-like stroke, and, accompanying the bleeding scraps of flesh that had been the guard, tore on past the walls of the space ship and out into the hypervoid.

The guard holding his tridents in Crane and Shiro had not much more warning. He saw his fellow obliterated, true; but that was all he lived to see, and he had time to do exactly nothing. One more quick flip of Seaton's singularly efficient weapon and the remains of that officer also disappeared into hyperspace. More of the chain went along, this time, but that did not matter. Dropping to the floor the remaining links of his hyperflail, Seaton sprang to Dorothy, reaching her side just as the punishing trident, released by the slain guard, fell away from her.

She recovered her senses instantly and turned a surprised face to the man, who, incoherent in his relief that she was alive and apparently unharmed, was taking her into his arms.

'Why, surely, Dick, I'm all right – how could I be any other way?' she answered his first agonized question in amazement. She studied his worn face in puzzled wonder and went on: 'But you certainly are not. What has happened, dear, anyway; and how could it have, possibly?'

'I hated like sin to be gone so long, Dimples, but it couldn't be helped,' Seaton, in his eagerness to explain his long absence, did not even notice the peculiar implications in his wife's speech and manner. 'You see, it was a long trip, and we didn't get a chance to break away from those meat hooks of theirs until after they got us into their city and examined us. Then, when we finally did break away, we found that we couldn't travel at night. Their days are bad enough, with this thick blue light, but during the nights there's absolutely no light at all, of any kind. No moon, no stars, no nothing . . .'

'Nights! What are you talking about, Dick, anyway?' Dorothy had been trying to interrupt since his first question and had managed at last to break in. 'Why, you haven't been gone at all, not even a second. We've all been right here, all the time!'

'Huh?' ejaculated Seaton. 'Are you completely nuts, Red-Top, or what . . . ?'

'Dick and I were gone at least a week, Dottie,' Margaret, who had been embracing Crane, interrupted in turn, 'and it was awful!'

'Just a minute, folks!' Seaton listened intently and stared

upward. 'We'll have to let the explanations ride a while longer. I thought they wouldn't give up that easy – here they come! I don't know how long we were gone – it seemed like a darn long time – but it was long enough so that I learned how to mop up on these folks, believe me! You take that sword and buckler of Peg's, Mart. They don't look so hot, but they're big medicine in these parts. All we've got to do is swing them fast enough to keep those stingaroos of theirs out of our gizzards and we're all set. Be careful not to hit too hard, though, or you'll bust that grating into forty pieces – it's hyperstuff, nowhere near as solid as anything we're used to. All it'll stand is about normal fly-swatting stroke, but that's enough to knock any of these fan-tailed humming birds into an outside loop. Ah, they've got guns or something! Duck down, girls, so we can cover you with these shields; and, Shiro, you might pull that piece of chain apart and throw the links at them – that'll be good for what ails them!'

The hypermen appeared in the control room, and battle again was joined. This time, however, the natives did not rush to the attack with their tridents; nor did they employ their futile rays of death. They had guns, shooting pellets of metal; they had improvised, cross-bowlike slings and catapults; they had spears and javelins made of their densest materials, which their strongest men threw with all their power. But pellets and spears alike thudded harmlessly against four-dimensional shields – shields once the impenetrable, unbreakable doors of their mightiest prison – and the masses of metal and stone vomited forth by the catapults were caught by Seaton and Crane and hurled back through the ranks of the attackers with devastating effect. Shiro also was doing untold damage with his bits of chain and with such other items of four-dimensional matter as came to hand.

Still the hypermen came pressing in, closer and closer. Soon the three men were standing in a triangle, in the center of which were the women, their flying weapons defining a volume of space to enter which meant hideous dismemberment and death to any hypercreature. But on they came, willing, it seemed, to spend any number of lives to regain their lost control over the Terrestrials; realizing, it seemed, that even those supernaturally powerful beings must in time weaken.

While the conflict was at its height, however, it seemed to Seaton that the already tenuous hypermen were growing even more wraithlike; and at the same time he found himself fighting with greater and greater difficulty. The lethal grating, which he had been driving with such speed that it had been visible only as a solid barrier, moved more and ever more slowly, to come finally to a halt in spite of his every effort.

He could not move a muscle, and despairingly he watched a now almost-invisible warden who was approaching him, controlling trident outthrust. But to his relieved surprise the hyperforceps did not touch him, but slithered *past him* without making contact; and hyperman and hyperweapon disappeared altogether, fading out slowly into nothingness.

Then Seaton found himself moving in space. Without volition he was floating across the control room, toward the switch whose closing had ushered the Terrestrials out of their familiar space of three dimensions and into this weirdly impossible region of horror. Nor was he alone in his movement. Dorothy, the Cranes, and Shiro were all in motion, returning slowly to the identical positions they had occupied at the instant when Seaton had closed his master switch.

And as they moved, they *changed*. The *Skylark* herself changed, as did every molecule, every atom of substance, in or of the spherical cruiser of the void.

Seaton's hand reached out and grasped the ebonite handle of the switch. Then, as his entire body came to rest, he was swept by wave upon wave of almost-unbearable relief as the artificial and unnatural extension into the fourth dimension began to collapse. Slowly, as had progressed the extrusion into that dimension, so progressed the de-extrusion from it. Each ultimate particle of matter underwent an indescribable and incomprehensible foreshortening; a compression; a shrinking together; a writhing and twisting reverse rearrangement, each slow increment of which was poignantly welcome to every outraged unit of human flesh.

Suddenly seeming, and yet seemingly only after untold hours, the return to three-dimensional space was finished. Seaton's hand drove through the remaining fraction of an inch of its travel with the handle of the switch; his ears heard the click and snap of the plungers driving home against their stop blocks – the closing of the relay switches had just been completed. The familiar fittings of the control room stood out in their normal three dimensions, sharp and clear.

Dorothy sat exactly as she had sat before the transition. She was leaning slightly forward in her seat – her gorgeous red-bronze hair in perfect order, her sweetly curved lips half parted, her violet eyes widened in somewhat fearful anticipation of what the dimensional translation was to bring. She was unchanged – but Seaton!

He also sat exactly as he had sat an instant – or was it a month? – before; but his face was thin and heavily lined, his normally powerful body was now gauntly eloquent of utter fatigue. Nor was Margaret in better case. She was haggard, almost emaciated. Her clothing, like that of Seaton, had been forced to return to a semblance of order by the exigencies of interdimensional and inter-time translation, and for a moment appeared sound and whole.

The translation accomplished, however, that clothing literally fell apart. The dirt and grime of their long, hard journey and the sticky sap of the hyperplants through which they had fought their way had of course disappeared – being four-dimensional material, all such had perforce remained behind in four-dimensional space – but the thorns and sucking disks of the hypervegetation had taken toll. Now each rent and tear reappeared, to give mute but eloquent testimony to the fact that the sojourn of those two human beings in hyperland had been neither peaceful nor uneventful.

Dorothy's glance flashed in amazement from Seaton to Margaret, and she repressed a scream as she saw the ravages wrought by whatever it was that they had gone through. She could not understand it, could not reconcile it with what she herself had experienced while in the hyperspace–hypertime continuum, but moved by the ages-old instinct of all true women, she reached out to take her abused husband into the shelter of her arms. But Seaton's first thought was for the bodiless foes whom they might not have left behind.

'Did we get away, Mart?' he demanded, hand still upon the switch. Then, without waiting for a reply, he went on: 'We must've made it, though, or we'd've been dematerialized before this. Three rousing cheers! We made it – we made it!'

For several minutes all four gave way to their mixed but profound emotions, in which relief and joy predominated. They had escaped from the intellectuals; they had come alive through hyperspace!

'But Dick!' Dorothy held Seaton off at arm's length and studied his gaunt, lined face. 'Lover, you look actually thin.'

'I *am* thin,' he replied. 'We were gone a week, we told you. I'm just about starved to death, and I'm thirstier even than that. Not being able to eat is bad; but going without water is worse, believe me! My whole insides feel like a mess of desiccated blotters. Come on, Peg; let's empty us a couple of water tanks.'

They drank; lightly and intermittently at first, then deeply.

At last Seaton put down the pitcher. 'That isn't enough, by any means; but we're damp enough inside so that we can swallow food, I guess. While you're finding out where we are, Mart, Peg and I'll eat six or eight meals apiece.'

While Seaton and Margaret ate – ate as they had drunk, carefully, but with every evidence of an insatiable bodily demand for food – Dorothy's puzzled gaze went from the worn faces of the diners to a mirror which reflected her own vivid, unchanged self.

'But I don't understand it at all, Dick!' she burst out at last. '*I'm* not thirsty, nor hungry, and I haven't changed a bit. Neither has Martin; and yet you two have lost pounds and pounds and look as though you had been pulled through a knot hole. It didn't seem to us as though you were away from us at all. You were going to tell me about that back there, when we were interrupted. Now go ahead and explain things, before I explode. What happened, anyway?'

Seaton, hunger temporarily assuaged, gave a full but concise summary of everything that had happened while he and Margaret were away from the *Skylark*. He then launched into a scientific dissertation, only to be interrupted by Dorothy.

'But, Dick, it doesn't sound reasonable that all that could *possibly* have happened to you and Peggy without our even knowing that any time at all had passed!' she expostulated. 'We weren't unconscious or anything, were we, Martin? We knew what was going on all the time, didn't we?'

'We were at no time unconscious, and we knew at all times what was taking place around us,' Crane made surprising but positive answer. He was seated at a visiplate, but had been listening to the story instead of studying the almost-sheer emptiness that was space. 'And since it is a truism of Norlaminian psychology that any lapse of consciousness, of however short duration, is impressed upon the conscious of a mind of even moderate power, I feel safe in saying that for Dorothy and me, at least, no lapse of time did occur or could have occurred.'

'There!' Dorothy exulted. 'You've got to admit that Martin knows his stuff. How are you going to get around that?'

'Search me – wish I knew.' Seaton frowned in thought. 'But Mart chirped it, I think, when he said "for Dorothy and me, at least," because for us two the time certainly lapsed, and lapsed plenty. However, Mart certainly *does* know his stuff; the old think tank is full of bubbles all the time. He doesn't make positive statements very often, and when he does you can sink the bank roll on 'em. Therefore, since you were both conscious and time did not lapse – for you – it must have been time itself that was cuckoo instead of you. It must have stretched, or must have been stretched, like the very dickens – for you.

'Where does that idea get us? I might think that their time was intrinsically variable, as well as being different from ours, if it was not for the regular alternation of night and day – of light and darkness, at least – that Peg and I saw, and which affected the whole country, as far as we could see. So that's out.

'Maybe they treated you two to a dose of suspended animation or something of the kind, since you weren't going anywhere ... Nope, that idea doesn't carry the right earmarks, and besides it would have registered as such on Martin's Norlaminianly psychological brain. So that's out, too. In fact, the only thing that could deliver the goods would be a sta – but that'd be a trifle strong, even for a hyperman, I'm afraid.'

'What would?' demanded Margaret. 'Anything that you would call strong ought to be worth listening to.'

'A stasis of time. Sounds a trifle far-fetched, of course, but...'

'But phooey!' Dorothy exclaimed. 'Now you *are* raving, Dick!'

'I'm not so sure of that, at all,' Seaton argued stubbornly. 'They really understand time, I think, and I picked up a couple of pointers. It would take a sixth-order field ... That's it, I'm pretty sure, and that gives me an idea. If they can do it in hypertime, why can't we do it in ours?'

'I fail to see how such a stasis could be established,' argued Crane. 'It seems to me that as long as matter exists time must continue, since it is quite firmly established that time depends upon matter – or rather upon the motion in space of that which we call matter.'

'Sure – that's what I'm going on. Time and motion are both relative. Stop all motion – relative, not absolute motion – and what have you? You have duration without sequence or succession, which is what?'

'That would be a stasis of time, as you say,' Crane conceded, after due deliberation. 'How can you do it?'

'I don't know yet whether I can or not – that's another question. We already know, though, how to set up a stasis of the ether along a spherical surface, and after I have accumulated a little more data on the sixth order it should not be impossible to calculate a volume-stasis in both ether and subether, far enough down to establish complete immobility and local cessation of time in gross matter so affected.'

'But would not all matter so affected assume at once the absolute zero of temperature and thus preclude life?'

'I don't think so. The stasis would be subatomic and instantaneous, you know; there could be no loss or transfer of energy. I don't see how gross matter could be affected at all. As far as I can see it would be an absolutely perfect suspension of animation. You and Dot lived through it, anyway, and I'm positive that that's what they did to you. And I still say that if anybody can do it, we can.'

' "And that," ' put in Margaret roguishly, 'as you so feelingly remark, "is a cheerful thought to dwell on – let's dwell on it!" '

'We'll do that little thing, too, Peg, some of these times; see if we don't!' Seaton promised. 'But to get back to our knitting, what's the good word, Mart – located us yet? Are we, or are we not, heading for that justly famed "distant galaxy" of the Fenachrone?'

'We are not,' Crane replied flatly, 'nor are we heading for any other point in space covered by the charts of Ravindau's astronomers.'

'Huh? Great Cat!' Seaton joined the physicist at his visiplate, and made complete observations upon the brightest nebulae visible.

He turned then to the charts, and his findings confirmed those of Crane. They were so far away from our own galaxy that the space in which they were was unknown, even to those masters of astronomy and of intergalactic navigation, the Fenachrone.

'Well, we're not lost, anyway, thanks to your cautious old bean.' Seaton grinned as he stepped over to an object-compass mounted upon the plane table.

This particular instrument was equipped with every refinement known to the science of four great solar systems. Its exceedingly delicate needle, swinging in an almost-perfect vacuum upon practically frictionless jeweled bearings, was focused upon the unimaginable mass of the entire First Galaxy, a mass so inconceivably great that mathematics had shown – and even Crane would have stated as a fact – that it would affect that needle from any point whatever, however distant in macrocosmic space.

Seaton actuated the minute force which set the needle in motion, but it did not oscillate. For minute after minute it revolved slowly but freely, coming ultimately to rest without any indication of having been affected in the least by any external influence. He stared at the compass in stark, unbelieving amazement, then tested its current and its every other factor. The instrument was in perfect order and in perfect adjustment. Grimly, quietly, he repeated the oscillatory test – with the same utterly negative result.

'Well, that is eminently, conclusively, definitely, and unqualifiedly that.' He stared at Crane, unseeing, his mind racing. 'The most sensitive needle we've got, and she won't even register!'

'In other words, we are lost.' Crane's voice was level and

calm. 'We are so far away from the First Galaxy that even that compass, supposedly reactive from any possible location in space, is useless.'

'But I don't get it, at all, Mart!' Seaton exclaimed, paying no attention to the grim meaning underlying his friend's utterance. 'With the whole mass of the galaxy as its object of attachment that needle absolutely will register from a distance greater than any possible diameter of the super-universe...' His voice died away.

'Go on; you are beginning to see the light,' Crane prompted.

'Yeah – no wonder I couldn't plot a curve to trace those Fenachrone torpedoes – our fundamental assumptions were unsound. The fact simply is that if space is curved at all, the radius of curvature is vastly greater than any figure as yet proposed, even by the Fenachrone astronomers. We certainly weren't out of our own space a thousandth of a second – more likely only a couple of millionths – do you suppose that there really are folds in the fourth dimension?'

'That idea has been advanced, but folds are not strictly necessary, nor are they easy to defend. It has always seemed to me that the hypothesis of linear departure is much more tenable. The planes need not be parallel, you know – in fact, it is almost a mathematical certainty that they are *not* parallel.'

'That's so, too; and that hypothesis would account for everything of course. But how are...'

'What *are* you two talking about?' demanded Dorothy. 'We simply couldn't have come that far – why, the *Skylark* was stuck in the ground the whole time!'

'As a physicist, Red-Top, you're a fine little beauty-contest winner.' Seaton grinned. 'You forget that with the velocity she had, the *Lark* wouldn't have been stopped within three months, either – yet she seemed to stop. How about that, Mart?'

'I have been thinking about that. It is all a question of relative velocities, of course; but even at that, the angle of departure of the two spaces must have been extreme indeed to account for our present location in three-dimensional space.'

'Extreme is right; but there's no use yapping about it now, any more than about any other spilled milk. We'll just have to go places and do things; that's all.'

'Go where and do what?' asked Dorothy pointedly.

'Lost – lost in space!' Margaret breathed.

As the dread import of their predicament struck into her consciousness she had seized the arm rests of her chair in a spasmodic clutch; but she forced herself to relax and her deep brown eyes held no sign of panic.

'But we have been lost in space before, Dottie, apparently as badly as we are now. Worse, really, because we did not have Martin and Dick with us then.'

'At-a-girl, Peg!' Seaton cheered. 'We may be lost – guess we are, temporarily, at least – but we're not licked, not by seven thousand rows of apple trees!'

'I fail to perceive any very solid basis for your optimism,' Crane remarked quietly, 'but you have an idea, of course. What is it?'

'Pick out the galaxy nearest our line of flight and brake down for it.' Seaton's nimble mind was leaping ahead. 'The *Lark*'s so full of uranium that her skin's bulging, so we've got power to burn. In that galaxy there are – there *must* be – suns with habitable, possibly inhabited, planets. We'll find one such planet and land on it. Then we'll do with our might what our hands find to do.'

'Such as?'

'Along what lines?' queried Dorothy and Crane simultaneously.

'Space ship, probably – *Two*'s entirely too small to be of any account in intergalactic work,' Seaton replied promptly. 'Or maybe fourth-, fifth-, and sixth-order projectors; or maybe some kind of an ultra-ultra radio or projector. How do I know, from here? But there's thousands of things that maybe we can do – we'll wait until we get there to worry about which one to try first.'

14: Wanted – A Planet

Seaton strode over to the control board and applied maximum acceleration. 'Might as well start traveling, Mart,' he remarked to Crane, who for almost an hour had been devoting the highest telescopic power of number six visiplate to spectroscopic, interferometric, and spectrophotometric studies of half a dozen selected nebulae. 'No matter which one you pick out we'll have to have quite a lot of positive acceleration yet before we reverse to negative.'

'As a preliminary measure, might it not be a good plan to gain some idea as to our present line of flight?' Crane asked dryly, bending a quizzical glance upon his friend. 'You know a great deal more than I do about the hypothesis of linear departure of incompatible and incommensurable spaces, however, and so perhaps you already know our true course.'

'Ouch! Pals, they got me!' Seaton clapped a hand over his heart; then, seizing his own ear, he led himself up to the switchboard and shut off the space drive, except for the practically negligible superimposed thirty-two feet per second which gave to the *Skylark*'s occupants a normal gravitational force.

'Why, Dick, how perfectly silly!' Dorothy chuckled. 'What's the matter? All you've got to do is...'

'Silly, says you?' Seaton, still blushing, interrupted her. 'Woman, you don't know the half of it! I'm just plain dumb, and Mart was tactfully calling my attention to the fact. Them's soft words that the slatlike string bean just spoke, but believe me, Red-Top, he packs a wicked wallop in that silken glove!'

'Keep still a minute, Dick, and look at the bar!' Dorothy protested. 'Everything's on zero, so we must still be going straight up, and all you have to do to get us back somewhere near our own galaxy is to turn it around. Why didn't one of you brilliant thinkers – or have I overlooked a bet?'

'Not exactly. You don't know about those famous linear departures, but I do. I haven't that excuse – I simply went off half cocked again. You see, it's like this: Even if those gyroscopes retained their orientation unchanged through the fourth-dimensional translation, which may or may not be the case, that line wouldn't mean a thing as far as getting back is concerned.

'We took one gosh-awful jump in going through hyperspace, you know, and we have no means at all of determining whether we jumped up, down, or side wise. Nope, he's right, as usual – we can't do anything intelligently until he finds out, from the shifting of spectral lines and so on, in what direction we actually are traveling. How're you coming with it, Mart?'

'For really precise work we shall require photographs, but I have made six preliminary observations, as nearly on rectangular coordinates as possible, from which you can calculate a first-approximation course which will serve until we can obtain more precise data. Here are my rough notes upon the spectra.'

'All right, while you're taking your pictures I'll run them off on the calculator. From the looks of those shifts I'd say I could hit our course within five degrees, which is close enough for a few days, at least.'

Seaton soon finished his calculations. He then read off from the great graduated hour- and declination-circles of the gyroscope cage the course upon which the power bar was then set, and turned with a grin to Crane, who had just opened the shutter for his first time exposure.

'We were off plenty, Mart,' he admitted. 'About ninety degrees minus declination and something like plus seven hours' right ascension, so we'll have to forget all our old data and start right from scratch. That won't hurt us much, though, since we haven't any idea where we are, anyway.

'We're heading about ten degrees or so to the right of that nebula over there, which is certainly a mighty long ways off from where I thought we were going. I'll put on full positive and point ten degrees to the left of it. Probably you'd better read it now, and by taking a set of observations, say a hundred hours apart, we can figure when we'll have to reverse acceleration.

'While you're doing that I thought I'd start seeing what I could do about a fourth-order projector. It'll take a long time to build, and we'll need one bad when we get inside that galaxy. What do you think?'

'I think that both of those ideas are sound,' Crane assented,

131

and each man bent to his task.

Crane took his photographs and studied each of the six key nebulae with every resource of his ultrarefined instruments. Having determined the *Skylark*'s course and speed, and knowing her acceleration, he was able at last to set upon the power bar an automatically varying control of such a nature that her resultant velocity was directly toward the lenticular nebula nearest her line of flight.

That done, he continued his observations at regular intervals – constantly making smaller his limit of observational error, constantly so altering the power and course of the vessel that the selected galaxy would be reached in the shortest possible space of time consistent with a permissible final velocity.

And in the meantime Seaton labored upon the projector. It had been out of the question, of course, to transfer to tiny *Two* the immense mechanism which had made of *Three* a sentient, almost living, thing; but, equally of course, he had brought along the force-band transformers and selectors, and as much as possible of the other essential apparatus. He had been obliged to leave behind, however, the very heart of the fifth-order installation – the precious lens of neutronium – and its lack was now giving him deep concern.

'What the matter, Dickie? You look as though you had lost your best friend.' Dorothy intercepted him one day as he paced about the narrow confines of the control room, face set and eyes unseeing.

'Not quite that, but ever since I finished that fourth-order outfit I've been trying to figure out something to take the place of that lens we had in *Three*, so that I can go ahead on the fifth, but that seems to be one thing for which there is absolutely no substitute. It's like trying to unscrew the inscrutable – it can't be done.'

'If you can't get along without it, why didn't you bring it along, too?'

'Couldn't.'

'Why?' she persisted.

'Nothing strong enough to hold it. In some ways it's worse than atomic energy. It's so hot and under such pressure that if that lens were to blow up in Omaha it would burn up the whole

United States, from San Francisco to New York City. It takes either thirty feet of solid inoson or else a complete force-bracing to stand the pressure. We had neither, no time to build anything, and couldn't have taken it through hyperspace even if we could have held it safely.'

'Does that mean . . .'

'No. It simply means that we'll have to start at the fourth again and work up. I did bring along a couple of good big faidons, so that all we've got to do is find a planet heavy enough and solid enough to anchor a full-sized fourth-order projector on, within twenty light-years of a white dwarf star.'

'Oh, is that all? You two'll do that, all right.'

'Ain't it wonderful, the confidence some women have in their husbands?' Seaton asked Crane, who was studying through number six visiplate and the fourth-order projector the enormous expanse of the strange galaxy at whose edge they now were. 'I think maybe we'll be able to pull it off, though, at that. Of course we aren't close enough yet to find such minutiae as planets, but how are things shaping up in general?'

'Quite encouraging! This galaxy is certainly of the same order of magnitude as our own, and . . .'

'Encouraging, huh?' Seaton broke in. 'If such a dyed-in-the-wool pessimist as you are can permit himself to use such a word as that, we're practically landed on a planet right now!'

'And shows the same types and varieties of stellar spectra,' Crane went on, unperturbed. 'I have identified with certainty no less than six white dwarf stars, and some forty yellow dwarfs of type G.'

'Fine! What did I tell you?' exulted Seaton.

'Now go over that again, in English, so that Peggy and I can feel relieved about it, too,' Dorothy directed. 'What's a type-G dwarf?'

'A sun like our own Sol, back home,' Seaton explained. 'Since we are looking for a planet as much as possible like our own Earth, it is a distinctly cheerful fact to find so many suns similar to our own. And as for the white dwarfs, I've got to have one fairly close to the planet we land on, because to get in touch with Rovol I've got to have a sixth-order projector; to build which I've first got to have one of the fifth order; for the construction of which I've got to have neutronium; to get which I'll have to be close to a white dwarf star. See?'

'Uh-huh! Clear and lucid to the point of limpidity – not.' Dorothy grimaced, then went on: 'As for me, I'm certainly glad to see those stars. It seems that we've been out there in absolutely empty space for ages, and I've been scared a pale lavender all the time. Having all these nice stars around us again is the next-best thing to being on solid ground.'

At the edge of the strange galaxy though they were, many days were required to reduce the intergalactic pace of the vessel to a value at which maneuvering was possible, and many more days passed into time before Crane announced the discovery of a sun which not only possessed a family of planets, but was also within the specified distance of a white dwarf star.

To any Earthly astronomer, whose most powerful optical instruments fail to reveal even the closest star as anything save a dimensionless point of light, such a discovery would have been impossible, but Crane was not working with Earthly instruments. For the fourth-order projector, although utterly useless at the intergalactic distances with which Seaton was principally concerned, was vastly more powerful than any conceivable telescope.

Driven by the full power of a disintegrating uranium bar, it could hold a projection so steadily at a distance of twenty light-years that a man could manipulate a welding arc as surely as though it was upon a bench before him – which, in effect, it was – and in cases in which delicacy of control was not an object, such as the present quest for such vast masses as planets, the projector was effective over distances of many hundreds of light-years.

Thus it came about that the search for a planetiferous sun near a white dwarf star was not unduly prolonged, and *Skylark Two* tore through the empty ether toward it.

Close enough so that the projector could reveal details, Seaton drove projections of all four voyagers down into the atmosphere of the first planet at hand. That atmosphere was heavy and of a pronounced greenish-yellow cast, and through it that fervent sun poured down a flood of lurid light upon a peculiarly dead and barren ground – but yet a ground upon which grew isolated clumps of a livid and monstrous vegetation.

'Of course detailed analysis at this distance is impossible, but what do you make of it, Dick?' asked Crane. 'In all our travels, this is only the second time we have encountered such an atmosphere.'

'Yes; and that's exactly twice too many.' Seaton, at the spectroscope, was scowling in thought. 'Chlorin, all right, with some fluorin and strong traces of oxide of nitrogen, nitrosyl chloride, and so on – just about like that one we saw in our own galaxy that time. I thought then and have thought ever since that there was something decidedly fishy about that planet, and I think there's something equally screwy about this one.'

'Well, let's not investigate it any further, then,' put in Dorothy. 'Let's go somewhere else, quick.'

'Yes, let's,' Margaret agreed, 'particularly if, as you said about that other one, it has a form of life on it that would make our grandfathers' whiskers curl up into a ball.'

'We'll do that little thing; we haven't got *Three*'s equipment now, and without it I'm no keener on smelling around this planet than you are,' and he flipped the projection across a few hundred million miles of space to the neighboring planet. Its air, while somewhat murky and smoky, was colorless and apparently normal, its oceans were composed of water, and its vegetation was green. 'See, Mart? I told you something was fishy. It's all wrong – a thing like that can't happen even once, let alone twice.'

'According to the accepted principles of cosmogony it is of course to be expected that all the planets of the same sun would have atmospheres of somewhat similar composition,' Crane conceded, unmoved. 'However, since we have observed two cases of this kind, it is quite evident that there are not only many more suns having planets than has been supposed, but also that suns capture planets from each other, at least occasionally.'

'Maybe – that would explain it, of course. But let's see what this world looks like – see if we can find a place to sit down on. It'll be nice to live on solid ground while I do my stuff.'

He swung the viewpoint slowly across the daylight side of the strange planet, whose surface, like that of Earth, was partially obscured by occasional masses of cloud. Much of that surface was covered by mighty oceans, and what little land there was seemed strangely flat and entirely devoid of topographical features.

The immaterial conveyance dropped straight down upon the largest visible mass of land, down through a towering jungle of fernlike and bamboolike plants, halting only a few feet above the ground. Solid ground it certainly was not, nor did it resemble the watery muck of our Earthly swamps. The huge stems of the vegetation rose starkly from a black and seething field of viscous mud – mud unrelieved by any accumulation of humus or of debris – and in that mud there swam, crawled, and slithered teeming hordes of animals.

'What funny-looking mud-puppies!' Dorothy exclaimed. 'And isn't that the thickest, dirtiest, gooiest mud you ever saw?'

'Just about,' Seaton agreed, intensely interested. 'But those things seem perfectly adapted to it. Flat, beaver tails; short, strong legs with webbed feet; long, narrow heads with rooting noses, like pigs; and heavy, sharp incisor teeth. Bet they live on those ferns and stuff – that's why there's no underbrush or dead stuff. Look at that bunch working on the roots of that big bamboo over there. They'll have it down in a minute – there she goes!'

The great trunk fell with a crash as he spoke, and was almost instantly forced beneath the repellent surface by the weight of the massed 'mud-puppies' who flung themselves upon it.

'Ah, I thought so!' Crane remarked. 'Their molar teeth do not match their incisors, being quite Titanotheric in type. Probably they can assimilate lignin and cellulose instead of requiring our usual nutrient carbohydrates. However, this terrain does not seem to be at all suitable for our purpose.'

'I'll say it doesn't. I'll scout around and see if we can't find some high land somewhere, but I've got a hunch that we won't care for that, either. This murky air and the strong absorption lines of SO_2 seem to whisper in my ear that we'll find some plenty hot and plenty sulphurous volcanoes when we find the mountains.'

A few large islands or small continents of high and solid land were found at last, but they were without exception volcanic. Nor were those volcanoes quiescent. Each was in constant and furious eruption; not the sporadic and comparatively mild outbursts of violence which we of green Terra know, but the uninterrupted, world-shaking cataclysmic paroxysms of primeval forces embattled – an inexhaustible supply of cold water striving to quench a world-filling core of incandescent magma. Each conical peak and rugged vent where once a cone had been spouted incredible columns of steam, of smoke, of dust, of molten and vaporized rock, and of noxious vapor. Each volcano was working steadily and industriously at its appointed task of building up a habitable world.

'Well, I don't see any place around here either fit to live in or solid enough to anchor an observatory onto,' Seaton concluded, after he had surveyed the entire surface of the globe. 'I think we'd better flit across to the next one, don't you, folks?'

Suiting action to word, he shot the beam to the next nearest planet, which chanced to be the one whose orbit was nearest the blazing sun, and a mere glance showed that it would not serve the purposes of the Terrestrials. Small it was, and barren: waterless, practically airless, lifeless; a cratered, jagged, burned-out ember of what might once have been a fertile little world.

The viewpoint then leaped past the flaming inferno of the luminary and came to rest in the upper layers of an atmosphere.

'Aha!' Seaton exulted, after he had studied his instruments briefly. 'This looks like home, sweet home to me. Nitrogen, oxygen, some CO_2, a little water vapor, and traces of the old familiar rare gases. And see them oceans, them clouds, and them there hills? Hot dog!'

As the projection dropped toward the new world's surface, however, making possible a detailed study, it became evident that there was something abnormal about it. The mountains were cratered and torn; many of the valleys were simply desolate expanses of weathered lava, tuff, and breccia; and, while it seemed that climatic conditions were eminently suitable, of animal life there was none.

Everywhere there were signs of ravishment, as though that fair world had been torn and ravaged by cataclysmic storms of violence unthinkable; ravages which for centuries Nature had been trying to heal.

And it was not only the world itself that had been outraged. Near a large inland lake there spread the ruins of what once had been a great city; ruins so crumbled and razed as to be almost unrecognizable. What had been stone was dust, what had been metal was rust; and dust and rust alike were now almost completely overgrown by vegetation. For centuries Nature undisturbed had slowly but implacably been reducing to nought the once ordered and purposeful works of a high intelligence.

'Hm-m-m!' Seaton mused, subdued. 'There *was* a near-collision of planet-bearing suns, Mart; and that chlorin planet *was* captured. This world was ruined by the strains set up – but surely they must have been scientific enough to have seen it coming? Surely they must have made plans so that *some* of them could have lived through it?'

He fell silent, driving the viewpoint hither and thither, like a hound in quest of a scent. 'I thought so!' Another ruined city lay beneath them; a city whose building, works, and streets had been fused together into one vast agglomerate of glaringly glassy slag, through which could be seen unmelted fragments of strangely designed structural members. 'Those ruins are fresh – that was done with heat beams, Mart. But who did it, and why? I've got a hunch – wonder if we're too late – if they've killed them all off already?'

Hard-faced now and grim, Seaton combed the continent, finding at last what he sought.

'Ah, I thought so!' he exclaimed, his voice low but deadly. 'I'll bet my shirt that the chlorins are wiping out the civilization of that planet – probably people more or less like us. What d'you say, folks – do we declare ourselves in on this, or not?'

'I'll tell the cockeyed world ... I believe that we should ... By all means ...' came from Dorothy, Margaret, and Crane.

'I knew you'd back me up. Humanity *über alles* – *homo sapiens* against all the vermin of the universe! Let's go, *Two* – do your stuff!'

As *Two* hurtled toward the unfortunate planet with her every iota of driving power, Seaton settled down to observe the strife and to see what he could do. That which lay beneath the viewpoint had not been a city, in the strict sense of the word. It had been an immense system of concentric fortifications, of which the outer circles had long since gone down under the irresistible attack of the two huge structures of metal which hung poised in the air above. Where those outer rings had been there was now an annular lake of boiling, seething lava. Lava from which arose gouts and slender pillars of smoke and fume; lava being volatilized by the terrific heat of the offensive beams and being hurled away in flaming cascades by the almost constant detonations of high-explosive shells; lava into which from time to time another portion of the immense fortress slagged down – put out of action, riddled, and finally fused by the awful forces of the invaders.

Even as the four Terrestrials stared in speechless awe, an intolerable blast of flame burst out above one of the flying forts and down it plunged into the raging pool, throwing molten slag far and wide as it disappeared beneath the raging surface.

'Hurray!' shrieked Dorothy, who had instinctively taken sides with the defenders. 'One down, anyway!'

But her jubilation was premature. The squat and monstrous fabrication burst upward through that flaming surface and, white-hot lava streaming from it in incandescent torrents, it was again in action, apparently uninjured.

'All fourth-order stuff, Mart,' Seaton, who had been frantically busy at his keyboard and instruments, reported to Crane. 'Can't find a trace of anything on the fifth or sixth, and that gives us a break. I don't know what we can do yet, but we'll do something, believe me!'

'Fourth-order? Are you sure?' Crane doubted. 'A fourth-order screen would be a zone of force, opaque and impervious to gravitation, whereas those screens are transparent and are not affecting gravity.'

'Yeah, but they're doing something that we never tried, since we never use the fourth-order stuff in fighting. They've both left the gravity band open – it's probably too narrow for them to work through, at least with anything very heavy – and that gives us the edge.'

'Why? Do you know more about it than they do?' queried Dorothy.

'Who and what are they, Dick?' asked Margaret.

'Sure I know more about it than they do. I understand the fifth and sixth orders and you can't get the full benefit of any order until you know all about the next one. Just like mathematics – nobody can really handle trigonometry until after he has had calculus. And as to who they are, the folks in that fort are of course natives of the planet, and they may well be people more or less like us. It's dollars to doughnuts, though, that those vessels are manned by the inhabitants of that interloping planet – that form of life I was telling you about – and it's up to us to pull their corks if we can. There, I'm ready to go, I think. We'll visit the ship first.'

The visible projection disappeared and, their images now invisible patterns of force, they stood inside the control room of one of the invaders. The air bore the faint, greenish-yellow tinge of chlorin; the walls were banked and tiered with controlling dials, meters, and tubes; and sprawling, lying, standing, or hanging before those controls were denizens of the chlorin planet. No two of them were alike in form. If one of them was using eyes he had eyes everywhere; if hands, hands by the dozen, all differently fingered, sprouted from one, two, or a dozen supple and snaky arms.

But the inspection was only momentary. Scarcely had the unseen visitors glanced about the interior when the visibeam was cut off sharply. The peculiar beings had snapped on a full-coverage screen, and their vessel, now surrounded by the opaque spherical mirror of a zone of force, was darting upward and away – unaffected by gravity, unable to use any of her weapons, but impervious to any form of matter or to any ether-borne wave.

'Huh! "We didn't come over here to get peeked at," says they,' Seaton snorted. 'Amoebic! Must be handy, though, at that, to sprout eyes, arms, ears, and so on whenever and wherever you want to – and when you want to rest, to pull in all such impedimenta and subside into a senseless green blob. Well, we've seen the attackers, now let's see what the natives look like. They can't cut us off without sending their whole works skyhooting off into space.'

Nor could they. The visibeam sped down into the deepest

sanctum of the fortress without hinderance, revealing a long, narrow control table at which were seated men – men not exactly like the humanity of Earth, of Norlamin, of Osnome, or of any other planet, but undoubtedly men, of the genus *homo*.

'You were right, Dick.' Crane the anthropologist now spoke. 'It seems that on planets similar to Earth in mass, atmosphere, and temperature, wherever situated, man develops. The ultimate genes must permeate universal space itself.'

'Maybe – sounds reasonable. But did you see that red light flash on when we came in? They've got detectors set on the gravity band – look at the expression on their faces.'

Each of the seated men had ceased his activity and was slumped down into his chair. Resignation, hopeless yet bitter, sat upon lofty, domed brows and stared out of large and kindly eyes. Fatigue, utter and profound, was graven upon lined faces and upon emaciated bodies.

'Oh, I get it!' Seaton exclaimed. 'They think the chlorins are watching them – as they probably do most of the time – and they can't do anything about it. Should think they could do the same – or could broadcast an interference – I could help them on that if I could talk to them – wish they had an educator, but I haven't seen any ...' He paused, brow knitted in concentration. 'I'm going to make myself visible to try a stunt. Don't talk to me; I'll need all the brain power I've got to pull this off.'

As Seaton's image thickened into substance its effect upon the strangers was startling indeed. First they shrank back in consternation, supposing that their enemies had at last succeeded in working a full materialization through the narrow gravity band. Then, as they perceived that Seaton's figure was human, and of a humanity different from their own, they sprang to surround him, shouting words meaningless to the Terrestrials.

For some time Seaton tried to make his meaning clear by signs, but the thoughts he was attempting to convey were far too complex for that simple medium. Communication was impossible and the time was altogether too short to permit of laborious learning of language. Therefore streamers of visible force shot from Seaton's imaged eyes, sinking deeply into the eyes of the figures at the head of the table.

'Look at me!' he commanded, and his fists clenched and

drops of sweat stood out on his forehead as he threw all the power of his brain into that probing, hypnotic beam.

The native resisted with all his strength, but not for nothing had Seaton superimposed upon his already-powerful mind a large portion of the phenomenal brain of Drasnik, the First of Psychology of Norlamin. Resistance was useless. The victim soon sat relaxed and passive, his mind completely subservient to Seaton's, and as though in a trance he spoke to his fellows.

'This apparition is the force-image of one of a group of men from a distant Solar System,' he intoned in his own language. 'They are friendly and intend to help us. Their space ship is approaching us under full power, but it cannot get here for several days. They can, however, help us materially before they arrive in person. To that end, he directs that we cause to be brought into this room a full assortment of all our fields of force, transmitting tubes, controllers, force-converters – in short, the equipment of a laboratory of radiation ... No, that would take too long. He suggests that one of us escort him to such a laboratory.'

15 : Valeron

As Seaton assumed, the near-collision of suns which had affected so disastrously the planet Valeron did not come unheralded to overwhelm a world unwarned, since for many hundreds of years her civilization had been of a high order indeed. Her astronomers were able, her scientists capable, the governments of her nations strong and just. Years before its occurrence the astronomers had known that the catastrophe was inevitable and had calculated dispassionately its every phase – to the gram, the centimeter, and the second.

With all their resources of knowledge and of power, however, it was pitifully little that the people of Valeron could do; for of what avail are the puny energies of man compared to the practically infinite forces of cosmic phenomena? Any attempt of the humanity of the doomed planet to swerve from their courses the incomprehensible masses of those two hurtling suns was as surely doomed to failure as would be the attempt of an ant to thrust from its rails an onrushing locomotive.

But what little could be done was done; done scientifically and logically; done, if not altogether without fear, at least in as much as was humbly possible without favor. With mathematical certainty were plotted the areas of least strain, and in those areas were constructed shelters. Shelters buried deeply enough to be unaffected by the coming upheavals of the world's crust; shelters of unbreakable metal, so designed, so latticed and braced as to withstand the seismic disturbances to which they were inevitably to be subjected.

Having determined the number of such shelters that could be built, equipped, and supplied with the necessities of life in the time allowed, the board of selection began its cold-blooded and heartless task. Scarcely one in a thousand of Valeron's teeming millions was to be given a chance for continued life, and they were to be chosen only from the children who would be in the prime of young adulthood at the time of the catastrophe.

These children were the pick of the planet : flawless in mind, body, and heredity. They were assembled in special schools near their assigned refuges, where they were instructed intensively in everything that they would have to know in order that civilization should not disappear utterly from the universe.

Such a thing could not be kept a secret long, and it is best to touch as lightly as possible upon the scenes which ensued after the certainty of doom became public knowledge. Humanity both scaled the heights of self-sacrificing courage and plumbed the very depths of cowardice and depravity.

Characters already strong were strengthened, but those already weak went to pieces entirely in orgies to a normal mind unthinkable. Almost overnight a peaceful and law-abiding world went mad – became an insane hotbed of crime, rapine, and pillage unspeakable. Martial law was declared at once, and after a few thousand maniacs had been ruthlessly shot down, the soberer inhabitants were allowed to choose between two alternatives. They could either die then and there before a firing squad, or they could wait and take whatever slight chance there might be of living through what was to come – but devoting their every effort meanwhile to the end that through those selected few the civilization of Valeron should endure.

Many chose death and were executed summarily and without formality, without regard to wealth or station. The rest worked. Some worked devotedly and with high purpose, some worked hopelessly and with resignation. Some worked stolidly and with thoughts only of the present, some worked slyly and with thoughts only of getting themselves, by hook or by crook, into one of those shelters. All, however, from the highest to the lowest, worked.

Since the human mind cannot be kept indefinitely at high tension, the new condition of things came in time to be regarded almost as normal, and as months lengthened into years the routine was scarcely broken. Now and then, of course, one went mad and was shot; another refused to continue his profitless labor and was shot; still another gave up the fight and shot himself. And always there were the sly – the self-seekers, the bribers, the corruptionists – willing to go to any lengths whatever to avoid their doom. Not openly did they carry on their machinations, but like loathsome worms eating at the heart of an outwardly fair fruit. But the scientists, almost to a man, were loyal. Trained to think, they thought clearly and logically, and surrounded themselves with soldiers and guards of the same stripe. Old men or weaklings would have no place in the post-cataclysmic world and there were accommodations for only the exactly predetermined number; therefore only those selected children and no others could be saved or would. And as for bribery, threats, blackmail, or any possible form of racketry or corruption – of what use is wealth or power to a man under sentence of death? And what threat or force could sway him? Wherefore most of the sly were discovered, exposed, and shot.

Time went on. The shelters were finished. Into them were taken stores, libraries, tools and equipment of every sort necessary for the rebuilding of a fully civilized world. Finally the 'children,' now in the full prime of young manhood and young womanhood, were carefully checked in. Once inside those massive portals they were of a world apart.

They were completely informed and completely educated; they had for long governed themselves with neither aid nor interference; they knew precisely what they must face; they knew exactly what to do and exactly how to do it. Behind them the mighty, multi-ply seals were welded into place and broken rock by the cubic mile was blasted down upon their refuges.

Day by day the heat grew more and more intense. Cyclonic storms raged ever fiercer, accompanied by an incessant blaze of lightning and a deafeningly continuous roar of thunder. More and ever more violent became the seismic disturbances as Valeron's very core shook and trembled under the appalling might of the opposing cosmic forces.

Work was at an end and the masses were utterly beyond control. The devoted were butchered by their frantic fellows; the hopeless were stung to madness; the stolid were driven to frenzy by the realization that there was to be no future; the remaining sly ones deftly turned the unorganized fury of the mob into a purposeful attack upon the shelters, their only hope of life.

But at each refuge the rabble met an unyielding wall of guards loyal to the last, and of scientists who, their work now done, were merely waiting for the end. Guards and scientists fought with rifles, ray guns, swords, and finally with clubs, stones, fists, feet, and teeth. Outnumbered by thousands they fell and the howling mob surged over their bodies. To no purpose. Those shelters had been designed and constructed to withstand the attacks of Nature gone berserk, and futile indeed were the attempts of the frenzied hordes to tear a way into their sacred recesses.

Thus died the devoted and high-souled band who had saved their civilization; but in that death each man was granted the boon which, deep in his heart, he craved. They had died quickly and violently, fighting for a cause they knew to be good. They did not die as did the members of the insanely terror-stricken, senseless mob ... in agony ... lingeringly ... but it is best to draw a kindly veil before the horrors attendant upon that riving, that tormenting, that cosmic outraging of a world.

The suns passed, each other upon his appointed way. The cosmic forces ceased to war and to the tortured and ravaged planet there at last came peace. The surviving children of Valeron emerged from their subterranean retreats and undauntedly took up the task of rebuilding their world. And to such good purpose did they devote themselves to the problems of rehabilitation that in a few hundred years there bloomed upon Valeron a civilization and a culture scarcely to be equaled in the universe.

For the new race had been cradled in adversity. In its ancestry there was no physical or mental taint or weakness, all dross having been burned away by the fires of cosmic catastrophe which had so nearly obliterated all the life of the planet. They were as yet perhaps inferior to the old race in point of numbers, but were immeasurably superior to it in physical, mental, moral, and intellectual worth.

Immediately after the Emergence it had been observed that the two outermost planets of the system had disappeared and that in their stead revolved a new planet. This phenomenon was recognized for what it was, an exchange of planets; something to give concern only to astronomers.

No one except sheerest romancers even gave thought to the possibility of life upon other worlds, it being an almost mathematically demonstrable fact that the Valeronians were the only life in the entire universe. And even if other planets might possibly be inhabited, what of it? The vast reaches of empty ether intervening between Valeron and even her nearest fellow planet formed an insuperable obstacle even to communication, to say nothing of physical passage. Little did anyone dream, as generation followed generation, of what hideously intelligent life that interloping planet bore, nor of how the fair world of Valeron—was to suffer from it.

When the interplanetary invaders were discovered upon Valeron, Quedrin Vornel, the most brilliant physicist of the planet, and his son Quedrin Radnor, the most renowned, were among the first to be informed of the visitation.

Of these two, Quedrin Vornel had for many years been engaged in researches of the most abstruse and fundamental character upon the ultimate structure of matter. He had delved deeply into those which we know as matter, energy, and ether, and had studied exhaustively the phenomena characteristic of or associated with atomic, electronic, and photonic rearrangements.

His son, while a scientist of no mean attainments in his own right, did not possess the phenomenally powerful and profoundly analytical mind that had made the elder Quedrin the outstanding scientific genius of his time. He was, however, a synchronizer *par excellence*, possessing to a unique degree the abilty to develop things and processes of great utilitarian value from concepts and discoveries of a purely scientific and academic nature.

The vibrations which we know as Hertzian waves had long been known and had long been employed in radio, both broadcast and tight-beam, in television, in beam-transmission of power, and in receiverless visirays and their blocking screens. When Quedrin the elder disrupted the atom, however, successfully and safely liberating and studying not only its stupendous energy but also an entire series of vibrations and particles theretofore unknown to science, Quedrin the younger began forthwith to turn the resulting products to the good of mankind.

Intra-atomic energy soon drove every prime mover of Valeron and shorter and shorter waves were harnessed. In beams, fans, and broadcasts Quedrin Radnor combined and heterodyned them, making of them tools and instruments immeasurably

147

superior in power, precision, and adaptability to anything that his world had ever before known.

Due to the signal abilities of brilliant father and famous son, the laboratory in which they labored was connected by a private communication beam with the executive office of the Bardyle of Valeron. 'Bardyle,' freely translated, means 'coordinator.' He was neither king, emperor, nor president; and, while his authority was supreme, he was not a dictator.

A paradoxical statement this, but a true one; for the orders – rather, requests and suggestions – of the Bardyle merely guided the activities of men and women who had neither government nor laws, as we understand the terms, but were working of their own volition for the good of all mankind. The Bardyle could not conceivably issue an order contrary to the common weal, nor would such an order have been obeyed.

Upon the wall of the laboratory the tuned buzzer of the Bardyle's beam-communicator sounded its subdued call and Klynor Siblin, the scientist's capable assistant, took the call upon his desk instrument. A strong, youthful face appeared upon the screen.

'Radnor is not here, Siblin?' The pictured visitor glanced about the room as he spoke.

'No, sir. He is out in the space ship, making another test flight. He is merely circling the world, however, so that I can easily get him on the plate here if you wish.'

'That would perhaps be desirable. Something very peculiar has occurred, concerning which all three of you should be informed.'

The connections were made and the Bardyle went on:

'A semicircular dome of force has been erected over the ruins of the ancient city of Mocelyn. It is impossible to say how long it has been in place, since you know the ruins lie in an entirely unpopulated area. It is, however, of an unknown composition and pattern, being opaque to vision and to our visibeams. It is also apparently impervious to matter. Since this phenomenon seems to lie in your province I would suggest that you three men investigate it and take such steps as you deem necessary.'

'It is noted, Bardyle,' and Klynor Siblin cut the beam.

He then shot out their heaviest visiray beam, poising its view-

148

point directly over what, in the days before the cataclysm, had been the populous city of Mocelyn.

Straight down the beam drove, upon the huge hemisphere of greenly glinting force; urged downward by the full power of the Quedrins' mighty generators. By the very vehemence of its thrust it tore through the barrier, but only for an instant. The watchers had time to perceive only fleetingly a greenish-yellow haze of light, but before any details could be grasped their beam was snapped – the automatically reacting screens had called for and had received enough additional power to neutralize the invading beam.

Then, to the amazement of the three physicists, a beam of visible energy thrust itself from the green barrier and began to feel its way along their own invisible visiray. Siblin cut off his power instantly and leaped toward the door.

'Whoever they are, they know something!' he shouted as he ran. 'Don't want them to find this laboratory, so I'll set up a diversion with a rocket plane. If you watch at all, Vornel, do it from a distance and with a spy ray, not a carrier beam. I'll get in touch with Radnor on the way.'

Even though he swung around in a wide circle, to approach the strange stronghold at a wide angle to his former line, such was the power of the plane that Siblin reached his destination in little more than an hour. Keying Radnor's visibeam to the visiplates of the plane, so that the distant scientist could see everything that happened, Siblin again drove a heavy beam into the unyielding pattern of green force.

This time, however, the reaction was instantaneous. A fierce tongue of green flame licked out and seized the flying plane in mid-air. One wing and side panel were sliced off neatly and Siblin was thrown out violently, but he did not fall. Surrounded by a vibrant shell of energy, he was drawn rapidly toward the huge dome. The dome merged with the shell as it touched it, but the two did not coalesce. The shell passed smoothly through the dome, which as smoothly closed behind it. Siblin inside the shell, the shell inside the dome.

16: Within the Chloran Dome

Siblin never knew exactly what happened during those first few minutes, nor exactly how it happened. One minute, in his sturdy plane, he was setting up his 'diversion' by directing a powerful beam of force upon the green dome of the invaders. Suddenly his rocket ship had been blasted apart and he had been hurled away from the madly spinning, gyrating wreckage.

He had a confused recollection of sitting down violently upon something very hard, and perceived dully that he was lying asprawl upon the inside of a greenishly shimmering globe some twenty feet in diameter. Its substance had the hardness of chilled steel, yet it was almost perfectly transparent, seemingly composed of cold green flame, pale almost to invisibility. He also observed, in an incurious, foggy fashion, that the great dome was rushing toward him at an appalling pace.

He soon recovered from his shock, however, and perceived that the peculiar ball in which he was imprisoned was a shell of force, of formula and pattern entirely different from anything known to the scientists of Valeron. Keenly alive and interested now, he noted with high appreciation exactly how the wall of force that was the dome merged with, made way for, and closed smoothly behind the relatively tiny globe.

Inside the dome he stared around him, amazed and not a little awed. Upon the ground, the center of that immense hemisphere, lay a featureless, football-shape structure which must be the vessel of the invaders. Surrounding it there were massed machines and engineering structures of unmistakable form and purpose; drills, derricks, shaft heads, skips, hoists, and other equipment for boring and mining. From the lining of the huge dome there radiated a strong, lurid, yellowish-green light which intensified to positive ghastliness the natural color of the gaseous chlorin which replaced the familiar air in that walled-off volume so calmly appropriated to their own use by the Outlanders.

As his shell was drawn downward toward the strange scene Siblin saw many moving things beneath him, but was able neither to understand what he saw nor to correlate it with anything in his own knowledge or experience. For those beings were amorphous. Some flowed along the ground, formless blobs of matter; some rolled, like wheels or like barrels; many crawled rapidly, snakelike; others resembled animated pancakes, undulating flatly and nimbly about upon a dozen or so short, tentacular legs; only a few, vaguely manlike, walked upright.

A glass cage, some eight feet square and seven high, stood under the towering bulge of the great ship's side; and as his shell of force engulfed it and its door swung invitingly open, Siblin knew that he was expected to enter it.

Indeed, he had no choice – the fabric of cold flame that had been his conveyance and protection vanished, and he had scarcely time to leap inside the cage and slam the door before the noxious vapors of the atmosphere invaded the space from which the shell's impermeable wall had barred it. To die more slowly, but just as surely, from suffocation? No, the cage was equipped with a thoroughly efficient oxygen generator and air purifier; there were stores of Valeronian food and water; there were a chair, a table, and a narrow bunk; and wonder of wonders, there were even kits of toilet articles and of changes of clothing.

Far above a great door opened. The cage was lifted and, without any apparent means either of support or of propulsion, it moved through the doorways and along various corridors and halls, coming finally to rest upon the floor in one of the innermost compartments of the sky rover. Siblin saw masses of machinery, panels of controlling instruments, and weirdly multiform creatures at station; but he had scant time even to glance at them, his attention being attracted instantly to the middle of the room where, lying in a heavily reenforced shallow cup of metal upon an immensely strong, low table, he saw a – a *something*; and for the first time an inhabitant of Valeron saw at close range one of the invaders.

It was in no sense a solid, nor a liquid, nor yet a jelly; although it seemed to partake of certain properties of all three. In part it was murkily transparent, in part greenishly translucent, in part turbidly opaque; but in all it was intrinsically horrible. In every physical detail and in every nuance of radiant aura of conscious power it was disgusting and appalling; sickeningly, nauseously revolting to every human thought and instinct.

But that it was sentient and intelligent there could be no doubt. Not only could its malign mental radiations be felt, but its brain could be plainly seen; a huge, intricately convolute organ suspended in an unyielding but plastic medium of solid jelly. Its skin seemed thin and frail, but Siblin was later to learn that that tegument was not only stronger than rawhide, but was more pliable, more elastic, and more extensible than the finest rubber.

As the Valeronian stared in helpless horror that peculiar skin stretched locally almost to vanishing thinness and an enormous Cyclopean eye developed. More than an eye, it was a special organ for a special sense which humanity has never possessed, a sense combining ordinary vision with something infinitely deeper, more penetrant and more powerful. Vision, hypnotism, telepathy, thought-transference – something of all these, yet in essence a thing beyond any sense or faculty known to us or describable in language, had its being in the almost-visible, almost-tangible beam of force which emanated from the single, temporary 'eye' of the Thing and bored through the eyes and deep into the brain of the Valeronian. Siblin's very senses reeled under the impact of that wave of mental power, but he did not quite lose consciousness.

'So *you* are one of the ruling intelligences of this planet – one of its most advanced scientists?' The scornful thought formed itself, coldly clear, in his mind. 'We have always known, of course, that we are the highest form of life in the universe, and the fact that you are so low in the scale of mentality only confirms that knowledge. It would be surprising indeed if such a noxious atmosphere as yours could nurture any real intelligence. It will be highly gratifying to report to the Council of Great Ones that not only is this planet rich in the materials we seek, but that its inhabitants, while intelligent enough to do our bidding in securing those materials, are not sufficiently advanced to cause us any trouble.'

'Why did you not come in peace?' Siblin thought back. Neither cowed nor shaken, he was merely amazed at the truculently overbearing mien of the strange entity. 'We would have been glad to cooperate with you in every possible way. It would seem self-evident that all intelligent races, whatever their outward form or mental status, should work together harmoniously for their mutual advancement.'

'Bah!' snapped the amoebus savagely. 'That is the talk of a weakling – the whining, begging reasoning of a race of low intelligence, one which knows and acknowledges itself inferior. Know you, feeble brain, that we of Chlora' – to substitute an intelligible word for the unpronounceable and untranslatable thought-image of his native world – 'neither require nor desire cooperation. We are in no need either of assistance or of instruction from any lesser and lower form of life. We instruct. Other races, such as yours, either obey or are obliterated. I brought you aboard this vessel because I am about to return to my own planet, and had decided to take one of you with me, so that the other Great Ones of the Council may see for themselves what form of life this Valeron boasts.

'If your race obeys our commands implicitly and does not attempt to interfere with us in any way, we shall probably permit most of you to continue your futile lives in our service; such as in mining for us certain ores which, relatively abundant upon your planet, are very scarce upon ours.

'As for you personally, perhaps we shall destroy you after the other Great Ones have examined you, perhaps we shall decide to use you as a messenger to transmit our orders to your fellow creatures. Before we depart, however, I shall make a demonstration which should impress upon even such feeble minds as those of your race the futility of any thought of opposition to us. Watch carefully – everything that goes on outside is shown in the view box.'

Although Siblin had neither heard, felt, nor seen the captain issue any orders, all was in readiness for the take-off. The mining engineers were all on board, the vessel was sealed for flight, and the navigators and control officers were at their panels. Siblin stared intently into the 'view box,' the three-dimensional visiplate that mirrored faithfully every occurrence in the neighborhood of the Chloran vessel.

The lower edge of the hemisphere of force began to contract, passing smoothly through or around – the spectator could not decide which – the ruins of Mocelyn, hugging or actually penetrating the ground, allowing not even a whiff of its precious chlorin content to escape into the atmosphere of Valeron. The ship then darted into the air and the shrinking edge became an ever-decreasing circle upon the ground beneath her. That circle disappeared as the meeting edge fused and the wall of force, now a hollow sphere, contained within itself the atmosphere of the invaders.

High over the surface of the planet sped the Chloran raider toward the nearest Valeronian city, which happened to be only a small village. Above the unfortunate settlement the callous monstrosity poised its craft, to drop its dread curtain of strangling, choking death.

Down the screen dropped, rolling out to become again a hemispherical wall, sweeping before it every milliliter of the life-giving air of Valeron and drawing behind it the noxious atmosphere of Chlora. For those who have ever inhaled even a small quantity of chlorin it is unnecessary to describe in detail the manner in which those villagers of Valeron died; for those who have not, no possible description could be adequate. Suffice it to say, therefore, that they died – horribly.

Again the wall of force rolled up, coming clear up to the outer skin of the cruiser this time, in its approach liquefying the chlorin and forcing it into storage chambers. The wall then disappeared entirely, leaving the marauding vessel starkly outlined against the sky. Then, further and even more strongly to impress the raging but impotent Klynor Siblin:

'Beam it down!' the amoebus captain commanded, and various officers sent out thin, whiplike tentacles toward their controls.

Projectors swung downward and dense green pillars of flaming energy erupted from the white-hot refractories of their throats. And what those green pillars struck subsided instantly into a pool of hissing, molten glass. Methodically they swept the entire area of the village. All organic matter – vegetation, bodies, humus – burst instantly into wildly raging flame and in that same instant was consumed; only the incombustible ash being left behind to merge with the metal and stone of the buildings and with the minerals of the soil as they melted to form a hellish lake.

'You monster!' shrieked Siblin, white, shaken, almost beside himself. 'You vile, unspeakable monster! Of what use is such a slaughter of innocent men? They had not harmed you . . .'

'Indeed they have not, nor could they,' the Chloran interrupted callously. 'They mean nothing whatever to me, in any way. I have gone to the trouble of wiping out this city to give you and the rest of your race an object lesson; to impress upon you how thoroughly unimportant you are to us and to bring home to you your abject helplessness. Your whole race is, as you have just shown yourself to be, childish, soft, and sentimental, and therefore incapable of real advancement. On the contrary we, the masters of the universe, do not suffer from silly inhibitions or from foolish weaknesses.'

The eye faded out, its sharp outlines blurring gradually as its highly specialized parts became transformed into or were replaced by the formless gel composing the body of the creature. The amoebus then poured himself out of the cup, assumed the shape of a doughnut, and rolled rapidly out of the room.

When the Chloran captain had gone, Siblin threw himself upon his narrow bunk, fighting savagely to retain his self-control. He *must* escape – he *must* escape – the thought repeated itself endlessly in his mind – but how? The glass walls of his prison were his only defense against hideous death. Nowhere in any Chloran thing, nowhere in any nook or cranny of the noisome planet toward which he was speeding, could he exist for a minute except inside the cell which his captors were keeping supplied with oxygen. No tools – nothing from which to make a protective covering – no way of carrying air – nowhere to go – helpless, helpless – even to break that glass meant death . . .

At last he slept, fitfully, and when he awoke the vessel was deep in interplanetary space. His captors paid no further attention to him – he had air, food, and water, and if he chose to kill himself that was of no concern to them – and Siblin, able to think more calmly now, studied every phase of his predicament.

There was absolutely no possibility of escape. Rescue was out of the question. He could, however, communicate with Valeron, since in his belt were tiny sender and receiver, attached by tight

155

beams to instruments in the laboratory of the Quedrins. Detection of that pencil beam might well mean instant death, but that was a risk which, for the good of humanity, must be run. Lying upon his side, he concealed one ear plug under his head and manipulated the tiny sender in his belt. 'Quedrin Radnor – Quedrin Vornel ...' he called for minutes, with no response. However, person-to-person communication was not really necessary; his messages would be recorded. He went on to describe in detail, tersely, accurately, and scientifically, everything that he had observed and deduced concerning the Chlorans, their forces, and their mechanisms.

'We are now approaching the planet,' he continued, now an observer reporting what he saw in the view box. 'It is apparently largely land. It has two polar ice caps, the larger of which I call north. A dark area, which I take to be an ocean, is the most prominent feature visible at this time. It is diamond-shaped and its longer axis, lying north and south, is about one quarter of a circumference in length. Its shorter axis, about half that length, lies almost upon the equator. We are passing high above this ocean, going east.

'East of the ocean and distant from it about one fifth of a circumference lies quite a large lake, roughly elliptical in shape, whose major axis lies approximately northeast and southwest. We are dropping toward a large city upon the southeast shore of this lake, almost equally distant from its two ends. Since I am to be examined by a so-called "Council of Great Ones," it may be that this city is their capital.

'No matter what happens, do not attempt to rescue me, as it is entirely hopeless. Escape is likewise impossible, because of the lethal atmosphere. There is a strong possibility, furthermore, that I may be returned to Valeron as a messenger to our race. This possibility is my only hope of returning. I am sending this data and will continue to send it as long as is possible, simply to aid you in deciding what shall be done to defend civilization against these monsters.

'We are now docking, near a large, hemispherical dome of force ... My cell is being transported through the atmosphere toward that dome ... It is opening. I do not know whether my beam can pass out through it, but I shall keep on sending ...

Inside the dome there is a great building, toward which I am floating ... I am inside the building, inside a glass compartment which seems to be filled with air ... Yes, it *is* air, for the creatures who are entering it are wearing protective suits of some transparent substance. Their bodies are now globular and they are walking, each upon three short legs. One of them is developing an eye, similar to the one I descr...'

Siblin's message stopped in the middle of a word. The eye had developed and in its weirdly hypnotic grip the Valeronian was helpless to do anything of his own volition. Obeying the telepathic command of the Great One, he stepped out into the larger room and divested himself of his scanty clothing. One of the monstrosities studied his belt briefly, recognized his communicator instruments for what they were, and kicked them scornfully into a corner – thus rendering it impossible for either captive or captors to know it when that small receiver throbbed out its urgent message from Quedrin Radnor.

The inspection and examination finished, it did not take long for the monstrosities to decide upon a course of action.

'Take this scum back to its own planet as soon as your cargo is unloaded,' the Great One directed. 'You must pass near that planet on your way to explore the next one, and it will save time and inconvenience to let it carry our message to its fellows.'

Out in space, speeding toward distant Valeron, the captain again communicated with Siblin:

'I shall land you close to one of your inhabited cities and you will at once get in touch with your Bardyle. You already know what your race is to do, and you have in your cage a sample of the ore with which you are to supply us. You shall be given twenty of your days in which to take from the mine already established by us enough of that ore to load this ship – ten thousand tons. The full amount – and pure mineral, mind you, no base rock – must be in the loading hoppers at the appointed time or I shall proceed to destroy every populated city, village, and hamlet upon the face of your globe.'

'But that particular ore is rare!' protested Siblin. 'I do not believe that it will prove physically possible to recover such a vast amount of it in the short time you are allowing us.'

'You understand the orders – obey them or die!'

17: Quedrin Radnor Retaliates

Very near to Valeron, as space distances go, yet so far away in terms of miles that he could take no active part whatever in the proceedings, Quedrin Radnor sat tense at his controls, staring into his visiplate. Even before Klynor Siblin had lifted his rocket plane off the ground, Radnor had opened his throttle wide. Then, his ship hurtling at full drive toward home, everything done that he could do, he sat and watched.

Watched, a helpless spectator. Watched while Siblin made his futilely spectacular attack; watched the gallant plane's destruction; watched the capture of the brave but foolhardy pilot; watched the rolling up and compression of the Chloran dome; watched in agony the obliteration of everything, animate and inanimate, pertaining to the outlying village; watched in horrified relief the departure of the invading space ship.

Screaming through the air, her outer plating white hot from its friction, her forward rocket tubes bellowing a vicious crescendo, Radnor braked his ship savagely to a landing in the dock beside the machine shop in which she had been built. During that long return voyage his mind had not been idle. Not only had he decided what to do, he had also made rough sketches and working drawings of the changes which must be made in his peaceful space ship to make of her a superdreadnought of the void.

Nor was this as difficult an undertaking as might be supposed. She already had power enough and to spare, her generators and converters being able to supply, hundreds of times over, her maximum present drain; and, because of the ever-present danger of collision with meteorites, she was already amply equipped with repeller screens and with automatically tripped zones of force. Therefore all that was necessary was the installation of the required offensive armament – beam projectors, torpedo tubes, fields of force, controls, and the like – the designing of which was a simple matter for the brain which had tamed to man's everyday use the ultimately violent explosiveness of intra-atomic energy.

Radnor first made sure that the machine-shop superintendent, master mechanic, and foreman understood the sketches fully and knew precisely what was to be done. Then, confident that the new projectors would project and that the as yet non-existent oxygen bombs would explode with their theoretical violence, he hurried to the office of the Bardyle. Already gathered there was a portentous group. Besides the coordinator there were scientists, engineers, architects, and beam specialists, as well as artists, teachers, and philosophers. The group, while not large, was thoroughly representative of Valeron's mental, intellectual, and scientific culture. Each member of the Council Extraordinary was unwontedly serious of mien, for each knew well what horror his world was facing. Warned by the utter, unreasoning wantonness of the destruction wrought by the Chlorans, each knew that the high civilization of Valeron, so long attuned to the arts of peace that strife had become almost unthinkable, must now devote its every effort to the grim and hateful business of war.

'Greetings, Quedrin Radnor!' began the Bardyle. 'Your plan for the defense of Valeron has been adopted, with a few minor alterations and additions suggested by other technical experts. It has been decided, however, that your proposed punitive visit to Chlora cannot be approved. As matters now stand it can be only an expedition of retaliation and vengeance, and as such can in no wise advance our cause.'

'Very well, Oh Bardyle! It is...' Radnor, trained from infancy in cooperation, was accepting the group decision as a matter of course when he was interrupted by an emergency call from his own laboratory. An assistant, returning to the temporarily deserted building had found the message of Klynor Siblin and had known that it should be given immediate attention.

'Please relay it to us here, at once,' Radnor instructed; and, when the message had been delivered:

'Fellow councilors, I believe that this word from Klynor Siblin will operate to change your decision against my proposed flight to Chlora. With these incomplete facts and data to guide me I shall be able to study intelligently the systems of offense and of defense employed by the enemy, and shall then be in position to strengthen immeasurably our own armament. Furthermore, Siblin was alive within the hour – there may yet be some slight chance of saving his life in spite of what he has said.'

The Bardyle glanced once around the circle of tense faces, reading in them the consensus of opinion without having recourse to speech.

'Your point is well taken, Councilor Quedrin, and for the sake of acquiring knowledge your flight is approved,' he said slowly. 'Provided, however – and this is a most important proviso – that you can convince us that there is a reasonable certainty of your safe return. Klynor Siblin had, of course, no idea that he would be captured. Nevertheless, the Chlorans took him, and his life is probably forfeit. You must also agree not to jeopardize your life in any attempt to rescue your friend unless you have every reason to believe that such an attempt will prove successful. We are insisting upon these assurances because your scientific ability will be of inestimable value to Valeron in this forthcoming struggle, and therefore your life must at all hazards be preserved.'

'To the best of my belief my safe return is certain,' replied Radnor positively. 'Siblin's plane, used only for low-speed atmospheric flying, had no defenses whatever and so fell easy prey to the Chlorans' attack. My ship, however, was built to navigate space, in which it may meet at any time meteorites traveling at immensely high velocities, and is protected accordingly. She already had four courses of high-powered repeller screens, the inside course of which, upon being punctured, automatically throws around her a zone of force.

'This zone, as most of you know, sets up a stasis in the ether itself, and thus is not only absolutely impervious to and unaffected by any material substance, however applied, but is also opaque to any vibration or wave-form propagated through the ether. In addition to these defenses I am now installing screens capable of neutralizing any offensive force with which I am familiar, as well as certain other armament, the plans of all of which are already in your possession, to be employed in the general defense.

'I agree also to your second condition.'

'Such being the case your expedition is approved,' the Bardyle said, and Radnor made his way back to the machine shop.

His first care was to tap Siblin's beam, but his call elicited no response. Those ultrainstruments were then lying neglected in a corner of an air-filled room upon far Chlora, where the almost soundless voice of the tiny receiver went unheard. Setting upon his receiver a relay alarm to inform him of any communication from Siblin, Radnor joined the men who were smoothly and efficiently re-equipping his vessel.

In a short time the alterations were done, and, armed now to the teeth with vibratory and with solid and gaseous destruction, he lifted his warship into the air, grimly determined to take the war into the territory of the enemy.

He approached the inimical planet cautiously knowing that their cities would not be undefended, as were those of his own world, and fearing that they might have alarms and detector screens of which he could know nothing. Poised high above the outermost layer of that noxious atmosphere he studied for a long time every visible feature of the world before him.

In this survey he employed an ordinary, old-fashioned telescope instead of his infinitely more powerful and maneuverable visirays, because the use of the purely optical instrument obviated the necessity of sending out forces which the Chlorans might be able to detect. He found the diamond-shaped ocean and the elliptical lake without difficulty, and placed his vessel with care. He then cut off his every betraying force and his ship plunged downward, falling freely under the influence of gravity.

Directly over the city Radnor actuated his braking rockets, and as they burst into their staccato thunder his hands fairly flashed over his controls. Almost simultaneously he scattered broadcast his cargo of bombs, threw out a vast hemisphere of force to confine the gas they would release, activated his spy ray, and cut in the generators of his awful offensive beams.

The bombs were simply large flasks of metal, so built as to shatter upon impact, and they contained only oxygen under pressure – but what a pressure! Five thousand Valeronian atmospheres those flasks contained. Well over seventy-five thousand pounds to the square inch in our ordinary terms, that pressure was one handled upon Earth only in high-pressure laboratories. Spreading widely to cover almost the whole circle of the city's expanse, those terrific canisters hurtled to the ground and exploded with all the devastating might of the high-explosive shells which in effect they were.

But the havoc they wrought as demolition bombs was neither their only nor their greatest damage. The seventy-five million cubic feet of free oxygen, driven downward and prevented from escaping into the open atmosphere by Radnor's forces, quickly diffused into a killing concentration throughout the Chloran city save inside that one upstanding dome. Almost everywhere else throughout that city the natives died exactly as had died the people of the Valeronian village in the strangling chlorin of the invaders; for oxygen is as lethal to that amoebic race as is their noxious halogen to us.

Long before the bombs reached the ground Radnor was probing with his spy ray at the great central dome from within which Klynor Siblin's message had in part been sent. But now he could not get through it; either they had detected Siblin's beam and blocked that entire communication band or else they had already put up additional barriers around their head-quarters against his attack, quickly though he had acted.

Snapping off the futile visiray, he concentrated his destructive beam into a cylinder of the smallest possible diameter and hurled it against the dome; but even that frightful pencil of annihilation, driven by Radnor's every resource of power, was utterly ineffective against that greenly scintillant hemisphere of force. The point of attack flared into radiant splendor, but showed no sign of overloading or of failure.

Knowing now that there was no hope at all of rescuing Siblin and that he himself had only a few minutes left in which to work, Radnor left his beam upon the dome only long enough for his recording photometers to analyze the radiations emanating from the point of contact. Then, full-driven still, but now operating at maximum aperture he drove it in a dizzying spiral outwardly from the dome, fusing the entire unprotected area of the metropolis into a glassily fluid slag of seething, smoking desolation. Those of the monstrosities who were beneath the protective hemisphere he could not touch, but all the others died. Some were riven asunder by the fragmentation of the bombs, many expired in the flood of lethal oxygen, the rest were cremated instantly in the unimaginable fury of Radnor's ravening beams.

But beneath that dome of force there was a mighty fortress indeed. It is true that her offensive weapons had not seen active service for many years; not since the last rebellion of the slaves had been crushed. It is also true that the Chloran officers whose duty it was to operate these weapons had been caught napping – as thoroughly surprised at that fierce counterattack as would be a group of Earthly hunters were the lowly rabbits to turn upon them with repeating rifles in their furry paws.

But it did not take long for those officers to tune in their offensive armament, and that armament was driven by no such puny engines as Radnor's space ship bore. Being stationary and a part of the regular equipment of a fortress, their size and mass were of course much greater than anything ordinarily installed in any vessel, of whatever class or tonnage. Also, in addition to being superior in size and number, the Chloran generators were considerably more efficient in the conversion and utilization of interatomic energy than were any then known to the science of Valeron.

Therefore, as Radnor had rather more than expected, he was not long allowed to wreak his will. From the dome there reached out slowly, almost caressingly, a huge arm of force incredible, at whose blighting touch his first or outer screen simply vanished – flared through the visible spectrum and went down, all in the veriest twinkling of an eye. That first screen, although the weakest by far of the four, had never even radiated under the heaviest test loads that Radnor had been able to put upon it. Now he sat at his instruments, tense but intensely analytical, watching with bated breath as that Titanic beam crashed through his second screen and tore madly at his third.

Well it was for Valeron that day that Radnor had armed and powered his vessel to withstand not only whatever forces he expected her to meet, but had, with the true scientific spirit and in so far as he was able, provided against any conceivable emergency. Thus, the first screen was, as has been said, sufficiently powerful to cope with anything the vessel was apt to encounter. Nevertheless, the power of the other defensive courses increased in geometrical progression; and, as a final precaution, the fourth screen, in the almost unthinkable contingency of its being overloaded, threw on automatically in the moment of its failure an ultimately impenetrable zone of force.

That scientific caution was now to save not only Radnor's life, but also the whole civilization of Valeron. For even that mighty fourth screen, employing in its generation as it did the unimaginable sum total of the power possible of production by the massed converters of the space flyer, failed to stop that awful thrust. It halted it for a few minutes, in a blazingly, flamingly pyrotechnic display of incandescence indescribable, but as the Chlorans meshed in additional units of their stupendous power plant it began to radiate higher and higher into the ultra-violet and was certainly doomed.

It failed, and in the instant of its going down, actuated a zone of force – a complete stasis in the ether itself, through which no possible manifestation, either of matter or of energy in any form, could in any circumstance pass. Or could it? Radnor clenched his teeth and waited. Whether or not there was a sub-ether – something lying within and between the discrete particles which actually composed the ether – was a matter of theoretical controversy and of some academically scientific interest.

But, postulating the existence of such a medium and even that of vibrations of such infinitely short period that they could be propagated therein, would it be even theoretically possible to heterodyne upon them waves of ordinary frequencies? And could those amorphous monstrosities be so highly advanced that they had reduced to practical application something that was as yet known to humanity only in the vaguest, most tenuous of hypotheses?

Minute after minute passed, however, during which the Valeronian remained alive within an intact ship which, he knew, was hurtling upward and away from Chlora at the absolute velocity of her inertia, unaffected by gravitation, and he began to smile in relief. Whatever might lie below the level of the ether, either of vibration or of substance, it was becoming evident that the Chlorans could no more handle it than he could.

For half an hour Radnor allowed his craft to drift within her impenetrable shield. Then, knowing that he was well beyond atmosphere, he made sure that his screens were full out and released his zone. Instantly his screens sprang into a dazzling, coruscant white under the combined attack of two space ships which had been following him. This time, however, the Chloran beams were stopped by the third screen. Either the enemy had not had time to measure accurately his power, or they had not considered such measurement worth while.

They were now to pay dearly for not having gauged his strength. Radnor's beam, again a stabbing stiletto of pure energy, lashed out against the nearer vessel; and that luckless ship mounted no such generators as powered her parent fortress. That raging spear, driven as it was by all the power that Radnor had been able to pack into his cruiser, tore through screens and metal alike as though they had been so much paper; and in mere seconds what had once been a mighty space ship was merely a cloud of drifting, expanding vapor. The furious shaft was then directed against the other enemy, but it was just too late – the canny amoebus in command had learned his lesson and had already snapped on his zone of force.

Having learned many facts vital to the defense of Valeron and knowing that his return homeward would now be unopposed, Radnor put on full touring acceleration and drove toward his native world. Motionless at his controls, face grim and hard, he devoted his entire mind to the problem of how Valeron could best wage the inevitable war of extinction against the implacable denizens of the monstrous, interloping planet Chlora.

As has been said, Radnor's reply to Siblin's message was un-heard, for his ultraphones were not upon his person, but were lying disregarded in a corner of the room in which their owner had undergone examination by his captors. They still lay there as the Valeronian in his cage was wafted lightly back into the space ship from which he had been taken such a short time before; lay there as that vehicle of vacuous space lifted itself from its dock and darted away toward distant Valeron.

During the earlier part of that voyage Radnor was also in the ether, traveling from Valeron to Chlora. The two vessels did not meet, however, even though each was making for the planet which the other had left and though each pilot was following the path for him the most economical of time and of power. In fact, due to the orbits, velocities, and distances involved, they were separated by such a vast distance at the time of their closest approach to each other that neither ship even affected the ultra-sensitive electromagnetic detector screens of the other.

Not until the Chloran vessel was within Valeron's atmosphere did her commander deign again to notice his prisoner.

'As I told you when last I spoke to you, I am about to land you in one of your established cities,' the amoebus informed Siblin then. 'Get in touch with your Bardyle at once and convey our instructions to him. You have the sample and you know what you are to do. No excuses for non-performance will be accepted. If, however, you anticipate having any difficulty in convincing your fellow savages that we mean precisely what we say, I will take time now to destroy one or two more of your cities.'

'It will not be necessary – my people will believe what I tell them,' Siblin thought back. Then deciding to make one more effort, hopeless although it probably would be, to reason with that highly intelligent but monstrously callous creature, he went on:

'I wish to repeat, however, that your demand is entirely be-yond reason. That ore is rare, and in the time you have allowed us I really fear that it will be impossible for us to mine the required amount of it. And surely, even from your own point of view, it would be more logical to grant us a reasonable extension of time than to kill us without further hearing simply because we have failed to perform a task that was from the very first impossible. You must bear it in mind that a dead community cannot work your mines at all.'

'We know exactly how abundant that ore is, and we know equally well your intelligence, and your ability,' the captain replied coldly – and mistakenly. 'With the machinery we have left in the mine and by working every possible man at all times, you can have it ready for us. I am now setting out to explore the next planet, but I shall be at the mine at sunrise, twenty of your mornings from tomorrow. Ten thousand tons of that mineral must be ready for me to load or else your entire race shall that day cease to exist. It matters nothing to us whether you live or die, since we already have slaves enough. We shall permit you to keep on living if you obey our orders in every particular, otherwise we shall not so permit.'

The vessel came easily to a landing. Siblin in his cage was picked up by the same invisible means, transported along corridors and through doorways, and was deposited, not ungently, upon the ground in the middle of a public square. When the raider darted away he opened the door of his glass prison and made his way through the gathering crowd of the curious to the nearest visiphone station, where the mere mention of his name cleared all lines of communication for an instant audience with the Bardyle of Valeron.

'We are glad indeed to see you again, Klynor Siblin.' The coordinator smiled in greeting. 'The more especially since Quedrin Radnor, even now on the way back from Chlora, has just reported that his attempt to rescue you was entirely in vain. He was met by forces of such magnitude that only by employing a zone of force was he himself able to win clear. But you undoubtedly have tidings of urgent import – you may proceed.'

Siblin told his story tersely and cogently, yet omitting nothing of importance. When he had finished his report the Bardyle said:

'Truly, a depraved evolution – a violent and unreasonable

race indeed.' He thought deeply for a few seconds, then went on: 'The council extraordinary has been in session for some time. I am inviting you to join us here. Quedrin Radnor should arrive at about the same time as you do, and you both should be present to clear up any minor points which have not been covered in your visiphone report. I am instructing the transportation officer there to put at your disposal any special equipment necessary to enable you to get here as soon as possible.'

The Bardyle was no laggard, nor was the transportation officer of the city in which Siblin found himself. Therefore when he came out of the visiphone station there was awaiting him a two-wheeled automatic conveyance bearing upon its windshield in letters of orange light the legend, 'Reserved for Klynor Siblin.' He stepped into the queer looking, gyroscopically stabilized vehicle, pressed down '9-2-6-4-3-8' – the location number of the airport – upon the banked keys of a numbering machine, and touched a red button, whereupon the machine glided off of itself.

It turned corners, dived downward into subways and swung upward onto bridges, selecting unerringly and following truly the guiding pencils of force which would lead it to the airport, its destination. Its pace was fast, mounting effortlessly upon the straightaways to a hundred miles an hour and more.

There were no traffic jams and very few halts, since each direction of traffic had its own level and its own roadway, and the only necessity for stopping came in the very infrequent event that a main artery into which the machine's way led was already so full of vehicles that it had to wait momentarily for an opening. There was no disorder, and there were neither accidents nor collisions; for the forces controlling those thousands upon thousands of speeding mechanisms, unlike the drivers of Earthly automobiles, were uniformly tireless, eternally vigilant, and – sober.

Thus Siblin arrived at the airport without incident, finding his special plane ready and waiting. It also was fully automatic, robot-piloted, sealed for high flight, and equipped with everything necessary for comfort. He ate a hearty meal, and then, as the plane reached its ninety-thousand-foot ceiling and leveled out at eight hundred miles an hour toward the distant capital, undressed and went to bed, to the first real sleep he had enjoyed for many days.

As has been indicated, Siblin lost no time; but, rapidly as he had traveled and instantly as he had made connections, Quedrin Radnor was already in his seat in the council extraordinary when Siblin was ushered in to sit with that august body. The visiphone reports had been studied exhaustively by every councilor, and as soon as the newcomer had answered their many questions concerning the details of his experiences the council continued its intense, but orderly and thorough, study of what should be done, what could be done, in the present crisis.

'We are in agreement, gentlemen,' the Bardyle at last announced. 'This new development, offering as it does only the choice between death and slavery of the most abject kind, does not change the prior situation except in setting a definite date for the completion of our program of defense. The stipulated amount of tribute probably could be mined by dint of straining our every resource, but in all probability that demand is but the first of such a never-ending succession that our lives would soon become unbearable.

'We are agreed that the immediate extinction of our entire race is preferable to a precarious existence which can be earned only by incessant and grinding labor for an unfeeling and alien race; an existence even then subject to termination at any time at the whim of the Chlorans.

'Therefore the work which was begun as soon as the strangers revealed their true nature and which is now well under way shall go on. Most of you know already what that work is, but for one or two who do not and for the benefit of the news broadcasts I shall summarize our position as briefly as is consistent with clarity.

'We intend to defend this, our largest city, into which is being brought everything needed of supplies and equipment, and as many men as can work without interfering with each other. The rest of our people are to leave their houses and scatter into widely separated temporary refuges until the issue has been decided. This evacuation may not be necessary, since the enemy will center their attack upon our fortress, knowing that until it has been reduced we are still masters of our planet.

'It was decided upon, however, not only in the belief that the enemy may destroy our unprotected centers of population, either wantonly or in anger at our resistance, but also because such a dispersion will give our race the greatest possible chance of survival in the not-at-all-improbable event of the crushing of our defenses here.

'One power-driven dome of force is to protect the city proper, and around that dome are being built concentric rings of fortifications housing the most powerful mechanisms of offense and defense possible for us to construct.

'Although we have always been a peaceful people our position is not entirely hopeless. The *sine qua non* of warfare is power, and of that commodity we have no lack. True, without knowledge of how to apply that power our cause would be already lost, but we are not without knowledge of the application. Many of our peace-time tools are readily transformed into powerful engines of destruction. Quedrin Radnor, besides possessing a unique ability in the turning of old things to new purposes, has studied exhaustively the patterns of force employed by the enemy and understands thoroughly their generation, their utilization, and their neutralization.

'Finally, the mining and excavating machinery of the Chlorans has been dismantled and studied, and its novel features have been incorporated in several new mechanisms of our own devising. Twenty days is none too long a time in which to complete a program of this magnitude and scope, but that is all the time we have. You wish to ask a question, Councilor Quedrin?'

'If you please. Shall we not have more than twenty days? The ship to be loaded will return in that time, it is true, but we can deal with her easily enough. Their ordinary space ships are no match for ours. That fact was proved so conclusively during our one engagement in space that they did not even follow me back here. They undoubtedly are building vessels of vastly greater power, but it seems to me that we shall be safe until those heavier vessels can arrive.'

'I fear that you are underestimating the intelligence of our foes,' replied the coordinator. 'In all probability they know exactly what we are doing, and were their present space ships superior to yours we would have ceased to exist ere this. It is practically certain that they will attack as soon as they have constructed craft of sufficient power to insure success. In fact, they may be able to perfect their attack before we can complete our defense, but that is a chance which we must take.

'In that connection, two facts give us ground for optimism. First, theirs is an undertaking of greater magnitude than ours, since they must of necessity be mobile and operative at a great distance from their base, whereas we are stationary and at home. Second, we started our project before they began theirs. This second fact must be allowed but little weight, however, for they may well be more efficient than we are in the construction of engines of war.

'The exploring vessel is unimportant. She may or may not call for her load of ore; she may or may not join in the attack which is now inevitable. One thing only is certain – we must and we will drive this program through to completion before she is due to dock at the mine. Everything else must be subordinated to the task; we must devote to it every iota of our mental, physical, and mechanical power. Each of you knows his part. The meeting is adjourned *sine die*.'

There ensued a world-wide activity unparalleled in the annals of the planet. During the years immediately preceding the cataclysm there had been hustle and bustle, misdirected effort, wasted energy, turmoil and confusion; and a certain measure of success had been wrested out of chaos only by the ability of a handful of men to think clearly and straight. Now, however, Valeron was facing a crisis infinitely more grave, for she had but days instead of years in which to prepare to meet it. But now, on the other hand, instead of possessing only a few men of vision, who had found it practically impossible either to direct or to control an out-and-out rabble of ignorant, muddled, and panic-stricken incompetents, she had a population composed entirely of clear thinkers, who, requiring a very little direction and no control at all, were able and eager to work together whole-heartedly for the common good.

Thus, while the city and its environs now seethed with activity, there was no confusion or disorder. Wherever there was room for a man to work, a man was working, and the workers were kept supplied with materials and with mechanisms. There were no mistakes, no delays, no friction. Each man knew his task and its relation to the whole, and performed it with a smoothly efficient speed born of a racial training in cooperation and coordination impossible to any member of a race of lesser mental attainments.

To such good purpose did every Valeronian do his part that at dawn of The Day everything was in readiness for the Chloran visitation. The immense fortress was complete and had been tested in every part, from the ranked batteries of gigantic converters and generators down to the most distant outlying visiray viewpoint. It was powered, armed, equipped, provisioned, garrisoned. Every once-populated city was devoid of life, its inhabitants having dispersed over the face of the globe, to live in isolated groups until it had been decided whether the proud civilization of Valeron was to triumph or to perish.

Promptly as that sunrise the Chloran explorer appeared at the lifeless mine, and when he found the loading hoppers empty he calmly proceeded to the nearest city and began to beam it down. Finding it deserted he cut off, and felt a powerful spy ray, upon which he set a tracer. This time the ray held up and he saw the immense fortress which had been erected during his absence; a fortress which he forthwith attacked viciously, carelessly, and with the loftily arrogant contempt which seemed to characterize his breed.

But was that innate contemptuousness the real reason for that suicidal attempt? Or had that vessel's commander been ordered by the Great Ones to sacrifice himself and his command so that they could measure Valeron's defensive power? If so, why did he visit the mine at all and why did he not know beforehand the location of the fortress? Camouflage? In view of what the Great Ones of Chlora must have known, why that commander did what he did that morning no one of Valeron ever knew.

The explorer launched a beam – just one. Then Quedrin Radnor pressed a contact and out against the invader there flamed a beam of such violence that the amoebus had no time to touch his controls, that even the automatic trips of his zone of force – if he had such trips – did not have time in which to react. The defensive screens scarcely flashed, so rapidly did that terrific beam drive through them, and the vessel itself disappeared almost instantly – molten, vaporized, consumed utterly. But there was no exultation beneath Valeron's mighty dome. From the Bardyle down, the defenders of their planet knew full well that the real attack was yet to come, and knew that it would not be long delayed.

Nor was it. Nor did those which came to reduce Valeron's farflung stronghold in any way resemble any form of space ship with which humanity was familiar. Two stupendous structures of metal appeared, plunging stolidly along, veritable flying fortresses, of such enormous bulk and mass that it seemed scarcely conceivable for them actually to support themselves in air.

Simultaneously the two floating castles launched against the towering dome of defense the heaviest beams they could generate and project. Under that awful thrust Valeron's mighty generators shrieked a mad crescendo and her imponderable shield radiated a fierce, eye-tearing violet, but it held. Not for nothing had the mightiest minds of Valeron wrought to convert their mechanisms and forces of peace into engines of war; not for nothing had her people labored with all their mental and physical might for almost two-score days and nights, smoothly and efficiently as one mind in one body. Not easily did even Valeron's Titanic defensive installations carry that frightful load, but they carried it.

Then, like mythical Jove hurling his bolt – like, that is, save that beside that Valeronian beam any possible bolt of lightning would have been as sweetly innocuous a caress as young love's first kiss – Radnor drove against the nearer structure a beam of concentrated fury; a beam behind which was every volt and every ampere that his stupendous offensive generators could yield.

The Chloran defenses in turn were loaded grievously, but in turn they also held; and for hours then there raged a furiously spectacular struggle. Beams, rods, planes, and needles of every known kind and of every usable frequency of vibratory energy wer driven against impenetrable neutralizing screens. Monstrous cannon, hurling shells with a velocity and of an explosive violence far beyond anything known to us of Earth, radio-beam-dirigible torpedoes, robot-manned drill planes, and many other lethal agencies of ultra-scientific war – all these were put to use by both sides in those first few frantic hours, but neither side was able to make any impression upon the other. Then, each realizing that the other's defenses had been designed to withstand his every force, the intensive combat settled down to a war of sheer attrition.

Radnor and his scientists devoted themselves exclusively to the development of new and ever more powerful weapons of offense; the Chlorans ceased their fruitless attacks upon the central dome and concentrated all their offensive power into two semicircular arcs, which they directed vertically downward upon the outer ring of the Valeronian works in an incessant and methodical flood of energy.

They could not pierce the defensive shields against Valeron's massed power, but they could and did bring into being a vast annular lake of furiously boiling lava, into which the outer ring of fortresses began slowly to crumble and dissolve. This method of destruction, while slow, was certain; and grimly, pertinaciously, implacably, the Chlorans went about the business of reducing Valeron's only citadel.

The Bardyle wondered audibly how the enemy could possibly maintain indefinitely an attack so profligate of energy, but he soon learned that there were at least four of the floating fortresses engaged in the undertaking. Occasionally the two creations then attacking were replaced by two precisely similar structures, presumably to return to Chlora in order to renew their supplies of the substance, whatever it was, from the atomic disintegration of which they derived their incomprehensible power.

And slowly, contesting stubbornly and bitterly every foot of ground lost, the forces of Valeron were beaten back under the relentless, never-ceasing attack of the Chloran monstrosities – back and ever back toward their central dome as ring after ring of the outlying fortifications slagged down into that turbulently seething, that incandescently flaming lake of boiling lava.

Valeron was making her last stand. Her back was against the wall. The steadily contracting ring of Chloran force had been driven inward until only one thin line of fortified works lay between it and the great dome covering the city itself. Within a week at most, perhaps within days, that voracious flood of lava would lick into and would dissolve that last line of defense. Then what of Valeron?

All the scientists of the planet had toiled and had studied, day and night, but to no avail. Each new device developed to halt the march of the encroaching constricting ban of destruction had been nullified in the instant of its first trial.

'They must know every move we make, to block us so promptly,' Quedrin Radnor had mused one day. 'Since they certainly have no visiray viewpoints of material substance within our dome, they must be able to operate a spy ray using only the narrow gravity band, a thing we have never been able to accomplish. If they can project such viewpoints of pure force through such a narrow band, may they not be able to project a full materialization and thus destroy us? But, no, that band is – must be – altogether too narrow for that.'

Stirred by these thoughts he had built detectors to announce the appearance of any nongravitational forces in the gravity band and had learned that his fears were only too well founded. While the enemy could not project through the open band any forces sufficiently powerful to do any material damage, they were thus in position to forestall any move which the men of Valeron made to ward off their inexorably approaching doom.

Far beneath the surface of the ground, in a room which was not only sealed but was surrounded with every possible safeguard, nine men sat at a long table, the Bardyle at its head.

'... and nothing can be done?' the coordinator was asking. 'There is no possible way of protecting the edges of the screens?'

'None.' Radnor's voice was flat, his face and body alike were eloquent of utter fatigue. He had driven himself to the point of collapse, and all his labor had proved useless. 'Without solid anchorages we cannot hold them – as the ground is fused they give way. When the fused area reaches the dome the end will come. The outlets of our absorbers will also be fused, and with no possible method of dissipating the energy being continuously radiated into the dome we shall all die, practically instantaneously.'

'But I judge you are trying something new, from the sudden cutting off of nearly all our weight,' stated another.

'Yes. I have closed the gravity band until only enough force can get through to keep us in place on the planet, in a last attempt to block their spy rays so that we can try one last resort . . .' He broke off as an intense red light suddenly flared into being upon a panel. 'No; even that is useless. See that red light? That is the pilot light of a detector upon the gravity band. The Chlorans are still watching us. We can do nothing more, for if we close that band any tighter we shall leave Valeron entirely and shall float away, to die in space.'

As that bleak announcement was uttered the councilors sat back limply in their seats. Nothing was said – what was there to say? After all, the now seemingly unavoidable end was not unexpected. Not a man at that table had really in his heart thought it possible for peaceful Valeron to triumph against the superior war-craftiness of Chlora.

They sat there, staring unseeing into empty air, when suddenly in that air there materialized Seaton's projection. Since its reception has already been related, nothing need be said of it except that it was the Bardyle himself who was the recipient of that terrific wave of mental force. As soon as the Terrestrial had made clear his intentions and his desires, Radnor leaped to his feet, a man transformed.

'A laboratory of radiation!' he exclaimed, his profound exhaustion forgotten in a blaze of new hope. 'Not only shall I lead him to such a laboratory, but my associates and I shall be only too glad to do his bidding in every possible way.'

Followed closely by the visitor, Radnor hurried buoyantly along a narrow hall and into a large room in which, stacked upon shelves, lying upon benches and tables, and even piled indiscriminately upon the floor, there was every conceivable type and kind of apparatus for the generation and projection of etheric forces.

Seaton's flashing glance swept once around the room, cataloguing and classifying the heterogeneous collection. Then, while Radnor looked on in a daze of incredulous astonishment, that quasi-solid figure of force made tangible wrought what was to the Valeronian a scientific miracle. It darted here and there with a speed almost impossible for the eye to follow, seizing tubes, transformers, coils, condensers, and other items of equipment, connecting them together with unbelievable rapidity into a mechanism at whose use the bewildered Radnor, able physicist though he was, could not even guess.

The mechanical educator finished, Seaton's image donned one of its sets of multiple headphones and placed another upon the unresisting head of his host. Then into Radnor's already reeling mind there surged an insistent demand for his language, and almost immediately the headsets were tossed aside.

'There, that's better!' Seaton – for the image was, to all intents and purposes, Seaton himself – exclaimed. 'Now that we can talk to each other we'll soon make those Chlorans wish that they had stayed at home.'

'But they are watching everything you do,' protested Radnor, 'and we cannot block them out without cutting off our gravity entirely. They will therefore be familiar with any mechanism we may construct and will be able to protect themselves against it.'

'They just think they will,' grimly. 'I can't close the gravity band without disaster, any more than you could, but I can find any spy ray they can use and send back along it a jolt that'll burn their eyes out. You see, there's a lot of stuff down on the edge of the fourth order that neither you nor the Chlorans know anything about yet, because you haven't had enough thousands of years to study it.'

While he was talking, Seaton had been furiously at work upon a small generator, and now he turned it on.

'If they can see through *that*,' he grinned, 'they're a lot smarter than I think they are. Even if they're bright enough to have figured out what I was doing while I was doing it, it won't do them any good, because this outfit will scramble any beam they can send through that band.'

'I must bow to your superior knowledge, of course,' Radnor said gravely, 'but I should like to ask one question. You are

177

working a full materialization through less than a tenth of the gravity band – something that has always been considered impossible. Is there no danger that the Chlorans may analyze your patterns and thus duplicate your feat?'

'Not a chance,' Seaton assured him positively. 'This stuff I am using is on a tight beam, so tight that it is proof against analysis or interference. It took the Norlaminians – and they're a race of real thinkers – over eight thousand years to go from the beams you and the Chlorans are using down to what I'm showing you. Therefore I'm not afraid that the opposition will pick it up in the next week or two. But we'd better get busy in a big way. Your most urgent need, I take it, is for something – anything – that will stop that surface of force before it reaches the skirt of your defensive dome and blocks your dissipators?'

'Exactly!'

'All right. We'll build you a four-way fourth-order projector to handle full materializations – four-way to handle four attackers in case they get desperate and double their program. With it you will send working images of yourselves into the power rooms of the Chloran ships and clamp a short-circuiting field across the secondaries of their converters. Of course they can bar you out with a zone of force if they detect you before you can kill the generators of their zones, but that will be just as good, as far as we're concerned – they can't do a thing as long as they're on, you know. Now put on the headset again and I'll give you the data on the projector. Better get a recorder, too, as there'll be some stuff that you won't be able to carry in your head.'

The recorder was brought in and from Seaton's brain there flowed into it and into the mind of Radnor the fundamental concepts and complete equations and working details of the new instrument. Upon the Valeronian's face was first blank amazement, then dawning comprehension, and lastly sheer, wondering awe as, the plan completed, he removed the headset. He began a confused panegyric of thanks, but Seaton interrupted him briskly.

'That's all right, Radnor, you'd do the same thing for us if things were reversed. Humanity has got to stick together against all the vermin of all the universes. But, say, I'd like to see this mess cleared up, myself – think I'll stick around and help you build it. You're worn out, but you won't rest until the Chlorans are whipped – I can't blame you for that, I wouldn't either – and I'm fresh as a daisy. Let's go!'

In a few hours the complex machine was done. Radnor and Siblin were seated at two of the sets of controls, associate physicists at the others.

'Since I don't know any more about their systems of conversion than you do, I can't tell you in detail what to do,' Seaton was issuing final instructions. 'But whatever you do, don't monkey with their primaries – shorting them might overload their liberators and blow this whole Solar System over into the next galaxy. Take time to be dead sure that you've got the secondaries of their main converters, and slap a short circuit on as many of them as you can before they cut you off with a zone. You'll probably find a lot of liberator-converter sets on vessels of that size, but if you can kill the ones that feed the zone generators they're cold meat.'

'You are much more familiar with such things than we are,' Radnor remarked. 'Would you not like to come along?'

'I'll say I would, but I can't,' Seaton replied instantly. 'This isn't me at all, you know. Um ... um ... m ... I could tag along, of course, but it would be ... but let's see ...'

'Oh, of course,' Radnor apologized. 'In working with you so long and so cordially I forgot for the moment that you are not here in person.'

'Can't be done, I'm afraid.' Seaton frowned, still immersed in the hitherto unstudied problem of the reprojection of a projected image. 'Need over two hundred thousand relays and – um – synchronization – neuro-muscular – not on this outfit. Wonder if it can be done at all? Have to look into it some time – but excuse me, Radnor, I was thinking and got lost. Ready to go? I'll follow you up and be ready to offer advice – not that you'll need it. Shoot!'

Radnor snapped on the power and he and his aid shot their projections into one of the opposing fortresses, Siblin and his associate going into the other. Through compartment after compartment of the immense structures the as yet invisible projections went, searching for the power rooms. They were not hard to find, extending as they did nearly the full length of the stupendous structures; vaulted caverns filled with linked pairs of mastodontic fabrications, the liberator-converters.

Springing in graceful arcs from heavily insulated ports in the ends of one machine of each pair were five great bus-bars, which Radnor and Siblin recognized instantly as secondary leads from the converters – the gigantic mechanisms which, taking the raw intra-atomic energy from the liberators, converted it into a form in which it could be controlled and utilized.

Neither Radnor nor Siblin had ever heard of five-phase energy of any kind, but those secondaries were unmistakable. Therefore all four images drove against the fivefold bars their perfectly conducting fields of force. Four converters shrieked wildly, trying to wrench themselves from their foundations; insulation smoked and burst wildly into yellow flame; the stubs of the bars grew white-hot and began to fuse; and in a matter of seconds a full half of each prodigious machine subsided to the floor, a semimolten, utterly useless mass.

Similarly went the next two in each fortress, and the next – then Radnor's two projections were cut off sharply as the Chloran's impenetrable zone of force went on, and that fortress, all its beams and forces inoperative, floated off into space.

Siblin and his partner were more fortunate. When the amoebus commanding their prey threw in his zone switch nothing happened. Its source of power had already been destroyed, and the two Valeronian images went steadily down the line of converters, in spite of everything the ragingly frantic monstrosities could do to hinder their progress.

The terrible beam of destruction held steadily upon that fortress by the beamers in Valeron's mighty dome had never slackened its herculean efforts to pierce the Chloran screens. Now, as more and more of the converters of that floating citadel were burned out those screens began to radiate higher and higher into the ultraviolet. Soon they went down, exposing defenseless metal to the blasting, annihilating fury of the beam, to which any conceivable substance is but little more resistant than so much vacuum.

There was one gigantic, exploding flash, whose unbearable brilliance darkened even the incandescent radiance of the failing screen, and Valeron's mighty beam bored on, unimpeded. And where that mastodontic creation had floated an instant before there were only a few curling wisps of vapor.

'Nice job of clean-up, boys – fine!' Seaton clapped a friendly hand upon Radnor's shoulder. 'Anybody can handle them now. You'd better take a week off and catch up on sleep. I could do with a little myself, and you've been on the job a lot longer than I have.'

'But hold on – don't go yet!' Radnor exclaimed in consternation. 'Why, our whole race owes its very existence to you – wait at least until our Bardyle can have a word with you!'

'That isn't necessary, Radnor. Thanks just the same, but I don't go in for that sort of thing, any more than you would. Besides, we'll be here in the flesh in a few days and I'll talk to him then. So long!' and the projection disappeared.

In due time *Skylark Two* came lightly to a landing in a parkway near the council hall, to be examined curiously by an excited group of Valeronians who wondered audibly that such a tiny space ship should have borne their salvation. The four Terrestrials, sure of their welcome, stepped out and were greeted by Siblin, Radnor, and the Bardyle.

'I must apologize, sir, for my cavalier treatment of you at our previous meeting.' Seaton's first words to the coordinator were in sincere apology. 'I trust that you will pardon it, realizing that something of the kind was necessary in order to establish communication.'

'Speak not of it, Richard Seaton. I suffered only a temporary inconvenience, a small thing indeed compared to the experience of encountering a mind of such stupendous power as yours. Neither words nor deeds can express to you the profound gratitude of our entire race for what you have done for Valeron.

'I am informed that you personally do not care for extravagant praise, but please believe me to be voicing the single thought of a world's people when I say that no words coined by brain of man could be just, to say nothing of being extravagant, when applied to you. I do not suppose that we can do anything, however slight, for you in return, in token that these are not entirely empty words?'

'You certainly can, sir,' Seaton made surprising answer. 'We are so completely lost in space that without a great deal of material and of mechanical aid we shall never be able to return to, nor even to locate in space, our native galaxy, to say nothing of our native planet.'

A concerted gasp of astonishment was his reply, then he was assured in no uncertain terms that the resources of Valeron were at his disposal.

A certain amount of public attention had of course to be endured; but Seaton and Crane, pleading a press of work upon their new projectors, buried themselves in Radnor's laboratory, leaving it to their wives to bear the brunt of Valeronian adulation.

'How do you like being a heroine, Dot?' Seaton asked one evening as the two women returned from an unusually demonstrative reception in another city.

'We just revel in it, since we didn't do any of the real work – it's just too perfectly gorgeous for words,' Dorothy replied shamelessly. 'Especially Peggy.' She eyed staid Margaret mischievously and winked furtively at Seaton. 'Why, you ought to see her – she could just simply roll it up on a fork and eat it, as though it were that much soft fudge!'

Since the scientific and mechanical details of the construction of a fifth-order projector have been given in full elsewhere there is no need to repeat them here. Seaton built his neutronium lens in the core of the near-by white dwarf star, precisely as Rovol had done it from distant Norlamin. He brought it to Valeron and around it there began to come into being a duplicate of the immense projector which the Terrestrials had been obliged to leave behind when they abandoned gigantic *Skylark Three* to plunge through the fourth dimension in tiny *Two*.

'Maybe it's none of my business, Radnor,' Seaton turned to the Valeronian curiously during a lull in their work, 'but how come you're still simply shooing away those Chloran vessels by making them put out their zones of force? Why didn't you hop over there on your projector and blow their whole planet over into the next solar system? I would have done that long ago if it had been me, I think.'

'We did visit Chlora once, with something like that in mind, but our attempt failed lamentably,' Radnor admitted sheepishly.

'You remember that peculiar special sense, that mental force that Siblin tried to describe to you? Well, it was altogether too strong for us. My father, possessing one of the strongest minds of Valeron, was in the chair, but they mastered him so completely that we had to recall the projection by cutting off the power to prevent them from taking from his mind by force the methods of transmission which you taught us and which we were then using.'

'Hmmm! So that's it, huh?' Seaton was greatly interested. 'As soon as I get this fifth-order outfit done I'll have to see what it can do about them.'

True to his word, Seaton's first use of the new mechanism was to assume the offensive. He first sought out and destroyed the Chloran structure then in space – now an easy task, since zones of force, while impenetrable to any ether-borne phenomena, offer no resistance whatever to forces of the fifth order, propagated as they are in that inner medium, the subether. Then, with the Quedrins standing by, to cut off the power in case he should be overcome, he invaded the sanctum sanctorum of all Chlora – the private office of the Supreme Great One himself – and stared unabashed and unaffected into the enormous 'eye' of the monstrous ruler of the planet.

There ensued a battle royal. Had mental forces been visible, it would have been a spectacular meeting indeed! Larger and larger grew the 'eye' until it was transmitting all the terrific power generated by that frightful, visibly palpitating brain. But Seaton was not of Valeron, nor was he handicapped by the limitations of a fourth-order projector. He was now being projected upon a full beam of the fifth, by a mechanism able to do full justice to his stupendously composite brain.

The part of that brain he was now employing was largely the contribution of Drasnik, the First of Psychology of ancient Norlamin; and from it he was hurling along that beam the irresistible sum total of mental power accumulated by ten thousand generations of the most profound students of the mind that our galaxy has ever known.

The creature, realizing that at long last it had met its mental master, must have emitted radiations of distress, for into the room came crowding hordes of the monstrosities, each of whom sought to add his own mind to those already opposing the intruder. In vain – all their power could not turn Seaton's penetrating glare aside, nor could it wrest from that glare's unbreakable grip the mind of the tortured Great One.

And now, mental means failing, they resorted to the purely physical. Hand rays of highest power blasted at that figure uselessly; fiercely driven bars, spears, axes, and all other weapons rebounded from it without leaving a mark upon it, rebounded bent, broken, and twisted. For that figure was in no sense matter as we understand the term. It was pure force – force made palpable and coherent by the incomprehensible power of disintegrating matter; force against which any possible application of mechanical power would be precisely as effective as would wafted thistledown against Gibraltar.

Thus the struggle was brief. Paying no attention to anything, mental or physical, that the other monstrosities could bring to bear, Seaton compelled his victim to assume the shape of the heretofore-despised human being. Then, staring straight into that quivering brain through those hate-filled, flaming eyes, he spoke aloud, the better to drive home his thought:

'Learn, so-called Great One, once and for all, that when you attack any race of humanity anywhere, you attack not only that one race, but all the massed humanity of all the planets of all the galaxies! As you have already observed, I am not of the planet Valeron, nor of this solar system, nor even of this galaxy; but I and my fellows have come to the aid of this race of humanity whom you were bold enough to attack.

'I have proved that we are your masters, mentally as well as scientifically and mechanically. Those of you who have been attacking Valeron have been destroyed, ships and crews alike. Those en route there have been destroyed in space. So also shall be destroyed any and all expeditions you may launch beyond the limits of your own foul atmosphere.

'Since even such a repellent civilization as yours must have its place in the great Scheme of Things, we do not intend to destroy your planet nor such of your people as remain upon it or near it, unless such destruction shall become necessary for the welfare of the human race. While we are considering what we shall do about you, I advise you to heed well this warning!'

20: The First Universe is Mapped

The four Tellurians had discussed at some length the subject of Chlora and her outlandish population.

'It looks as though you were perched upon the horns of a first-class dilemma,' Dorothy remarked at last. 'If you let them alone there is no telling what harm they will do to these people here, and yet it would be a perfect shame to kill them all – they can't help being what they are. Do you suppose you can figure a way out of it, Dick?'

'Maybe – I've got a kind of hunch, but it hasn't jelled into a workable idea yet. It's tied in with the sixth-order projector that we'll have to have, anyway, to find our way back home. Until we get that working I guess we'll just let the amoebuses stew in their own juice.'

'Well, and then what?' Dorothy prompted.

'I told you it's nebulous yet, with a lot of essential details yet to be filled in...' Seaton paused, then went on, doubtfully: 'It's pretty wild – I don't know whether...'

'Now you *must* tell us about it, Dick,' Margaret urged.

'I'll say you've got to,' Dorothy agreed. 'You've had a lot of ideas wild enough to make any sane creature's head spin around in circles, but not one of them was so hair-raising that you were backward in talking about it. This one must be the prize brain-storm of the universe – spill it to Red-Top!'

'All right, but remember that it's only half baked and that you asked for it. I'm doping out a way to send them back to their own solar system, planet and all.'

'What!' exclaimed Margaret.

Dorothy simply whistled – a long, low whistle highly eloquent of incredulity.

'Maintenance of temperature? Time? Power? Control?' Crane, the imperturbable, picked out unerringly the four key factors of the stupendous feat.

'Your first three objections can be taken care of easily enough,' Seaton replied positively. 'No loss of temperature is possible through a zone of force – our own discovery. We can

185

stop time with a stasis – we learned that from watching those four-dimensional folks work. The power of cosmic radiation is practically infinite and eternal – we learned how to use that from pure intellectuals. Control is the sticker, since it calls for computations and calculations at present impossible; but I believe that when we get our mechanical brain done, it will be able to work out even such a problem as that.'

'What d'you mean, mechanical brain?' demanded Dorothy.

'The thing that is going to run our sixth-order projector,' Seaton explained. 'You see, it'll be altogether too big and too complicated to be controlled manually, and thought – human thought, at least – is on one band of the sixth order. Therefore the logical thing to do is to build an artificial brain capable of thinking on *all* bands of the order instead of only one, to handle the whole projector. See?'

'No,' declared Dorothy promptly, 'but maybe I will, though, when I see it work. What's next on the program?'

'Well, it's going to be quite a job to build that brain and we'd better be getting at it, since without it there'll be no *Skylark Four* ...'

'Dick, I object!' Dorothy protested vigorously. 'The *Skylark of Space* was a nice name ...'

'Sure, you'd think so, since you named her yourself,' interrupted Seaton in turn, with his disarming grin.

'Keep still a minute, Dickie, and let me finish. *Skylark Two* was pretty bad, but I stood it; and by gritting my teeth all out of shape, I did manage to keep from squawking about *Skylark Three*, but I certainly am not going to stand for *Skylark Four*. Why, just think of giving a name like that to such a wonderful thing as she is going to be – as different as can be from anything that has ever been dreamed of before – just as though she were going to be simply one more of a long series of cup-challenging motor boats or something! Why, it's – it's just too perfectly idiotic for words!'

'But she's *got* to be some kind of a *Skylark*. Dot – you know that.'

'Yes, but give her a name that means something – that sounds like something. Name her after this planet, say – *Skylark of Valeron* – how's that?'

'O.K. by me. How about it, Peg? Mart?'

The Cranes agreed to the suggestion with enthusiasm and Seaton went on:

'Well, an onion by any other name would smell as sweet, you know, and it's going to be just as much of a job to build the *Skylark of Valeron* as it would have been to build *Skylark Four*. Therefore, as I have said before and am about to say again, we'd better get at it.'

The fifth-order projector was moved to the edge of the city, since nowhere within its limits was there room for the structure to be built, and the two men seated themselves at its twin consoles and their hands flew over its massed banks of keyboards. For a few minutes nothing happened; then on the vast, level plain before them – a plain which had been a lake of fluid lava a few weeks before – there sprang into being an immense foundation-structure of trussed and latticed girder frames of inoson, the hardest, strongest, and toughest form of matter possible to molecular structure. One square mile of ground it covered and it was strong enough, apparently, to support a world.

When the foundation was finished, Seaton left the framework to Crane, while he devoted himself to filling the interstices and compartments as fast as they were formed. He first built one tiny structure of coils, fields, and lenses of force – one cell of the gigantic mechanical brain which was to be. He then made others, slightly different in tune, and others, and others.

He then set forces to duplicating these cells, forces which automatically increased in number until they were making and setting five hundred thousand cells per second, all that his connecting forces could handle. And everywhere, it seemed, there were projectors, fields of force, receptors and converters of cosmic energy, zones of force, and many various shaped lenses and geometric figures of neutronium incased in sheaths of faidon.

From each cell led tiny insulated wires, so fine as to be almost invisible, to the 'nerve centers' and to one of the millions of projectors. From these in turn ran other wires, joining together to form larger and larger strands until finally several hundred enormous cables, each larger than a man's body, reached and merged into an enormous, glittering, hemispherical, mechano-electrical inner brain.

187

For forty long Valeronian days – more than a thousand of our Earthly hours – the work went on ceaselessly, day and night. Then it ceased of itself and there dangled from the center of the glowing, gleaming hemisphere a something which is only very vaguely described by calling it either a heavily wired helmet or an incredibly complex headset. It was to be placed over Seaton's head, it is true – it *was* a headset, but one raised to the millionth power.

It was the energizer and controller of the inner brain, which was in turn the activating agency of that entire cubic mile of as yet inert substance, that assemblage of thousands of billions of cells, so soon to become the most stupendous force ever to be conceived by the mind of man.

When that headset appeared Seaton donned it and sat motionless. For hour after hour he sat there, his eyes closed, his face white and strained, his entire body eloquent of a concentration so intense as to be a veritable trance. At the end of four hours Dorothy came up resolutely, but Crane waved her back.

'This is far and away the most crucial point of the work, Dorothy,' he cautioned her gravely. 'While I do not think that anything short of physical violence could distract his attention now, it is best not to run any risk of disturbing him. An interruption now would mean that everything would have to be done over again from the beginning.'

Something over an hour later Seaton opened his eyes, stretched prodigiously, and got up. He was white and trembling, but tremendously relieved and triumphant.

'Why, Dick, what have you been doing? You look like a ghost!' Dorothy was now an all solicitous wife.

'I've been *thinking*, Rufus, and if you don't believe that it's hard work you'd better try it some time! I won't have to do it any more though – got a machine to do my thinking for me now.'

'Oh, is it all done?'

'Nowhere near, but it's far enough along so that it can finish itself. I've just been telling it what to do.'

'*Telling* it! Why, you talk as though it were human!'

'Human? It's a lot more than that. It can outthink and outperform even those pure intellectuals – "and that," as the poet feelingly remarked, "is going some"! And if you think that riding in that fifth-order projector was a thrill, wait until you see what this one can do. Think of it' – even the mind that had conceived the thing was awed – 'it is an extension of my own brain, using waves that traverse even intergalactic distances practically instantaneously. With it I can see anything I want to look at, anywhere; can hear anything I want to hear. It can build, make, do, or perform anything that my brain can think of.'

'That is all true, of course,' Crane said slowly, his sober mien dampening Dorothy's ardor instantly, 'but still – I can not help wondering...' He gazed at Seaton thoughtfully.

'I know it, Mart, and I'm working up my speed as fast as I possibly can,' Seaton answered the unspoken thought, rather than the words. 'But let them come – we'll take 'em. I'll have everything on the trips, ready to spring.'

'What *are* you two talking about?' Dorothy demanded.

'Mart pointed out to me the regrettable fact that my mental processes are in the same class as the proverbial molasses in January, or as a troop of old and decrepit snails racing across a lawn. I agreed with him, but added that I would have my thoughts all thunk up ahead of time when the pure intellectuals tackle us – which they certainly will.'

'Slow!' she exclaimed. 'When you planned the whole *Skylark of Valeron* and nobody knows what else, in five hours?'

'Yes, dear heart, *slow*. Remember when we first met our dear departed friend Eight, back in the original *Skylark*? You saw him materialize exact duplicates of each of our bodies, clear down to the molecular structures of our chemistry, in less than one second, from a cold standing start. Compared to that job, the one I have just done is elementary. It took me over five hours – he could have done it in nothing flat.

'However, don't let it bother you too much. I'll never be able to equal their speed, since I'll not live enough millions of years to get the required practice, but our being material gives us big advantages in other respects that Mart isn't mentioning because, as usual, he is primarily concerned with our weaknesses – yes? No?'

'Yes; I will concede that being material does yield advantages which may perhaps make up for our slower rate of thinking,' Crane conceded.

'Hear that? If he admits that much, you know that we're as good as in, right now,' Seaton declared. 'Well, while our new brain is finishing itself up, we might as well go back to the hall and chase the Chlorans back where they belong – the Brain worked out the equations for me this morning.'

From the ancient records of Valeron, Radnor and the Bardyle had secured complete observational data of the cataclysm, which had made the task of finding the present whereabouts of the Chlorans' original sun a simple task. The calculations and computations involved in the application of forces of precisely the required quantities to insure the correct final orbit were complex in the extreme; but, as Seaton had foretold, they had presented no insurmountable difficulties to the vast resources of the Brain.

Therefore, everything in readiness, the two Terrestrial scientists surrounded the inimical planet with a zone of force and with a stasis of time. They then erected force-control stations around it, adjusted with such delicacy and precision thay they would direct the planet into the exact orbit it had formerly occupied around its parent sun. Then, at the instant of correct velocity and position, the control stations would go out of existence and the forces would disappear.

As the immense ball of dazzlingly opaque mirror which now hid the unwanted world swung away with ever-increasing velocity, the Bardyle, who had watched the proceedings in incredulous wonder, heaved a profound sigh of relaxation.

'What a relief – what a relief!' he exclaimed.

'How long will it take?' asked Dorothy curiously.

'Quite a while – something over four hundred years of our time. But don't let it bother you – they won't know a thing about it. When the forces let go they'll simply go right on, from exactly where they left off, without realizing that any time at all has lapsed – in fact, for them, no time at all shall have lapsed. All of a sudden they will find themselves circling around a different sun, that's all.

'If their old records are clear enough they may be able to recognize it as their original sun and they'll probably do a lot of

190

wondering as to how they got back there. One instant they were in a certain orbit around this sun here, the next instant they will be in another orbit around an entirely different sun! They'll know, of course, that we did it, but they'll have a sweet job figuring out how and what we did – some of it is really deep stuff. Also, they will be a few hundred years off in their time, but since nobody in the world will know it, it won't make any difference.'

'How perfectly weird!' Dorothy exclaimed. 'Just think of losing a four-hundred-year chunk right out of the middle of your life and not even knowing it!'

'I would rather think of the arrest of development,' meditated Crane. 'Of the opportunity of comparing the evolution of the planets already there with that of the returned wanderer.'

'Yeah, it would be interesting – it's a shame we won't be alive then,' Seaton responded, 'but in the meantime we've got a lot of work to do for ourselves. Now that we've got this mess straightened out I think we had better tell these folks good-bye, get into *Two,* and hop out to where Dot's *Skylark of Valeron* is going to materialize.'

The farewell to the people of Valeron was brief, but sincere.

'This is in no sense good-bye,' Crane concluded. 'By the aid of these newly discovered forces of the sixth order there shall soon be worked out a system of communication by means of which all the inhabited planets of the galaxies shall be linked as closely as are now the cities of any one world.'

Skylark Two shot upward and outward, to settle into an orbit well outside that of Valeron. Seaton then sent his projection back to the capital city, fitted over his imaged head the controller of the inner brain, and turned to Crane with a grin.

'That's timing it, old son – she finished herself up less than an hour ago. Better cluster around and watch this, folks, it's going to be good.'

At Seaton's signal the structure which was to be the nucleus of the new space traveler lifted effortlessly into the air its millions of tons of dead weight and soared, as lightly as little *Two* had done, out into the airless void. Taking up a position a few hundred miles away from the Terrestrial cruiser, it shot out a spherical screen of force to clear the ether of chance bits of debris. Then inside that screen there came into being a structure of gleaming inoson, so vast in size that to the startled onlookers it appeared almost of planetary dimensions.

'Good heavens – it's stupendous!' Dorothy exclaimed. 'What did you boys make it so big for – just to show us you could, or what?'

'Hardly! She's just as small as she can be and still do the work. You see, to find our own galaxy we will have to project a beam to a distance greater than any heretofore assigned diameter of the universe, and to control it really accurately its working base and the diameter of its hour and declination circles would each have to be something like four light-years long. Since a ship of that size is of course impracticable, Mart and I did some figuring and decided that with circles one thousand kilometers in diameter we could chart galaxies accurately enough to find the one we're looking for – if you think of it, you'll realize that there are a lot of hundredth-millimeter marks around the circumference of circles of that size – and that they would probably be big enough to hold a broadcasting projection somewhere near a volume of space as large as that occupied by the Green System. Therefore we built the *Skylark of Valeron* just large enough to contain those thousand-kilometer circles.'

As *Skylark Two* approached the looming planetoid the doors of vast airlocks opened. Fifty of those massive gates swung aside before her and closed behind her before she swam free in the cool, sweet air and bright artificial sunlight of the interior. She then floated along above an immense grassy park toward two well-remembered and beloved buildings.

'Oh, Dick!' Dorothy squealed. 'There's our house – and Martin's! It's funny, though, to see them side by side. Are they the same inside, too – and what's that funny little low building between them?'

'They duplicate the originals exactly, except for some items of equipment which would be useless here. The building between them is the control room, in which are the master headsets of the Brain and its lookouts. The Brain itself is what you would think of as underground – inside the shell of the planetoid.'

The small vessel came lightly to a landing and the wanderers disembarked upon the close-clipped, springy turf of a perfect lawn. Dorothy flexed her knees in surprise.

'How come we aren't weightless, Dick?' she demanded. 'This gravity isn't – *can't* be – natural. I'll bet you did that too!'

'Mart and I together did, sure. We learned a lot from the intellectuals and a lot more in hyperspace, but we could neither derive the fundamental equations nor apply what knowledge we already had until we finished this sixth-order outfit. Now, though, we can give you all the gravity you want – or as little – whenever and wherever you want it.'

'Oh marvelous – this is glorious, boys!' Dorothy breathed. 'I have always just simply despised weightlessness. Now, with these houses and everything, we can have a perfectly wonderful time!'

'Here's the dining room,' Seaton said briskly. 'And here's the headset you put on to order dinner or whatever is appropriate to the culinary department. You will observe that the kitchen of this house is purely ornamental – never to be used unless you want to.'

'Just a minute, Dick,' Dorothy's voice was tensely serious. 'I have been really scared ever since you told me about the power of that Brain, and the more you tell me of it the worse scared I get. Think of the awful damage a wild, chance thought would do – and the more an ordinary mortal tries to avoid any thought the surer he is to think it, you know that. Really, I'm not ready for that yet, dear – I'd much rather not go near the headset.'

'I know, sweetheart,' his arm tightened around her. 'But you didn't let me finish. These sets around the house control forces which are capable of nothing except duties pertaining to the part of the house in which they are. This dining-room outfit, for instance, is exactly the same as the Norlaminian one you used so much, except that it is much simpler.

'Instead of using a lot of keyboards and force-tubes, you simply think into that helmet what you want for dinner and it appears. Think that you want the table cleared and it is cleared – dishes and all simply vanish. Think of anything else you want done around this room and it's done – that's all there is to it.

'To relieve your mind I'll explain some more. Mart and I both realized that that Brain could very easily become the most terrible, the most frightfully destructive thing that the universe has ever seen. Therefore, with two exceptions, every controller on this planetoid is of a strictly limited type. Of the two master controls, which are unlimited and very highly reactive, one responds only to Crane's thoughts, the other only to mine. As soon as we get some loose time we are going to build a couple of auxiliaries, with automatic stops against stray thoughts, to break you girls in on – we know as well as you do, Red-Top, that you haven't had enough practice yet to take an unlimited control.'

'I'll say *I* haven't!' she agreed feelingly. 'I feel a lot better now – I'm sure I can handle the rest of these things very nicely.'

'Sure you can, Well, let's call the Cranes and go into the control room,' Seaton suggested. 'The quicker we get started the quicker we'll get done.'

Accustomed as she was to the banks and tiers of keyboards, switches, dials, meters, and other operating paraphernalia of the control rooms of the previous *Skylark*s, Dorothy was taken aback when she passed through the thick, heavily insulated door into that of the *Skylark of Valeron*. For there were four gray walls, a gray ceiling, and a thick gray rug. There were low, broad double chairs and headsets. There was nothing else.

'This is your seat, Dottie, here beside me, and this is your headset – it's just a visiset, so you can see what is going on, not a controller,' he hastened to reassure her. 'You have a better illusion of seeing if your eyes are open, that's why everything is neutral in color. But better still for you girls, we'll turn off the lights.'

The illumination, which had seemed to pervade the entire room instead of emanating from any definite sources, faded out; but in spite of the fact that the room was in absolute darkness Dorothy saw with a clarity and a depth of vision impossible to any Earthly eyes. She saw at one and the same time, with infinite precision of detail, the houses and their contents; the whole immense sphere of the planetoid, inside and out; Valeron and her sister planets circling their sun; and the stupendous full sphere of the vaulted heavens.

She knew that her husband was motionless at her side, yet she saw him materialize in the control room of *Skylark Two*. There he seized the cabinet which contained the space chart of the

Fenachrone – that library of films portraying all the galaxies visible to the wonderfully powerful telescopes and projectors of that horrible but highly scientific race.

That cabinet became instantly a manifold scanner, all its reels flashing through as one. Simultaneously there appeared in the air above the machine a three-dimensional model of all the galaxies there listed. A model upon such a scale that the First Galaxy was but a tiny lenticular pellet, although it was still disproportionately large; upon such a scale that the whole vast sphere of space covered by the hundreds of Fenachrone scrolls was compressed into a volume but little larger than a basketball. And yet each tiny galactic pellet bore its own peculiarly individual identifying marks.

Then Dorothy felt as though she herself had been hurled out into the unthinkable reaches of space. In a fleeting instant of time she passed through thousands of star clusters, and not only knew the declination, right ascension, and distance of each galaxy, but saw it duplicated in miniature in its exact place in an immense, three-dimensional model in the hollow interior of the space-flyer in which she actually was.

The mapping went on. To human brains and hands the task would have been one of countless years. Now, however, it was to prove only a matter of hours, for this was no human brain. Not only was it reactive and effective at distances to be expressed intelligibly in light-years or parsecs; because of the immeasurable sixth-order velocity of its carrier wave it was equally effective across reaches of space so incomprehensibly vast that the rays of visible light emitted at the birth of a sun so far away would reach the point of observation only after that sun had lived through its entire cycle of life and had disappeared.

'Well, that's about enough of that for you, for a while,' Seaton remarked in a matter-of-fact voice. 'A little of that stuff goes a long ways at first – you have to get used to it.'

'I'll say you do! Why ... I ... it ...' Dorothy paused, even her ready tongue at a loss for words.

'You can't describe it in words – don't try,' Seaton advised. 'Let's go outdoors and watch the model grow.'

To the awe, if not to the amazement of the observers, the model had already begun to assume a lenticular pattern. Galaxies, then, really were arranged in general as were the stars composing them; there really *were* universes, and they really were lenticular – the vague speculations of the hardiest and most exploratory cosmic thinkers were being confirmed.

For hour after hour the model continued to grow and Seaton's face began to take on a look of grave concern. At last, however, when the chart was three fourths done or more, a deep-toned bell clanged out the signal for which he had been waiting – the news that there was now being plotted a configuration of galaxies identical with that portrayed by the space chart of the Fenachrone.

'Gosh!' Seaton sighed hugely. 'I was beginning to be afraid that we had escaped clear out of our own universe, and that would have been bad – very, *very* bad, believe me! The rest of the mapping can wait – let's go!'

Followed by the others he dashed into the control room, threw on his helmet, and hurled a projection into the now easily recognizable First Galaxy. He found the Green System without difficulty, but he could not hold it. It was so far away that the utmost delicacy of control of which the gigantic sixth-order installation was capable could not keep the viewpiont from leaping erratically, in fantastic bounds of hundreds of millions of miles, all through and around its objective.

But Seaton had half expected this development and was prepared for it. He had already sent out a broadcasting projection; and now, upon a band of frequencies wide enough to affect every receiving instrument in use throughout the Green System and using power sufficient to overwhelm any transmitter, however strong, that might be in operation, he sent out in a mighty voice his urgent message to the scientists of Norlamin.

21 : Dunark takes a Hand

In the throne room of Kondal, with its gorgeously resplendent jeweled ceiling and jeweled metallic-tapestry walls, there were seated in earnest consultation the three most powerful men of the planet Osnome – Roban, the Emperor; Dunark, the Crown Prince; and Tarnan, the Commander-in-Chief. Their 'clothing' was the ordinary Osnomian regalia of straps, chains, and metallic bands, all thickly bestudded with blazing gems and for the most part supporting the full assortment of devastatingly powerful hand weapons without which any man of that race would have felt stark naked. Their fierce green faces were keenly hawklike; the hard, clean lines of their bare green bodies bespoke the rigid physical training that every Osnomian undergoes from birth until death.

'Father, Tarnan may be right,' Dunark was saying soberly. 'We are too savage, too inherently bloodthirsty, too deeply interested in killing, not as a means to some really worth-while end, but as an end in itself. Seaton the Overlord thinks so, the Norlaminians think so, the Dasorians think so, and I am beginning to think so myself. All really enlightened races look upon us as little better than barbarians, and in part I agree with them. I believe, however, that if we were really to devote ourselves to study and to productive effort we could soon equal or surpass any race in the System, except of course the Norlaminians.'

'There may be something in what you say,' the emperor admitted dubiously, 'but it is against all our racial teachings. What, then, of an outlet for the energies of all manhood?'

'Constructive effort instead of destructive,' argued the Karbix. 'Let them build – study – learn – advance. It is all too true that we are far behind other races of the System in all really important things.'

'But what of Urvan and his people?' Roban brought up his last and strongest argument. 'They are as savage as we are, if not more so. As you say, the necessity for continuous warfare ceased with the destruction of Mardonale, but are we to leave our whole planet defenseless against an interplanetary attack from Urvania?'

'They dare not attack us,' declared Tarnan, 'any more than we dare attack them. Seaton the Overlord decreed that the people of us two first to attack the other dies root and branch, and we all know that the word of the Overlord is no idle, passing breath.'

'But he has not been seen for long. He may be far away and the Urvanians may decide at any time to launch their fleets against us. However, before we decide this momentous question I suggest that you two pay a visit of state to the court of Urvan. Talk to Urvan and his Karbix as you have talked to me, of cooperation and of mutual advancement. If they will cooperate, we will.'

During the long voyage to Urvania, the third planet of the fourteenth sun, however, their new ardor cooled perceptibly – particularly that of the younger man – and in Urvan's palace it became clear that the love of peaceful culture inculcated upon those fierce minds by contact with more humane peoples could not supplant immediately the spirit of strife bred into bone and fiber during thousands of generations of incessant warfare.

For when the two Osomians sat down with the two Urvanians the very air seemed charged with animosity. Like strange dogs meeting with bared fangs and bristling manes, Osnomian and Urvanian alike fairly radiated hostility. Therefore Tarnan's suggestions as to cooperation and understanding were decidedly unconvincing, and were received with open scorn.

'Your race may well wish to cooperate with ours,' sneered the Emperor of Urvania, 'since but for the threats of that self-styled Overlord, you would have ceased to exist long since. And how do we know where that one is, what he is doing, whether he is paying any attention to us? Probably you have learned that he has left this System entirely and have already planned an attack upon us. In self-defense we shall probably have to wipe out your race to keep you from destroying ours. At any rate your plea is very evidently some underhanded trick of your weak and cowardly race...'

'Weak! Cowardly! *Us?* You conceited bloated toad!' stormed Dunark, who had kept himself in check thus far only by sheer power of will. He sprang to his feet, his stool flying backward. 'Here and now I demand a meeting of honor, if you know the meaning of the word honor.'

The four enraged men, all drawing weapons, were suddenly swept apart, then clutched and held immovably as a figure of force materialized among them – the form of an aged, white-bearded Norlaminian.

'Peace, children, and silence!' the image commanded sternly. 'Rest assured that there shall be no more warfare in this System and that the decrees of the Overlord shall be enforced to the letter. Calm yourselves and listen. I know well, mind you, that none of you really meant what has just been said. You of Osnome were so impressed by the benefits of mutual helpfulness that you made this journey to further its cause; you of Urvania are at heart also strongly in favor of it, but neither of you has strength enough to admit it.

'For know, vain and self-willed children, that it is weakness, not strength, which you have been displaying. It may well be, however, that your physical bravery and your love of strife can now be employed for the general good of all humanity. Would you join hands, to fight side by side in such a cause?'

'We would,' chorused the four, as one.

Each was heartily ashamed of what had just happened, and was glad indeed of the opportunity to drop it without losing face.

'Very well! We of Norlamin fear greatly that we have inadvertently given to one of the greatest foes of universal civilization weapons equal in power to the Overlord's own, and that he is even now working to undo all that has been done. Will you of Osnome and you of Urvania help in conducting an expedition against that foe?'

'We will!' they exclaimed.

Dunark added: 'Who is that enemy, and where is he to be found?'

'He is Dr. Marc C. DuQuesne, of Earth.'

'DuQuesne!' barked Dunark. 'Why, I thought the Fenachrone killed him! But we shall attend to it at once – when I kill any one he *stays* killed!'

'Just a moment, son,' the image cautioned. 'He has surrounded Earth with defenses against which your every arm would be entirely impotent. Come you to Norlamin, bringing each of you one hundred of his best men. We shall have prepared for you certain equipment which, although it may not enable you to emerge victorious from the engagement, will at least insure your safe return. It might be well also to stop at Dasor, which is not now far from your course of flight, and bring along Sacner Carfon, who will be of great assistance, being a man both of action and learning.'

'But *DuQuesne*!' raved Dunark, who realized immediately what must have happened. 'Why didn't you ray him on sight? Didn't you know what a liar and a thief he is, by instinct and training?'

'We had no suspicion then who he was, thinking, as did you, that DuQuesne had passed. He came under another name, as Seaton's friend. He came as one possessing knowledge, with fair and plausible words. But of that we shall inform you later. Come at once – we shall place upon your controls forces which shall pilot you accurately and with speed.'

Upon the aqueous world of Dasor they found its amphibious humanity reveling in an activity which, although dreamed of for centuries, had been impossible of realization until the *Skylark* had brought to them a supply of Rovolon, the metal of power. Now cities of metal were arising here and there above her waves, airplanes and helicopters sped through and hovered in her atmosphere, barges and pleasure craft sailed the almost unbroken expanse of ocean which was her surface, immense submarine freighters bored their serenely stolid ways through her watery depths.

Sacner Carfon, the porpoiselike, hairless, naked Dasorian councilor, heaved his six and a half feet of height and his five hundredweight of mass into Dunark's vessel and greeted the Osnomian prince with a grave and friendly courtesy.

'Yes, friend, everything is wonderfully well with Dasor,' he answered Dunark's query. 'Now that our one lack, that of power, has been supplied, our lives can at last be lived to the full, unhampered by the limitations which we have hitherto been compelled to set upon them. But this from Norlamin is terrible news. What know you of it?'

During the trip to Norlamin the three leaders not only discussed and planned among themselves, but also had many conferences with the Advisory Five of the planet toward which they were speeding, so that they arrived upon that ancient world with a complete knowledge of what they were to attempt. There Rovol and Drasnik instructed them in the use of fifth-order forces, each according to his personality and ability.

To Sacner Carfon was given command, and he was instructed minutely in every detail of the power, equipment, and performance of the vessel which was to carry the hope of civilization. To Tarnan, the best balanced of his race, was given a more limited knowledge. Dunark and Urvan, however, were informed only as to the actual operation of the armament, with no underlying knowledge of its nature or construction.

'I trust that you will not resent this necessary caution,' Drasnik said carefully. 'Your natures are as yet essentially savage and bloodthirsty; your reason is all too clouded by passion. You are, however, striving truly, and that is a great good. With a few mental operations, which we shall be glad to give you at a later time, you shall both be able to take your places as leaders in the march of your peoples toward civilization.'

Fodan, majestic chief of the Five, escorted the company of warriors to their battleship of space, and what a ship she was! Fully twice the size of *Skylark Three* in every dimension she lay there, surcharged with power and might, awaiting only her commander's touch to hurl herself away toward distant and inimical Earth.

But the vengeful expedition was too late by far. DuQuesne had long since consolidated his position. His chain of interlinked power stations encircled the globe. Governments were in name only. World Steel now ruled the entire Earth and DuQuesne's power was absolute. Nor was that rule as yet unduly onerous. The threat of war was gone, the tyranny of gangsterism was done, everybody was working for high wages – what was there to kick about? Some men of vision of course perceived the truth and were telling it, but they were being howled down by the very people they were trying to warn.

It was thus against an impregnably fortified world that Dunark and Urvan directed every force with which their flying superdreadnought was armed. Nor was she feeble, this monster of the skyways, but DuQuesne had known well what form the attack would take and, having the resources of the world upon which to draw, he had prepared to withstand the massed assault of a hundred vessels – or a thousand.

Therefore the attack not only failed; it was repulsed crushingly. For from his massed generators DuQuesne hurled out upon the Norlaminian space ship a solid beam of such incredible intensity that in neutralizing its terrific ardor her store of power-uranium dwindled visibly, second by second. So rapidly did the metal disappear that Sacner Carfon, after waging the unequal struggle for some twenty hours, abandoned it and drove back toward the Central System, despite the raging protests of Dunark and of his equally tempestuous lieutenant.

And in his private office, which was also a complete control room, DuQuesne smiled at Brookings – a hard, cold smile. 'Now you see,' he said coldly. 'Suppose I hadn't spent all this time and money on my defenses?'

'Well, why don't you go out and chase 'em? Give 'em a scare anyway?'

'Because it would be useless,' DuQuesne stated flatly. 'That ship carries more stuff than anything we have ready to take off at present. Also, Dunark does not scare. You might kill him, but you can't scare him – it isn't in the breed.'

'Well, what is the answer, then? You have tried to take Norlamin with everything you've got – bombs, automatic ships, and projectors – and you haven't got to first base. You can't even get through their outside screens. What are you going to do – let it go on as a stalemate?'

'Hardly!' DuQuesne smiled thinly. 'While I do not make a practice of divulging my plans, I am going to tell you a few things now, so that you can go ahead with more understanding and hence with greater confidence. Seaton is out of the picture, or he would have been back here before this. The Fenachrone are all gone. Dunark and his people are unimportant. Norlamin is the only known obstacle between me and the mastery of the galaxy, therefore Norlamin must be either conquered or destroyed. Since the first alternative seems unduly difficult, I shall destroy her.'

'Destroy Norlamin – how?' The thought of wiping out that world, with all its ancient culture, did not appall – did not even affect – Brookings' callous mind. He was merely curious concerning the means to be employed.

'This whole job so far has been merely a preliminary toward that destruction,' DuQuesne informed him levelly. 'I am now ready to go ahead with the second step. The planet Pluto is, as you may or may not know, very rich in uranium. The ships which we are now building are to carry a few million tons of that metal to a large and practically uninhabited planet not too far from Norlamin. I shall install driving machinery upon that planet and, using it as a projectile which all their forces cannot stop, I shall throw Norlamin into her own sun.'

Raging but impotent, Dunark was borne back to Norlamin; and, more subdued now but still bitterly humiliated, he accompanied Urvan, Sacner Carfon, and the various Firsts to a consultation with the Five.

As they strolled along through the grounds, past fountains of flaming color, past fantastically geometric hedges intricately and ornately wrought of noble metal, past walls composed of self-luminous gems so moving as to form fleeting, blending pictures of exquisite line and color, Sacner Carfon eyed Drasnik in unobtrusive signal and the two dropped gradually behind.

'I trust that you were successful in whatever it was you had in mind to do while we set up the late diversion?' Carfon asked quietly, when they were out of earshot.

Dunark and Urvan, his fierce and fiery aids, had taken everything that had happened at its face value, but not so had the leader. Unlike his lieutenants, the massive Dasorian had known at first blast that his expedition against DuQuesne was hopeless. More, it had been clear to him that the Norlaminians had known from the first that their vessel, enormous as she was and superbly powerful, could not crush the defenses of Earth.

'We knew, of course, that you would perceive the truth,' the First of Psychology replied as quietly. 'We also knew that you would appreciate our reasons for not taking you fully into our confidence in advance. Tarnan of Osnome also had an inkling of it, and I have already explained matters to him. Yes; we succeeded. While DuQuesne's whole attention was taken up in resisting your forces and in returning them in kind, we were able to learn much that we could not have learned otherwise. Also, our young friends Dunark and Urvan, through being chastened, have learned a very helpful lesson. They have seen themselves in true perspective for the first time; and, having fought side by side in a common and so far as they know a losing cause, they have become friends instead of enemies. Thus it will now be possible to inaugurate upon those two backward planets a program leading toward true civilization.'

In the Hall of the Five the Norlaminian spokesman voiced thanks and appreciation for the effort just made, concluding:

'While as a feat of arms the expedition may not have been a success, in certain other respects it was far from being a failure. By its help we were enabled to learn much, and I can assure you now that the foe shall not be allowed to prevail – it is graven upon the Sphere that civilization is to go on.'

'May I ask a question, sir?' Urvan was for the first time in his bellicose career speaking diffidently. 'Is there no way of landing a real storming force upon Earth? Must we leave DuQuesne in possession indefinitely?'

'We must wait, son, and work,' the chief answered, with the fatalistic calm of his race. 'At present we can do nothing more, but in time...'

He was interrupted by a deafening blast of sound – the voice of Richard Seaton, tremendously amplified.

'This is the *Skylark* calling Rovol of Norlamin ... *Skylark* calling Rovol of Norlamin ...' it repeated over and over, rising to a roar and diminishing to a whisper as Seaton's broadcaster oscillated violently through space.

Rovol laid a beam to the nearest transmitter and spoke: 'I am here, son. What is it?'

'Fine! I'm away out here in...'

'Hold on a minute, Dick!' Dunark shouted. He had been humble and sober enough since his return to Norlamin, realizing as he never had before his own ignorance in comparison with the gigantic minds about him; the powerlessness of his entire race in comparison with the energies he had so recently seen in action. But now, as Seaton's voice came roaring in and

Rovol and his brain-brother were about to indulge so naïvely and so publicly in a conversation which certainly should not reach DuQuesne's ears, his spirits rose. Here was something he could do to help.

'DuQuesne is alive, has Earth completely fortified, and is holding everything we can give him,' Dunark went on rapidly. 'He's got everything we have, maybe more, and he's undoubtedly listening to every word we're saying. Talk Mardonalian – I know for a fact that DuQuesne can't understand that. They've got an educator here and I'll give it to Rovol right now – all right, go ahead.'

'I'm clear out of the galaxy,' Seaton's voice went on, now speaking the language of the Osnomian race which had so recently been destroyed. 'So many hundreds of millions of parsecs away that none of you except Orlon could understand the distance. The speed of transmission is due to the fact that we have perfected and I am using a sixth-order projector, not a fifth. Have you a ship fit for really long-distance flight – as big as *Three* was, or bigger?'

'Yes; we have a vessel twice her size.'

'Fine! Load her up and start. Head for the Great Nebula in Andromeda – Orlon knows what and where it is. That isn't very close to my line, but it will do until you get some apparatus up. I've got to have Rovol, Drasnik, and Orlon, and I would like to have Fodan; you can bring along anybody else that wants to come. I'll sign on again in an hour – you should be started by then.'

Besides the four Norlaminians mentioned, Caslor, First of Mechanism, and Astron, First of Energy, also elected to make the stupendous flight, as did many 'youngsters' from the Country of Youth. Dunark would not be left behind, nor would adventurous Urvan. And lastly there was Sacner Carfon the Dasorian, who remarked that he 'would have to go along to make the boys behave and to steer the ship in case the old professors forget to.' The space ship was well on its way when at the end of the hour Seaton's voice again was heard.

'All right, put me on a recorder and I'll give you the data,' he instructed, when he had made sure that his signal was being received.

'DuQuesne has been trying to put a ray on us and he may try to follow us,' Dunark put in.

'Let him,' Seaton shot back grimly, then spoke in English: 'DuQuesne, Dunark says that you're listening in. You have my urgent, if not cordial, invitation to follow this Norlaminian ship. If you follow it far enough, you'll take a long, long ride, believe me!'

Again addressing the voyagers, he recounted briefly everything that had occurred since the abandonment of *Skylark Three*, then dived abruptly into the fundamental theory and practical technique of sixth-order phenomena and forces.

Of that ultramathematical dissertation Dunark understood not even the first sentence; Sacner Carfon perhaps grasped dimly a concept here and there. The Norlaminians, however, sat back in their seats, relaxed and smiling, their prodigious mentalities not only absorbing greedily but assimilating completely the enormous doses of mathematical and physical science being thrust upon them so rapidly. And when that epoch-making, that almost unbelievable, tale was done, not one of the aged scientists even referred to the tape of the recorder.

'Oh, wonderful – wonderful!' exclaimed Rovol in ecstasy, his transcendental imperturbability broken at last. 'Think of it! Our knowledge extended one whole order farther in each direction, both into the small and into the large. Magnificent! And by one brain, and that of a youth. Extraordinary! And we may now traverse universal space in ordinary time, because that brain has harnessed the practically infinite power of cosmic radiation, a power which exhausted the store of uranium carried by *Skylark Three* in forty hours. Phenomenal! Stupendous!'

'But do not forget that the brain of that youth is a composite of many,' said Fodan thoughtfully, 'and that in it, among others, were yours and Drasnik's. Seaton himself ascribes to that peculiar combination his successful solution of the problem of the sixth order. You know, of course, that I am in no sense belittling the native power of that brain. I am merely suggesting that perhaps other noteworthy discoveries may be made by superimposing brains in other, but equally widely divergent, fields of thought.'

'An interesting idea, truly, and one which may be fruitful of result,' assented Orlon, the First of Astronomy, 'but I would suggest that we waste no more time. I, for one, am eager to behold with my own inner consciousness the vistas of the galaxies.'

Agreeing, the five white-bearded scientists seated themselves at the multiplex console of their fifth-order installation and set happily to work. Their gigantic minds were undaunted by the task they faced – they were only thrilled with interest at the opportunity of working with magnitudes, distances, forces, objects, and events at the very contemplation of which any ordinary human mind would quail.

Steadily and contentedly they worked on, while at the behest of their nimble and unerring fingers there came into being the forces which were to build into their own vessel a duplicate of the mechano-electrical brain which actuated and controlled the structure, almost of planetary proportions, in which Seaton was even then hurtling toward them. Hurtling with a velocity rapidly mounting to a value incalculable; driven by the power liberated by the disintegrating matter of all the suns of all the galaxies of all the universes of cosmic space!

22 : Trapping the Intellectuals

With all their might of brain and skill of hand and with all the resources of their fifth-order banks of forces, it was no small task for the Norlaminians to build the sixth-order controlling system which their ship must have if they were to traverse universal space in any time short of millennia. But finally it was done.

A towering mechano-electrical brain almost filled the mid-section of their enormous sky rover, the receptors and converters of the free energy of space itself had been installed, and their intra-atomic space-drive, capable of developing an acceleration of only five light-velocities, had been replaced by Seaton's newly developed sixth-order cosmic-energy drive which could impart to the ship and its entire contents, without jolt, jar, or strain, any conceivable, almost any calculable, acceleration.

For many days the Norlaminian vessel had been speeding through the void at her frightful maximum of power toward the *Skylark of Valeron*, which in turn was driving toward our galaxy at the same mad pace. Braking down now, since only a few thousand light-years of distance separated the hurtling flyers, Seaton materialized his image at the brain control of the smaller cruiser and thought into it for minutes.

'There, we're all set!' In the control room of the *Skylark* Seaton laid aside his helmet and wiped the perspiration from his forehead in sheer relief. 'The trap is baited and ready to spring – I've been scared to death for a week that they'd tackle us before we were ready for them.'

'What difference would it have made?' asked Margaret curiously. 'Since we have our sixth-order screens out they couldn't hurt us, could they?'

'No, Peg; but keeping them from hurting us isn't enough – we've got to capture them. And they'll have to be almost directly between Rovol's ship and ours to make that capture possible. You see, we'll have to send out from each vessel a hollow hemisphere of force and to surround them. If we had only one ship, or if they don't come between our two ships, we can't bottle them up, because they have exactly the same velocity of propagation that our forces have.

'Also, you can see that our projector can't work direct on more than a hemisphere without cutting its own beams, and that we can't work through relay stations because, fast as relays are, the Intellectuals would get away while the relays were cutting in. Any more questions?'

'Yes; I have one,' put in Dorothy. 'You told us that this artificial brain of yours could do anything that your own brain could think of, and here you've got it stuck already and have to have two of them. How come?'

'Well, this is a highly exceptional case,' Seaton replied. 'What I said would be true ordinarily, but now, as I explained to Peg, it's working against something that can think and act just as quickly as I can.'

'I know, dear, I was just putting you on the spot a little. What are you using for bait?'

'Thoughts. We're broadcasting them from a point midway between the two vessels. They're keen on investigating any sixth-order impulses they feel, you know – that's why we've kept all our stuff on tight beams heretofore, so that they probably couldn't detect it – so we're sending out a highly peculiar type of thought, that we are pretty sure will bring them in from wherever they are.'

'Let me listen to it, just for a minute?' she pleaded.

'W-e-l-l . . . I don't know.' He eyed her dubiously. 'Not for a minute – no. I haven't even tried to listen to the finished product, myself. Being of a type that not even a pure intellectual can resist, they'd burn out any human brain in mighty short order. Maybe you might for about a tenth of a second, though.'

He lowered a helmet over her expectant head and snatched it off again, but that moment had been enough for Dorothy. Her violet eyes widened terribly in an expression commingled of amazedly poignant horror and of dreadfully ecstatic fascination; her whole body trembled uncontrollably.

'Dick – Dick!' she shrieked; then, recovering slowly: 'How horrible – how ghastly – how perfectly, exquisitely damnable! What is it? Why, I actually heard babies begging to be born! And there were men who had died and gone to heaven and to hell; there were minds that had lost their bodies and didn't know what to do – were simply shrieking out their agony, despair, and utter, unreasoning terror for the whole universe to hear! And there were joys, pleasures, raptures, so condensed as to be almost as unbearable as the tortures. And there were other things – awful, terrible, utterly indescribable and unimaginable things! Oh, Dick, I was sure that I had gone stark, raving crazy!'

'Easy, dear,' Seaton reassured his overwrought wife. 'All those things are really there, and more. I told you it was bad medicine – that it would tear any human mind to pieces.'

Seaton paused, weighing in his mind how best to describe the utterly indescribable signal that was being broadcast, then went on, choosing his words with care:

'All the pangs and all the ecstasies, all the thoughts and all the emotions of all evolution of all things, animate and inanimate, are there; of all things that ever have existed from the unknowable beginning of infinite time and of all things that ever shall exist until time's unknowable end. It covers all animate life, from the first stirring of that which was to vitalize the first unicell in the slime of the first world ever to come into being in the cosmos, to the last cognition of the ultimately last intelligent entity ever to be.

'Our present humanity was of course included, from before conception through birth, through all of life, through death, and through the life beyond. It covers inanimate evolution from the ultimate particle and wave, through the birth, life, death, and rebirth of any possible manifestation of energy and of matter, up to and through the universe.

'Neither Mart nor I could do it all. We carried everything as far as we could, then the Brain went through with it to its logical conclusion, which of course we could not reach. Then the Brain systematized all the data and reduced it to a concentrated essence of pure thought. It is that essence which is being broadcast and which will certainly attract the Intellectuals. In the brief flash you got of it you probably could understand only the human part – but maybe it's just as well.'

'I'll say it's just as well!' Dorothy emphatically agreed. 'I wouldn't listen to that again, even for a millionth of a second, for a million dollars – but I wouldn't have missed it for another million, either. I don't know whether to beg you to listen to it, Peggy, or to implore you not to.'

'Don't bother,' Margaret replied positively. 'Anything that could throw you into such a hysterical tantrum as that did, I don't want any of at all. None at all, in fact, would be altogether too much for . . .'

'Got them, folks – all done!' Seaton exclaimed 'You can put on your headsets now.'

A signal lamp had flashed brightly and he knew that those two gigantic brains, working in perfect synchronism, had done instantaneously all that they had been set to do.

'Are you dead sure that they got them all, Dick?'

'Absolutely, and they got them in less time than it took the filament of the lamp to heat up. You can bank on it that all seven of them are in the can. I go off half cocked and make mistakes, but those Brains don't – they can't.'

Seaton was right. Though far away, even as universal distances go, the Intellectuals had felt that broadcast thought and had shot toward its source at their highest possible speed. For in all their long lives and throughout all their cosmic wanderings they had never encountered thoughts of such wide scope, such clear cogency, such tremendous power.

The discarnate entities approached the amazing pattern of mental force which was radiating so prodigally and addressed it; and in that instant there shot out curvingly from each of the mechano-electrical brains a gigantic, hemispherical screen.

Developing outwardly from the two vessels as poles with the unimaginable velocity possible only to sixth-order forces, the two cups were barriers impenetrable to any sixth-order force, yet neither affected nor were affected by the gross manifestations which human senses can perceive. Thus solar systems, even the neutronium cores of stars, did not hinder their instantaneous development.

Hundreds of light-years in diameter though they were, the open edges of those semiglobes of force met in perfect alignment and fused smoothly, effortlessly, instantaneously together to form a perfect, thought-tight sphere. The violently radiating thought-pattern which had so interested the Intellectuals disappeared, and at the same instant the ultra-sensitive organisms of the entities were assailed by the, to them, deafening and blinding crash and flash of the welding together along its equator of the far-flung hollow globe.

These simultaneous occurrences were the first intimations that everything was not what it appeared, and the disembodied intelligences flashed instantly into furious activity, too late by the smallest possible instant of time. The trap was sprung, the sphere was impervious at its every point, and, unless they could break through that wall, the Intellectuals were incarcerated until Seaton should release his screens.

Within the confines of the globe there were not a few suns and thousands of cubic parsecs of space upon whose stores of energy the Intellectuals could draw. Wherefore they launched a concerted attack upon the wall, hurling against it all the force they could direct. But they were not now contending against the power of any human, organic finite brain. For Seaton's mind, powerfully composite though it was of the mightiest intellects of the First Galaxy, was only the primary impulse which was being impressed upon the grids of, and was being amplified to any desirable extent by, the almost infinite power of those two cubic miles of coldly emotionless, perfectly efficient, mechano-electrical artificial Brains.

Thus against every frantic effort of the Intellectuals within it the sphere was contracted inexorably, and as it shrank, reducing the volume of space from which the prisoners could draw energy, their struggles became weaker and weaker. When the ball of force was only a few hundred miles in diameter and the two vessels were relatively at rest, Seaton erected auxiliary stations around it and assumed full control.

Rapidly then the prisoning sphere, little larger now than a toy balloon, was brought through the inoson wall of the *Skylark* and held motionless in the air above the Brain room. A complex structure of force was built around it, about which in turn there appeared a framework of inoson, supporting sixteen massive bars of uranium.

Seaton took off his helmet and sighed. 'There, that'll hold them for a while, I guess.'

'What are you going to do with them?' asked Margaret.

'Darned if I know, Peg,' he admitted ruefully. 'That's been worrying me ever since we figured out how to catch them. We can't kill them and I'm afraid to let them go, because they're entirely too hot to handle. So in the meantime, pending the hatching out of a feasible method of getting rid of them permanently, I have put them in jail.'

'Why, Dick, how positively brutal!' Dorothy exclaimed.

'Yeah? There goes your soft heart again, Red-Top, instead of your hard head. I suppose it would be positively O.K. to let them loose, so that they can dematerialize all four of us? But it isn't as bad as it sounds, because I've got a stasis of time around them. We can leave them in there for seventeen thousand million years and even their intellects won't know it, because for them no time at all shall have lapsed.'

'No-o-o – of course we can't let them go scot-free,' Dorothy admitted, 'but we – I should – well, maybe couldn't you make a bargain with them to give them their liberty if they will go away and let us alone? They're such free spirits, surely they'd rather do that than stay bottled up forever.'

'Since they are purely intellectual and hence immortal, I doubt very much if they'll dicker with us at all,' Seaton replied. 'Time doesn't mean a thing to them, you know; but since you insist I'll check the stasis and talk it over with them.'

A tenuous projection, heterodyned upon waves far below the band upon which the captives had their being, crept through the barrier screen and Seaton addressed his thoughts to the entity known as 'One.'

'Being highly intelligent, you have already perceived that we are vastly more powerful than you are. Living in the flesh possesses many advantages over an immaterial existence. One of these is that it permitted us to pass through the fourth dimension, which you cannot do because your patterns are purely three-dimensional and inextensible. While in hyperspace we learned many things. Particularly we learned much of the really fundamental natures and relationship of time, space, and matter, gaining thereby a basic knowledge of all nature which is greater, we believe, than any that has ever before been possessed by any three-dimensional being.

'Not only can we interchange matter and energy as you do in

your materializations and dematerializations, but we can go much farther than you can, working in levels which you cannot reach. For instance, I am projecting myself through this screen, which you cannot do because the carrier wave is far below your lowest attainable level.

'With all my knowledge, however, I admit that I cannot destroy you, since you can shrink as nearly to a mathematical point as I can compress this zone, and its complete coalescence would of course liberate you. Upon the other hand, you realize your helplessness inside that sphere. You can do nothing since it cuts off your sources of power.

'I can keep you imprisoned therein as long as I choose. I can set upon it forces which will keep you imprisoned until this two-hundred-kilogram ingot of uranium has dwindled down to a mass of less than one milligram. Knowing that the half-life period of that element is approximately five times ten to the ninth years, you can calculate for yourself how long you shall remain incarcerated.

'My wife, however, has a purely sentimental objection to confining you thus, and wishes to make an agreement with you whereby we may set you at liberty without endangering our own present existences. We are willing to let you go if you will agree to leave this universe forever. I realize, of course, that you are beyond either sentiment or passion and are possessed of no emotions whatever. Realizing this, I give you a choice, upon purely logical grounds, thus:

'Will you leave us and our universe alone, to work out our own salvation or our own damnation, as the case may be, or shall I leave you inside that sphere of force until its monitor bars are exhausted? Think well before you reply; for, know you, we all prefer to exist for a short time as flesh and blood rather than for all eternity as fleshless and immaterial intelligences. Not only that – we intend so to exist and we shall so exist!'

'We shall make no agreements, no promises,' One replied. 'Yours is the most powerful mind I have encountered – almost the equal of one of ours – and I shall take it.'

'You just *think* you will!' Seaton blazed. 'You don't seem to get the idea at all. I am going to surround you with an absolute stasis of time, so that you will not even be conscious of imprisonment, to say nothing of being able to figure a way out of it, until certain more pressing matters have been taken care of. I shall then work out a method of removing you from this universe in such a fashion and to such a distance that if you should desire to come back here the time required would be, as far as humanity is concerned, infinite. Therefore it must be clear to you that you will not be able to get any of our minds, in any circumstances.'

'I had not supposed that a mind of such power as yours could think so muddily,' One reproved him. 'In fact, you do not so think. You know as well as I do that the time with which you threaten me is but a moment. Your galaxy is insignificant, your universe is but an ultramicroscopic mote in the cosmic all. We are not interested in them and would have left them before this had I not encountered your brain, the best I have seen in substance. That mind is highly important and that mind I shall have.'

'But I have already explained that you can't get it, ever,' protested Seaton, exasperated. 'I shall be dead long before you get out of that cage.'

'More of your purposely but uselessly confused thinking,' retorted One. 'You know well that your mind shall never perish, nor shall it diminish in vigor throughout all time to come. You have the key to knowledge, which you will hand down through all your generations. Planets, solar systems, galaxies, will come and go, as they have since time first was; but your descendants will be eternal, abandoning planets as they age to take up their abodes upon younger, pleasanter worlds, in other systems and in other galaxies – even in other universes.

'And I do not believe that I shall lose as much time as you think. You are bold indeed in assuming that your mind, able as it is, can imprison mine for even the brief period we have been discussing. At any rate, do as you please – we will make neither promises nor agreements.'

23 : The Long, Long Ride

Immense as the Norlaminian vessel was, getting her inside the planetoid was a simple matter to the Brain. Inside the *Skylark* a dome bulged up, driving back the air, a circular section of the multilayered wall disappeared; Rovol's space-torpedo floated in; the wall was again intact; the dome vanished; the visitor settled lightly into the embrace of a mighty landing cradle which fitted exactly her slenderly stupendous bulk.

The Osnomian prince was the first to disembark, appearing unarmed; for the first time in his warlike life he had of his own volition laid aside his every weapon.

'Glad to see you, Dick,' he said simply, but seizing Seaton's hand in both his own, with a pressure that said far more than his words. 'We thought they got you, but you're bigger and better than ever – the worse jams you get into, the stronger you come out.'

Seaton shook the hands enthusiastically. 'Yeah, "lucky" is my middle name – I could fall into a cesspool and climb out covered with talcum powder and smelling like a bouquet of violets. But you've advanced more than I have,' glancing significantly at the other's waist, bare now of its wonted assortment of lethal weapons. 'You're going good, old son – we're all behind you!'

He turned and greeted the other newcomers in cordial and appropriate fashion, then all went into the control room.

During the long flight from Valeron to the First Galaxy no one paid any attention to course or velocity – a handful of cells in the Brain piloted the *Skylark* better than any human intelligence could have done it. Each Norlaminian scientist studied rapturously new vistas of his specialty: Orlon the charted galaxies of the First Universe, Rovol the minutely small particles and waves of the sixth order, Astron the illimitable energies of cosmic radiation, and so on.

Seaton spent day after day with the Brain, computing, calculating, thinking with a clarity and a cogency hitherto impossible, all to one end. What should he do, what *could* he do, with those confounded Intellectuals? Crane, Fodan, and Drasnik spent their time in planning the perfect government – planetary, systemic, galactic, universal – for all intelligent races, wherever situated.

Sacner Carfon studied quietly but profoundly with Caslor of Mechanism, adapting many of the new concepts to the needs of his aqueous planet. Dunark and Urvan, their fiery spirits now subdued and strangely awed, devoted themselves as sedulously to the arts and industries of peace as they formerly had to those of war.

Time thus passed quickly, so quickly that, almost before the travelers were aware, the vast planetoid slowed down abruptly to feel her cautious way among the crowded stars of our galaxy. Though a mere crawl in comparison with her inconceivable intergalactic speed, her present pace was such that the stars sped past in flaming lines of light. Past the double sun, one luminary of which had been the planet of the Fenachrone, she flew; past the Central System; past the Dark Mass, whose awful attraction scarcely affected her cosmic-energy drive – hurtling toward Earth and toward Earth's now hated master, DuQuesne.

DuQuesne had perceived the planetoid long since, and his robot-manned ships rushed out into space to do battle with Seaton's new and peculiar craft. But of battle there was none; Seaton was in no mood to trifle. Far below the level of DuQuesne's screens, the cosmic energies directed by the Brain drove unopposed upon the power bars of the space fleet of Steel and that entire fleet exploded in one space-filling flash of blinding brilliance. Then the *Skylark*, approaching the defensive screens, halted.

'I know that you're watching me, DuQuesne, and I know what you're thinking about, but you can't do it.' Seaton, at the Brain's control, spoke aloud. 'You realize, don't you, that if you clamp on a zone of force it'll throw the Earth out of its orbit?'

'Yes; but I'll do it if I have to,' came back DuQuesne's cold accents. 'I can put it back after I get done with you.'

'You don't know it yet, half-shot, but you are going to do exactly nothing at all!' Seaton snapped. 'You see, I've got a lot of stuff here that you don't know anything about because you haven't had a chance to steal it yet, and I've got you stopped cold. I'm just two jumps ahead of you, all the time. I could hypnotize you right now and make you do anything I say, but I'm not going to – I want you to be wide awake and aware of everything that goes on. Snap on your zone if you want to – I'll see to it that the Earth stays in its orbit. Well, start something, you big, black ape!'

The screens of the *Skylark* glowed redly as a beam carrying the full power of DuQuesne's installations was hurled against them – a beam behind which there was the entire massed output of Steel's world-girdling network of super-power stations. But Seaton's screens merely glowed; they did not radiate even under that Titanic thrust. For, as has been said, this new *Skylark* was powered, not by intra-atomic energy, but by cosmic energy. Therefore her screens did not radiate; in fact, the furious blasts of DuQuesne's projectors only increased the stream of power being fed to her receptors and converters.

The mighty shields of the planetoid took every force that DuQuesne could send, then Seaton began to compress his zones, leaving open only the narrow band in the fourth order through which the force of gravitation makes itself manifest. Not only did he leave that band open, he so blocked it open that not even DuQuesne's zones of force, full-driven though they were, could close it.

In their closing those zones brought down over all Earth a pall of darkness of an intensity theretofore unknown. It was not the darkness of any possible night, but the appalling, absolute blackness of the utter absence of every visible wave from every heavenly body. As that unrelieved and unheralded blackness descended, millions of Earth's humanity went mad in unspeakable orgies of fright, of violence, and of crime.

But that brief hour of terror, horrible as it was, can be passed over lightly, for it ended forever any hope of world domination by any self-interested man or group, paving the way as it did for the heartiest possible reception of the government of right instead of by might so soon to be given to Earth's peoples by the sages of Norlamin.

Through the barriers both of mighty space ship and of embattled planet Seaton drove his sixth-order projection. Although built to be effective at universal distances the installation was equally efficient at only miles, since its control was purely mental. Therefore Seaton's image, solid and visible, materialized in DuQuesne's inner sanctum – to see DuQuesne standing behind Dorothy's father and mother, a heavy automatic pistol pressed into Mrs. Vaneman's back.

'That'll be all from you, I think,' DuQuesne sneered. 'You can't touch me without hurting your beloved parents-in-law and you're too tender-hearted to do that. If you make the slightest move toward me all I've got to do is to touch the trigger. And I shall do that, anyway, right now, if you don't get out of this System and stay out. I am still master of the situation, you see.'

'You are master of nothing, you murderous baboon!'

Even before Seaton spoke the first word his projection had acted. DuQuesne was fast, as has been said, but how fast are the fastest human nervous and muscular reactions when compared with the speed of thought? DuQuesne's retina had not yet registered the fact that Seaton's image had moved when his pistol was hurled aside and he was pinioned by forces as irresistible as the cosmic might from which they sprang.

DuQuesne was snatched into the air of the room – was surrounded by a globe of energy – was jerked out of the building through a welter of crushed and broken masonry and concrete and of flailing, flying structural steel – was whipped through atmosphere, stratosphere, and empty space into the control room of the *Skylark of Valeron*. The enclosing shell of force disappeared and Seaton hurled aside his controlling helmet, for he knew that wave upon wave of passion, of sheer hate, was rising, battering at the very gates of his mind; knew that if he wore that headset one second longer the Brain, actuated by his own uncontrollable thoughts, would passionately but mercilessly exert its awful power and blast his foe into nothingness before his eyes.

Thus at long last the two men, physically so like, so unlike mentally, stood face to face; hard gray eyes staring relentlessly into unyielding eyes of midnight black. Seaton was in a towering rage; DuQuesne, cold and self-contained as ever, was calmly alert to seize any possible chance of escape from his present predicament.

'DuQuesne, I'm telling you something,' Seaton gritted

through clenched teeth. 'Prop back your ears and listen. You and I are going out in that projector. You are going to issue "cease firing" orders to all your stations and tell them that you're all washed up – that a humane government is taking things over.'

'Or else?'

'Or else I'll do, here and now, what I've been wanting to do to you ever since you shot up Crane's place that night – I will scatter your component atoms all the way from here to Valeron.'

'But, Dick...' Dorothy began.

'Don't butt in, Dot!' Stern and cold, Seaton's voice was one his wife had never before heard. Never had she seen his face so hard, so bitterly implacable. 'Sympathy is all right in its place, but this is the show-down. The time for dealing tenderly with this piece of mechanism in human form is past. He has needed killing for a long time, and unless he toes the mark quick and careful he'll get it, right here and right now.

'And as for you, DuQuesne,' turning again to the prisoner, 'for your own good I'd advise you to believe that I'm not talking just to make a noise. This isn't a threat, it's a promise – get me?'

'You couldn't do it, Seaton, you're too...' Their eyes were still locked, but into DuQuesne's there had crept a doubt. 'Why, I believe you *would*!' he exclaimed.

'A damned good way to find out is to say no. Yes or no?'

'Yes.' DuQuesne knew when to back down. 'You win – temporarily at least,' he could not help adding.

The projection went out and the required orders were given. Sunlight, moonlight, and starlight again bathed the world in wonted fashion. DuQuesne sat at ease in a cushioned chair, smoking Crane's cigarettes; Seaton stood scowling blackly, hands jammed deep into pockets, addressing the jury of Nor-laminians.

'You see what a jam I'm in?' he complained. 'I could be arrested for what I think of that bird. He ought to be killed, but I can't do it unless he gives me about half an excuse, and he's darn careful not to do that. So what?'

'The man has a really excellent brain, but it is slightly warped,' Drasnik offered. 'I do not believe, however, that it is beyond repair. It may well be that a series of mental operations might make of him a worth-while member of society.'

'I doubt it.' Seaton still scowled. 'He'd never be satisfied unless he was all three rings of the circus. Being a big shot isn't enough – he's got to be Poo-Bah. He's naturally antisocial – he would always be making trouble and would never fit into a really civilized world. He *has* got a wonderful brain; but he isn't human ... Say, that gives me an idea!' His corrugated brow smoothed magically, his boiling rage was forgotten.

'Blackie, how would you like to become a pure intellect? A bodiless intelligence, immaterial and immortal, pursuing pure knowledge and pure power throughout all cosmos and all time, in company with seven other such entities?'

'What are you trying to do, kid me?' DuQuesne sneered. 'I don't need any sugar coating on my pills. You are going to take me on a one-way ride – all right, go to it, but don't lie about it.'

'No; I mean it. Remember the one we met in the first *Skylark*? Well, we captured him and six others, and it's a very simple matter to dematerialize you so that you can join them. I'll bring them in, so that you can talk to them yourself.'

The Intellectuals were brought into the control room, the stasis of time was released, and DuQuesne – via projection – had a long conversation with One.

'That's the life!' he exulted. 'Better a million times over than any possible life in the flesh – the ideal existence! Think you can do it without killing me, Seaton?'

'Sure can – I know both the words and the music.'

DuQuesne and the caged Intellectuals poised in the air, Seaton threw a zone around cage and man, the inner zone of course disappearing as the outer one went on. DuQuesne's body disappeared – but not so his intellect.

'That was the first really bad mistake you ever made, Seaton,' the same sneering, domineering, icily cold DuQuesne informed Seaton's projection in level thought. 'It was bad because you can't ever remedy it – you *can't* kill me now! And now I *will* get you – what's to hinder me from doing anything I please?'

'I am, bucko,' Seaton informed him cheerfully. 'I told you quite a while ago that you'd be surprised at what I could do, and that still goes as it lays. But I'm surprised at your rancor and at the survival of your naughty little passions. What d'you make of it, Drasnik? Is it simply a hangover, or may it be permanent in his case?'

'Not permanent, no,' Drasnik decided. 'It is only that he has not yet become accustomed to his changed state of being. Such emotions are definitely incompatible with pure mentality and will disappear in a short time.'

'Well, I'm not going to let him think, even for a minute, that I slipped up on his case,' Seaton declared. 'Listen, you! If I hadn't been dead sure of being able to handle you I would have killed you instead of dematerializing you. And don't get too cocky about my not being able to kill you yet, either, if it comes to that. It shouldn't be impossible to calculate a zone in which there would be no free energy whatever, so that you would starve to death. But don't worry – I'm not going to do it unless I have to.'

'Just what do you think you *are* going to do?'

'See that miniature space ship there? I am going to compress you and your new playmates into this spherical capsule and surround you with a stasis of time. Then I am going to send you on a trip. As soon as you are out of the galaxy this bar here will throw in a cosmic-energy drive – not using the power of the bar itself, you understand, but only employing its normal radiation of energy to direct and to control the energy of space – and you will depart for scenes unknown with an acceleration of approximately three times ten to the twelfth centimeters per second. You will travel at that acceleration until this small bar is gone. It will last something more than one hundred thousand million years; which, as One will assure you, is but a moment.

'Then these large bars, which will still be big enough to do the work, will rotate your capsule into the fourth dimension. This is desirable, not only to give you additional distance, but also to destroy any orientation you may have remaining, in spite of the stasis of time and not inconsiderable distance already covered. When and if your capsule gets back into three-dimensional space you will be so far away from here that you will certainly need most of what is left of eternity to find your way back here.' Then, turning to the ancient physicist of Norlamin: 'O.K.,

Rovol?'

'An exceedingly scholarly bit of work,' Rovol applauded.

'It is well done, son,' majestic Fodan gravely added. 'Not only is it a terrible thing indeed to take away a life, but it is certain that the unknowable force is directing these disembodied mentalities in the engraving upon the Sphere of a pattern which must forever remain hidden from our more limited senses.'

Seaton thought into the headset for a few seconds, then again projected his mind into the capsule.

'All set to go, folks?' he asked. 'Don't take it too hard – no matter how many millions of years the trip lasts, you won't know anything about it. Happy landings!'

The tiny space-ship prison shot away, to transport its contained bodiless intelligences into the indescribable immensities of the superuniverse; of the cosmic all; of that ultimately infinite space which can be knowable, if at all, only to such immortal and immaterial, to such incomprehensibly gigantic mentalities as were theirs.

The erstwhile Overlord and his wife sat upon an ordinary davenport in their own home, facing a fireplace built by human labor, within which nature-grown logs burned cracklingly. Dorothy wriggled luxuriously, fitting her gorgeous auburn head even more snugly into the curve of Seaton's shoulder, her supple body even more closely into the embrace of his arm.

'It's funny, isn't it, lover, the way things turn out? Space ships and ordinary projectors and forces and things are all right, but I'm awfully glad that you turned that horrible Brain over to the Galactic Council in Norlamin and said you'd never build another. Maybe I shouldn't say it, but it's ever so much nicer to have you just a man again, instead of a – well, a kind of a god or something.'

'I'm glad of it, too, Dot – I couldn't hold the pose. When I got so mad at DuQuesne that I had to throw away the headset I realized that I never could get good enough to be trusted with that much dynamite.'

'We're both really human, and I'm glad of it. It's funny, too,' she went on dreamily, 'the way we jumped around and how much we missed. From here across thousands of solar systems to Osnome, and from Norlamin across thousands of galaxies to Valeron. And yet we haven't seen either Mars or Venus, our next-door neighbors, and there are lots of places on Earth, right in our own back yard, that we haven't seen yet, either.'

'Well, since we're going to stick around here for a while, maybe we can catch up on our local visitings.'

'I'm glad that you are getting reconciled to the idea; because where you go I go, and if I can't go you can't, either, so you've *got* to stay on Earth for a while, because Richard Ballinger Seaton Junior is going to be born right here, and not off in space somewhere!'

'Sure he is, sweetheart. I'm with you, all the way – you're a blinding flash and a deafening report; and, as I may have intimated previously, I love you.'

'Yes ... and I love you ... it's wonderful, how happy you and I are ... I wish more people could be like us ... more of them will be, too, don't you think, when they have learned what cooperation can do?'

'They're bound to. It'll take time, of course – racial hates and fears cannot be overcome in a day – but the people of good old Earth are not too dumb to learn.'

Auburn head close to brown, they stared into the flickering flames in silence; a peculiarly and wonderfully satisfying silence.

For these two the problems of life were few and small.